PLEASURES
of the
NIGHT

By Sylvia Day

PLEASURES OF THE NIGHT
ALLURING TALES *(anthology)*

Coming Soon

HEAT OF THE NIGHT

PLEASURES
of the
NIGHT

Sylvia Day

red

AVON

An Imprint of HarperCollinsPublishers

HarperCollins books may be purchased for educational, business, or sales promotional use. For information please write: Special Markets Department, HarperCollins Publishers, 10 East 53rd Street, New York, NY 10022.

FIRST EDITION

Interior text designed by Elizabeth M. Glover

Library of Congress Cataloging-in-Publication Data
Day, Sylvia.
    Pleasures of the night / by Sylvia Day.—1st ed.
        p. cm.
ISBN: 978-0-06-123098-1
ISBN-10: 0-06-123098-7
1. Dreams—Fiction. I. Title.

PS3604.A9875P56   2007
813´.6—dc22   2006032268

12 13 14 15 16   ❖/RRD   10 9 8 7 6 5 4

This book is gratefully dedicated to super agents Pamela Harty and Deidre Knight. Their mission, which they chose to accept, was to get me where I wanted to go. They did so beautifully. As my goals expand, they continue to do so.

Thank you so much, P & D.

Hugs!

This story was lovingly critiqued by the awesome Annette McCleave (*www.AnnetteMcCleave.com*). Thank you, Annette.

Lyssa was named after my test reader and friend, Alyssa Hurzeler. Thank you for your honesty.

Thank you, Rose Shapiro, for your editorial assistance and suggestions. You helped me tremendously.

Thanks to the Allure Authors (*www.AllureAuthors.com*) for cheering me on. This business can be tough. Your friendship and support make it easier.

And thank you to my editor, Erika Tsang, for signing on this series and having such enthusiasm for it. I'm grateful.

Prologue

The woman beneath Aidan Cross was only moments away from a stunning orgasm. Her throaty cries filled the air, urging their audience to draw closer.

After centuries of protecting women in this manner, he knew the signs and adjusted his thrusts accordingly. His lean hips rose and fell in tireless motion, stroking his cock through her creamy depths with unfailing skill. She gasped, scratched his skin, arched her back.

"Yes, yes, yes . . ."

The breathless pants made him smile, the power of her rapidly approaching climax filling the room with a glow only he could see. On the fringes of the Twilight, where the light of her passion met the dark of her inner fears, the Nightmares waited with palpable excitement. But he held them off.

He would deal with them in a moment.

Cupping her buttocks, Aidan angled her hips higher, so

that every deep thrust rubbed the root of his cock against her clit. She came with a cry, her cunt rippling in orgasm along the hard length of him, her body moving with a wild, reckless abandon she never displayed while awake.

He kept her there, suspended in rapture, absorbing the energy this dream created. He enhanced it, magnified it, sent it back through her. She began to sink into the deepest dream state, the most restful, far from the Twilight where she was vulnerable.

"Brad . . ." She sighed before drifting completely away.

Aidan was aware that this encounter was no more than a phantasm, a connection of minds. Their skin had touched only in her subconscious. For her, however, their lovemaking had seemed entirely real.

When he was certain she was safe, Aidan withdrew from her body and shed the skin of her fantasy. From beneath the façade of Brad Pitt, his true body emerged—growing taller, broader of shoulder, his hair changing to his natural close-cropped inky black, the blue of his irises darkening to their natural shade of translucent sapphire.

The Nightmares writhed in anticipation, their shadowy bodies undulating on the edge of the Dreamer's consciousness. There were several of them tonight, and only one of him. As he summoned his glaive, Aidan's grin was genuine. He loved it when they outnumbered him so greatly. Eons of fighting had left him with a grudge, and he relished every opportunity to take it out on Nightmares.

With practiced grace Aidan flexed his sword arm with sinuous movements, using the substantial weight of his blade to alter the focus of his muscles from sexual tension to the limberness of a warrior. Certain assets could be augmented in dreams, but facing multiple opponents required innate skill regardless.

When he was ready, he drawled, "Shall we?"

And with a powerful forward lunge, Aidan made the first fatal thrust.

"Did you have a good night, Captain Cross?"

Aidan shrugged and kept moving toward the Temple of the Elders, his black robes swirling around his ankles with every long stride. "Same as usual."

Waving his farewell to the Guardian who had called out to him, Aidan passed beneath the massive torii gate into the open-air center courtyard. As his bare feet carried him silently across the cool stone floor, a gentle breeze ruffled his hair and teased his senses with its fragrance. Energized as he was, he could have remained in the field and fought longer, but the Elders forbade it.

For an age now they had insisted that every Guardian return to the Temple complex at regular intervals. They claimed it was to give them time to rest, but Aidan knew this wasn't the entire reason. Guardians needed very little downtime. The archway behind him was the true purpose of the order to return. Huge and colored a shocking red, it was so imposing that it forced every Guardian to stare and read the warning engraved in the ancient language: *"Beware of the Key that turns the Lock."*

Due to lack of proof, he had begun to doubt the existence of the Key. Perhaps the legend was merely a tool to inspire fear, to urge the Guardians forward, to keep them on their toes and prevent them from becoming lax in their duties.

"Hi, Captain."

He turned his head at the soft purr and met the dark eyes of Morgan, one of the Playful Guardians whose job it was to fill in dreams of surfing on the beach or weddings, among countless other joyous activities. Slowing, he altered his course to meet her where she peeked out from behind a fluted column of alabaster stone.

"What are you doing?" he asked, his mouth curved in an indulgent smile.

"The Elders are looking for us."

"Oh?" His eyebrows rose. It was rarely a good thing to be summoned. "So you're hiding? Clever girl."

"Let's frolic by the stream," she suggested in a husky whisper, "and I'll tell you what I heard."

No fool he, Aidan nodded without hesitation. When a lovely Player was in the mood to be playful, one didn't question the offer.

He led her stealthily away, descending from the raised marble platform to the grass beyond. Steadying Morgan down the sloping path to the heated stream below, Aidan took a moment to enjoy the pristine beauty of the new day and the panoramic vista of rolling green hills, bubbling streams, and raging waterfalls. Over the rise, his home waited. An image of sliding shoji doors and tatami mats over hardwood floors came into his mind. It was sparsely furnished, the colors muted, everything chosen with peace and tranquillity in mind. Small and intimate, it was his refuge—albeit a lonely one.

With a careless wave of his hand, he silenced the water so that a breathless hush weighted the air. He had no wish to strain his hearing or shout to be heard.

Discarding the robes of their respective stations—his

black to display his elevated rank, hers multicolored in honor of her frivolity—they sank naked into the steaming water. Resting against a small shelf of rock, Aidan closed his eyes and tugged his companion closer.

"It's unusually quiet today," he murmured.

"Because of Dillon." Morgan curled into his side, her small breasts a delicious pressure against his skin. "He claimed to have found the Key."

The news didn't affect Aidan in any way. Every few centuries a Guardian fell prey to their desire to live the legend. It was nothing new, although the Elders took every mistaken discovery seriously.

"Which clue did he miss?" he asked, knowing that he personally would never miss one. Occasionally Dreamers would show some signs, but never all of them. If they had, he would kill them without question.

"His Dreamer couldn't actually see his features, as Dillon thought. Turns out the Dreamer's fantasy of how Dillon looked just happened to be very close in appearance to reality."

"Ah." The most common error, and one that was made more and more frequently. Dreamers didn't have the ability to see into the Twilight, so they couldn't discern the true features of the Guardians who spent time with them. Only the mythical Key could see them as they were. "But the other traits were there? Was he called by name?"

"Yes."

"The Dreamer controlled the dream?"

"Yes."

"The Nightmares seemed confused and disoriented?"

"Yep . . ." Turning her head, she licked his nipple, then

swam around to encase his hips between her widespread thighs.

He caught her by the waist and urged her against him. He was distracted, his physical actions more habitual than passion-driven. Deep affection for anyone was a luxury Elite Warriors could not afford. It was a weakness that made them vulnerable. "What does that have to do with you and me?"

Morgan ran damp fingers through his hair. "The Elders are now reinvigorated by the news. That so many mortals display such a proliferation of the traits leads them to believe the time has come."

"And?"

"They've decided to send Elite Warriors, like you, to enter the dreams of those who resist us. My task is to work with the Nurturers to heal them once you've gained entry."

Sighing his misery, Aidan dropped his head back gently against the stone. Some Dreamers shut away parts of themselves so securely, not even the Guardians could enter. Either they had been abused in some manner and blocked out the recollections, or they felt such guilt for certain past actions, they refused to recall them. Protecting Dreamers of that nature from the Nightmares was the most difficult task of all. Without a full understanding of their inner suffering, the ability of the Guardians to help them was severely limited.

And the horrors he had seen in their minds . . .

As memories resurfaced with a vengeance—wars, disease, tortures unparalleled—a shiver swept across his skin despite the warm water. Images that haunted him through centuries.

Fighting, action . . . he could handle. Sex, the blessed for-getfulness of orgasm . . . he sought with near desperation. A tactile man with insatiable desires, he fucked and fought well, and the Elders had no hesitation in using him to their best advantage. He knew his strengths and weaknesses, and took on the Dreamers who benefited from them.

To assign him to work exclusively with those who were damaged, with no reprieve . . . What the Elders asked of him now would be pure hell, not just for him but for his men.

"You must be excited," Morgan murmured, misunder-standing his sudden hurried breathing. "The Elite so love a good conflict."

He took a deep breath. If the weight of his calling seemed crushing, that was for him alone to know. Once he'd had boundless enthusiasm for his work, but lack of progress had a way of disheartening even the most hopeful.

Amid all the ancient legends and tall tales, there was nothing that said his work would ever end. The Night-mares could not be eliminated, only controlled. At any given moment, thousands in the mortal realm were suffer-ing from nightmares whose merciless grip they could not awaken from. Aidan was weary of the stalemate. He was a man who sought a result, and he had been denied one for centuries.

Morgan, sensing his preoccupation, brought his atten-tion back to her with a hand between his legs, talented fingers circling his cock. Aidan's mouth curved in the smile that promised her every desire. He would give her what she wanted. Then he'd give her more.

By concentrating on her, he could forget himself. For a

while. "How shall we begin, love? Hard and fast? Or slow and easy?"

With a quiet sound of anticipation, Morgan rubbed her hard nipples against his chest. "You know what I need," she breathed.

Sex was the closest he came to companionship, yet it soothed only his physical hunger, leaving him with a deeper craving. Despite the Dreamers he met and the innumerable Guardians he worked with, he was alone.

And would be for eternity.

"I figured I'd find you out here," rumbled a deep voice behind Aidan.

Continuing his exercises, he turned to face his best friend. They stood in the clearing at the rear of his house, knee-deep in wild grass, bathed in the magenta glow of the simulated approaching dusk. Sweat slid down his temples as he wielded his glaive, but despite the lengthening hour, he wasn't yet fatigued. "You figured right."

"Word of our new assignment is spreading rapidly through the ranks." Connor Bruce paused a few feet away, his crossed arms boasting massive biceps and brawny forearms. The blond giant didn't have the speed or agility that Aidan boasted, but he made up for it in pure brute strength.

"I know." Aidan lunged toward an imagined adversary, his sword leading the way in a mock fatal thrust.

He and Connor had been friends for centuries, ever since they were dorm mates at the Elite academy. While spending their days toiling through multiple classes and their nights indulging in women, they had forged a bond that held tight through the years.

The academy was a rigorous course, with an extremely high attrition rate. When times got rough, Aidan and Connor had goaded each other to continue on. Of the twenty students who started out in their class, they were among only three to graduate.

Those who didn't complete the training picked up other callings. They became Healers, or Players. Some chose to be Masters and teach. It was a worthy goal. Aidan's mentor, Master Sheron, had been a pivotal figure in his life, and he remembered the Guardian with admiration and affection, even after all these years.

"I can tell you're not happy about the Elders' decision," Connor said dryly. "But lately you're unhappy with everything they do."

Aidan paused, his sword arm falling to his side. "Maybe that's because I don't know what the hell it is that they're doing."

"You've got that look on your face," Connor muttered.

"What look?"

"The I've-got-one-hundred-questions-to-ask look."

Master Sheron had invented the nickname for Aidan's pensiveness. It was one of the many things the Elder-in-training had imparted that stayed with him to this day.

Aidan missed the hours he'd spent with his mentor at the stone table beneath the tree in the academy courtyard. He would ask a multitude of questions, and Sheron would enlighten him with laudable patience. Shortly after they graduated, Sheron had gone through Induction to become a full-fledged Elder, and Aidan had never seen him again.

Lifting his hand, Aidan fingered the stone pendant

Sheron had given him the day he'd graduated. He wore it always as a tangible reminder of those days and the eager youth he'd once been.

"Don't you ever wonder why anyone would want to become an Elder?" he asked Connor. Yes, the possibility of finding answers was tempting, but Induction changed Guardians in a way Aidan found alarming. Sheron had been youthful in appearance, with dark hair and eyes, and tawny skin. Now he would look like the other Elders—white-haired, with pale skin and eyes. For a nearly immortal race, a change that drastic had to signal something. Aidan was damn sure it wasn't good.

"No, I don't." Connor's jaw set stubbornly. "Tell me where the fighting is. That's all I want to know."

"Don't you want to know what we're fighting *for*?"

"Shit, Cross. The same thing we've always been fighting for—to contain the Nightmares while we search for the Key. You know we're the only barrier between them and the humans. Since we screwed up by letting the Nightmares in, we've got to stick with it until we find a way to keep them out."

Aidan blew out his breath. Unlike smarter parasites who knew from whence their meal came, Nightmares drained their hosts to death. Leaving the Dreamers unprotected would ensure the extinguishing of humanity, perhaps their entire plane of existence.

He could picture it. The endless nightmares they would suffer. Afraid to sleep, unable to work or eat. An entire species decimated by horror and fatigue. Madness would ensue.

"Okay." Aidan moved toward his house, and Connor fell

into step beside him. "So, hypothetically speaking, what if there was no Key?"

"No Key? Well, that would suck, because that's the only thing that keeps me going some days, knowing there's a light at the end of the tunnel." Connor shot him a narrowed sidelong glance. "What are you getting at?"

"I'm saying it's possible the legend of the Key is bullshit. Maybe we're taught it for just the reason you mentioned, to give hope and motivation when our task seems endless." Aidan slid open the shoji door to his living room and retrieved his scabbard, which rested against the wall. "If that's the case, we're screwing Dreamers with this new assignment. Instead of protecting them from the Nightmares, half of the Elite are going to be wasting their time looking for a miracle that may not exist."

"Man, I'd tell you to get laid," Connor muttered, striding past him and heading toward the kitchen, "but you were with Morgan this morning, so that's not what's eating you."

"Leaving Dreamers with subpar protection doesn't sit well with me, and it pisses me off that the Elders are so secretive about why we're doing it. I have trouble believing what I can't see."

"But you chose to hunt Nightmares for a career?" Connor snorted and rounded the corner, out of sight. A moment later he returned with two beers. "Our success is based entirely on what we can't see."

"Yeah, I know. Thanks." Aidan accepted the proffered drink and drank deep swallows while crossing the room to a wooden-framed chair. "It's not our glaives that kill Nightmares, but the power of our determination that in-

spires fear. It's something we have in common with the
bastards—killing through terror."

Which was the cause of the rift between him and his
parents—one a Healing Guardian, the other a Nurturer.
They couldn't understand the path he'd chosen, and the
constant questions they pestered him with had eventually driven him away. He couldn't seem to explain why he
needed to be working *against* the Nightmares, not cleaning
up after them. Since they were the only biological family he
had, that left him with only one emotional bond—Connor.
A man he loved and respected like a brother.

"So how do you explain how we ended up living in this
conduit," Connor queried, sinking into the matching chair
opposite him, "if there isn't a Key?"

According to legend, the Nightmares found a Key
into their old world—the world Aidan was too young to
remember—and then the Nightmares spread, killing everything. The Elders barely had time to create the fissure
within abbreviated space that allowed them to escape into
this conduit plane between the human dimension and the
one the Guardians had been forced to leave behind. It
took Aidan a while to fully grasp the concept of multiple
planes of existence and the space-time continuum—one
a product of metaphysics, the other a product of physics.
But the idea that a single being—the Key—was capable of
tearing those fissures open at will, spilling the contents of
one plane into another, was something he still didn't quite
comprehend.

He trusted things that could be proven, like the psy-
chological change this conduit had wrought in their species, making them nearly immortal and ephemeral like the

Nightmares. The Guardians had been defenseless before, but here they were on equal footing with their enemy.

"The Elders got us into this fissure without a Key," Aidan pointed out. "I'm sure the Nightmares could do the same."

"So you toss out a widely accepted answer, and replace it with conjecture." Connor crushed his empty beer container. "Wine, women, and kicking ass, Cross. The life of an Elite Warrior. Enjoy it. What more do you want?"

"Answers. I'm tired of the Elders talking to me in damn riddles. I want the truth, all of it."

Connor snorted. "You never quit. That persistence makes you a great warrior, but it also makes you a pain in the ass. I've got three words for you: Need. To. Know. How many missions have there been when you were the only person who knew what the hell was going on?"

"That's not the same," Aidan argued. "That scenario is a temporary delay of information. This is permanent avoidance."

"You used to be the most idealistic person I know. What happened to the trainee who swore he'd be the Guardian to find the Key and kill it?"

"That was teenage bravado talking. That kid grew up and got tired."

"I liked being a teenager. I could fuck all night and still tear up Nightmares the next day. Now it's one or the other."

Aidan understood that his friend was trying to lighten what was quickly becoming a volatile conversation, but he couldn't contain his disquiet any longer, and Connor was the only person he trusted with such matters.

Conner knew him well enough to sense his determination.

"Listen, Cross." He rested his forearms on his thighs, and stared at Aidan with narrowed eyes and a taut jaw. "I'm telling you—as a friend, not your lieutenant—that you have to forget your doubts and rally the troops."

"We're wasting valuable resources."

"Man, I'm *jazzed* that we're switching things up! What we were doing wasn't working, so now we're trying something new. That's progress. You're the one stagnating. Get over yourself and get with the program."

Shaking his head, Aidan pushed to his feet. "Consider what I'm saying."

"I did. It's stupid. End of subject."

"How's the smell?"

"Huh?"

"You've got your head shoved so far up your ass, it's got to stink."

"Them's fighting words." Connor stood.

"How can you dismiss something without even giving it a moment's thought?"

They stared each other down for long moments, each sweltering in the heat of his separate aggravations.

"What the hell is going on?" Connor growled. "What's this about?"

"I want someone—*you*—to consider the possibility that the Elders are hiding something."

"All right. But I want *you* to consider the possibility that they're not."

"Fine." Aidan ran a hand through the sweat-dampened

roots of his hair and heaved out his breath. "I'm going to get cleaned up."

Connor crossed his arms. "Then what?"

"I don't know. You figure something out."

"Whenever I do the planning, we get in trouble. That's why you're captain."

"No. I'm captain because I'm better than you."

Connor threw his golden head back and laughed his deep-timbered laugh, a sound that blew through the tension like a hard breeze in fog. "There's still some of that bravado left in you."

As Aidan went to take a shower, he hoped he had more than bravado left.

He'd need everything he had to make it through the hard assignments ahead. Assignments his instincts didn't agree with at all.

Chapter 1

Lyssa Bates glanced at the cat-shaped clock on the wall with its ticking tail and second-hand whiskers. It was finally nearing five o'clock. Almost time to start the weekend, and she couldn't wait.

Exhausted, she ran her hands through her long hair and yawned. It seemed she never got recharged enough, no matter how long she rested. Her days off passed in a blur of kicked-off sheets and buckets of coffee. Her social life had slowed to a drip as her time spent in bed grew longer and longer. None of the prescription insomnia medications helped. It wasn't that she couldn't sleep. In fact, she couldn't seem to *stop* sleeping.

She just wasn't getting any rest.

Standing, she held her arms above her head and stretched. Every sinew in her body protested. Flames from scented candles flickered on the tops of her metal filing cabinets, covering the medicinal odors of her clinic with the smell of sugar cookies. But the yummy scent failed to entice her hunger as it was meant to do. She was losing weight and growing weaker. Her doctor was prepared to send her to a sleep clinic to monitor her REM patterns, and she was about to agree. He said her lifelong lack of dream recollection was a mental manifestation of a physical malady, one he just hadn't pinpointed yet. Lyssa was just grateful that he didn't prescribe a straitjacket.

"That was your last patient, so you can go home if you want."

Turning, Lyssa managed a smile for Stacey, her receptionist, who stood in the office doorway.

"You look like shit, Doc. Are you coming down with something?"

"Hell if I know," Lyssa muttered. "I've been feeling under the weather for at least a month now."

She had actually been "sickly" most of her life, which was one of the reasons she had turned to medicine for a career. Now she spent as much time as her energy level would allow in her cheery clinic with its creamy marble floors and soft Victorian decor. Behind Stacey, the narrow wainscoted hallway led to the waiting area decorated with cooing lovebirds in antique cages. It was cozy and warm, a place where Lyssa enjoyed spending time. When she wasn't so damn tired.

Stacey leaned against the doorjamb and wrinkled her nose. Dressed in scrubs with cartoon animals on them, she looked cute and bubbly, which suited her personality. "God, I hate being sick. I hope you feel better soon. Your first patient on Monday is a Lab who just needs boosters. I'll reschedule them, if you want. Give you an extra hour to decide if you feel up to coming in or not."

"I love you," Lyssa said with a grateful smile.

"Nah, you just need someone to take care of you. Like a boyfriend. Man, the way the single guys look at you when they come in here . . ." Stacey whistled. "Half the time I think they bought dogs just to come see you."

"Didn't you just say I looked like shit?"

"Girl talk. You'd look better on your deathbed than most women do on their best day. These guys don't remember their pets' checkups because of the reminder postcards. Trust me."

Lyssa rolled her eyes. "I just gave you a raise. What do you want now?"

"For you to go home. I'll close up with Mike."

"I won't argue with that." She was dead on her feet, and although the clinic was still filled with the soothing cacophony of barking dogs, Mike's whirring grooming tools, and talking birds, everything was gradually winding down for the evening. "Let me put these charts away and I'll—"

"No way. If I let you start doing my job, what'll you need me for?" Stacey strode over, scooped up the files from the mahogany desktop, and moved out to the hallway. "See ya Monday, Doc."

Shaking her head with a smile, Lyssa retrieved her purse and fished out her keys before she exited the back of her clinic to the staff parking area. Her black BMW Roadster waited in the nearly empty lot. It was a beautiful day, both sunny and warm, and she lowered the top before heading home. During the twenty-minute drive, she guzzled the cold leftover coffee in her cup holder and blared the radio, trying to stay awake long enough to keep from killing herself or someone else on the highway.

Her sleek car wove easily through the slight traffic in her small Southern California town. An impulse buy when she had finally acknowledged she was destined to die young, the Roadster was a purchase she'd never regretted.

Over the last four years she had made a lot of similarly drastic changes, like moving to the Temecula Valley and leaving a hugely successful veterinary practice in San Diego behind. She'd thought her chronic fatigue was due to her stressful work schedule and outrageous cost-of-living, and for the first few years after the move, she had felt much better. Lately, however, her health seemed worse than ever.

A battery of tests had ruled out a variety of ailments, such as lupus and multiple sclerosis. Incorrect diagnoses like fibromyalgia and sleep apnea had her taking useless medications and wearing painful masks that prevented any shuteye whatsoever. The latest diagnosis of narcolepsy was depressing, suggesting no cure for the weariness that was ruining her life. Her ability to work the long hours she enjoyed had been diminished years ago, and she was slowly losing her mind.

The wrought-iron gate to her condo community swung open and she pulled inside, passing the communal pool area she had yet to use before hitting the remote to her garage door around the corner.

She pulled to an abrupt stop inside with pinpoint precision, hit the remote again, and was inside her granite-countered kitchen before the garage door had lowered all the way. Tossing her purse on the breakfast bar, Lyssa stripped out of her ivory silk shirt and blue slacks, then sank into her down-stuffed couch.

She was asleep before her head hit the cushion.

Aidan stared at the portal barring him from his latest assignment and scowled. The psyche inside was seriously fucked up to build a barrier like this. Metallic and broad, it stood alone in a sea of black. Rising upward so far he couldn't see where the damn thing ended, it was the strongest deterrent he had ever come across. No wonder the other half-dozen Guardians had met with failure.

He cursed and ran his hands through his hair, which was now graying slightly at the temples. Guardians didn't age. They were immortal, unless a Nightmare sucked the life out of them. But some of the whacked-out shit he'd seen over the years had scarred him visibly. Weary and disheartened, he gripped the hilt of his sword and banged hard on the door. It was going to be a long night.

"Who is it?" came a lilting voice from inside.

He paused mid-swing, his interest piqued.

"Hello?" she called out.

With his brain slowed by the unexpectedness of the conversation, he blurted the first thing that came to mind. "Who do you want it to be?"

"Oh, go away," she grumbled. "I'm sick of you wackos."

Aidan blinked at the door. "Excuse me?"

"No wonder I never get any sleep with you guys banging on the door with your riddles. If you won't tell me your name, you can go away."

"What name do you prefer?"

"Your real one, smart ass."

His brow arched as he suddenly felt as if he were the one who was mentally disturbed and not the other way around.

"Bye, whoever you are. Nice talking to you." Her voice grew distant, and he knew he was losing her.

"Aidan," he yelled.

"Oh." There was a pregnant pause. "I like that name."

"Good. I guess." He frowned, not sure what to do next. "Can I come in?"

The door swung open with torturous leisure, the hinges screeching and soft puffs of rust exploding from the cracks. He stared for a moment, startled at how easy it was to gain entry when he had been warned the task would be next to impossible. Then he was struck by the interior. Inside was just as pitch black as the outside. He'd never seen anything like it.

Stepping carefully into her "dream," he asked, "Why don't you turn the lights on?"

"You know," she said dryly, "I've been trying to do that for years."

Her voice floated across the darkness like a warm spring breeze. He searched through her memories and found nothing unusual. Lyssa Bates was an ordinary woman who lived an ordinary life. There was nothing in her past or present that could explain this emptiness.

The door behind him stood open. He could withdraw. Send for a Nurturer. Be grateful for the easiest assignment he'd had in a long, long time. Instead, he stayed, intrigued by the first flash of genuine interest in a Dreamer he had felt in many centuries.

"Well . . ." He scrubbed a hand along his jaw. "Try thinking of someplace you'd like to go and take us there."

"Close the door, please." He heard her padding away.

Aidan considered the wisdom of shutting himself inside here with her. "Can't we leave it open?"

"No. They'll come in if you don't shut it."

"Who'll come in?"

"The Shadows."

Aidan stood silently, absorbing the fact that she recognized the Nightmares as separate entities. "I can kill them for you," he offered.

"I abhor violence, if you must know."

"Yeah, I knew that. That's one of the reasons you became a vet."

She snorted. "Now I remember why I kicked you guys out. You pry too much."

Turning to shut the door, Aidan said, "You let me in quickly enough."

"I like your voice. Is that a brogue? Where are you from?"

"Where do you want me to be from?"

"Whatever." The footsteps padded farther away. "Show yourself out. I'm not talking to you anymore."

Aidan laughed softly and admired her spirit. She wasn't cowed, despite how miserable it must be to be alone in the dark. "You know what your problem is, Lyssa Bates?"

"You and your friends bugging me?"

"You don't know how to dream. All the endless possibilities of your mind—all the places you can go, the things you can do, the people you can be with—and you're not indulging in any of it."

"You think I *like* sitting here in the dark? I would love to be on a Caribbean beach right now, rolling around in the sand with a hot guy."

The door shut with a tremendous booming sound, and he heaved out a breath. He had no idea what to do now. Nurturing, healing, all that mushy stuff . . . he wasn't good at any of it.

"What would Hot Guy look like?" he asked. Sex he could do. And honestly, for the first time in a long time, he was actually looking forward to it. There was something about the irreverent way she spoke . . .

"Oh, I don't know," she said, her voice settling into one area. "Tall, dark, and handsome. Isn't that what all women want?"

"Not always." He moved toward her, sifting through her memories for past examples of what she considered hot.

"You sound like you know."

He shrugged, then remembered she couldn't see him. "I've had some experience. Keep talking so I can find you."

"Why can't we talk like this?"

"Because"—he altered his course to the left—"I would rather not raise my voice."

"It's a very luscious voice."

His brows rose. "Thank you."

Luscious was not a word he'd heard in regard to his voice before. The compliment made his cock twitch, and the damn thing was so jaded, it hardly ever did that without physical manipulation. It certainly had never done that without visual stimuli. "I like your voice, too. I picture you being very pretty."

Rifling through her mind, he saw that she was indeed attractive, but tired, with red-rimmed dark eyes and a slender frame.

"Well, we'll be sure to keep the lights out then." She

sounded sad. Normally he would be backing away quickly from such emotion. Lust and anger were all he could afford to experience. He couldn't care too deeply about anyone's fate. Not even his own.

"There are those of us who can help you," he said softly.

"Which one? The one who came last night and imitated the voice of my cheating ex-boyfriend?"

Aidan winced. "Bad choice, but with the door in the way, I've got to hand it to him for even picking up on that much."

She laughed, and the throaty sound was very different from what he had expected to hear. It was vibrant, full of life, a taste of the woman she'd been before whatever had happened to fuck her up.

"The other night they sounded like my mother."

He lowered to a crouch beside her. "To comfort you. That was smart, considering how close you are to her."

"I don't want comfort, Aidan," she said, yawning.

A heady floral fragrance filled his nostrils, and wanting more of it, he sat down with his legs crossed. "What *do* you want, Lyssa?"

"Sleep." Her sweet voice was so wearied. "God, I just want to go to sleep and rest. My mother talks too much to let that happen. And your people keep pounding on the damn door. The main reason I let you in was to shut you guys up."

"Come here," he murmured, reaching into the darkness and finding her warm, soft body.

As she curled against his chest, he created a wall behind him and settled, stretching his long legs out in front of them and holding her close.

"This is nice," she breathed, her breath hot as it gusted through the opening of his tunic and grazed his chest. Her weight was slight, but she was full-breasted, a discovery that both pleased and surprised him. "It was your voice, too."

"Hmm?"

"Why I let you in."

"Ah." He stroked the length of her spine, soothing her, whispering assurances that made no sense to him but sounded good.

"You're almost hard enough to be uncomfortable," she grumbled, wrapping her arms around his waist. "What the hell do you do for a living?"

He buried his nose in her hair and breathed her in. The scent was fresh and sweet. Innocent. While this woman had spent her life healing small creatures, he'd spent an eternity fighting and killing. "I keep the bad guys away."

"Sounds rough."

He said nothing. The urge to find solace with her was nearly overwhelming, but unlike how he felt with other women, he didn't wish to lose himself in her body. He just wanted to hold her, and take comfort in her caring. Her livelihood was healing, and he wanted, for just a fleeting instant, to be healed.

He squashed the desire ruthlessly.

"I'm so sleepy, Aidan."

"Rest, then," he murmured. "I'll make sure you're not disturbed."

"Are you an angel?"

His mouth curved, and he hugged her closer. "No, darling. I'm not."

Her reply was a gentle snore.

* * *

It was not-so-gentle kneading on her leg that woke her. Lyssa stretched, startled to find herself on the couch, then even more startled to realize she felt wonderful. The late afternoon sun lit her living room through the sliding glass door, and Jelly Bean, her tabby cat, was grumbling as he always did when she slept too long and didn't pay enough attention to him.

Sitting up, she rubbed her eyes and laughed as her stomach growled in protest. She was famished, truly hungry for the first time in weeks.

"I guess I should have tried sleeping overnight on the couch earlier," she told JB, scratching him behind the ears before rising to her feet. The ringing of the phone made her jump. She hurried to the breakfast bar to get it.

"Dr. Bates," she greeted breathlessly.

"Good afternoon, Doctor," her mother replied, laughing. "You sleeping all day again?"

"I guess." Lyssa looked at the clock. It was nearly one. "It must have worked this time, though. I feel better than I have in months."

"Good enough to go out to lunch?"

Her stomach rumbled its approval at the thought. "Definitely. How long before you get here?"

"I'm just around the corner."

"Cool." Reaching over, she sprinkled fish food in her salt-water tank. Eager clown fish rose to the surface, making her smile. "Let yourself in. I'm going to clean up."

Tossing the cordless handset on the couch before running up the stairs, Lyssa showered and dressed quickly in a comfortable chocolate velour jogging suit. She ran a comb through her wet hair and then clipped it up, noting that she still looked tired, even though she felt great.

Her mother, however, looked nothing less than fabulous dressed in red silk cigarette pants and matching shrunken jacket. With her chin-length blond hair and rouged lips, Cathryn Bates hadn't let two divorces dampen her desire to look hot and attract men.

While her mother rambled on about one thing or another, Lyssa rushed her out the kitchen door and into her Roadster. "Let's go, Mom. Talk in the car, I'm starved."

"You've said that before," Cathy muttered, "and then ate like a bird."

Lyssa ignored that quip and looked over her shoulder as she backed out of her garage. "Where to?"

"Soup Plantation?" Her mom raked her with an assessing glance. "Nah, you need some meat on your bones. Vincent's?"

"Pasta. Yum." Licking her lips, she turned the wheel and sped out of her condo complex. With the top down and a good night's rest, she felt ready to take on the world. It was nice to have energy and be happy. She had almost forgotten how wonderful it was.

Vincent's Italian restaurant was busy, as usual, but they didn't have any trouble securing a seat. Red and white gingham tablecloths and wooden chairs lent to the casual country interior. Soft candles burned on every tabletop, and Lyssa immediately broke into the fresh-baked rosemary bread with gusto.

"Well, look at you!" her mom said approvingly, gesturing for wine by holding her stemmed glass aloft. "I wonder if your sister is eating hardy, too. Her obstetrician says the baby is another boy. She's been trying to think of names."

"Yeah, she told me." Dipping another chunk of bread in olive oil, Lyssa shrugged and reached for the menu. An upbeat Italian tune struggled to be heard over the lunch crowd din, but the busy atmosphere was just what she needed to feel like part of civilization again. "I told her the best I could do was some pet names. She wasn't impressed."

"I suggested she pull out that baby book I bought her. Start with the A's and work her way down. Adam, Alden—"

"Aidan!" Lyssa cried mid-bite. Something tender warmed her insides and made her sigh. "I don't know why, but I really love that name."

It was a beautiful Twilight night. The sky above was an ebon blanket of stars, and in the distance, the roaring of the various waterfalls competed with laughter and hushed musical tones. Guardians who had worked the long night before were relaxing away the stresses of their day. For Aidan, however, his work was just beginning.

He passed beneath the massive archway at the Temple of the Elders and paused at the *chōzuya*. Dipping the waiting ladle into the fountain, he rinsed out his mouth and washed his hands before continuing on.

Grumbling under his breath, he then traversed the center courtyard and entered the *haiden* where the Elders awaited him. They sat before him in semicircular rows that faced the columned entryway he had just come through. Rising several stories above him, there were so many benches that

the Guardians had lost count of how many Elders occupied them long ago.

"Captain Cross," greeted one of them. Which one, Aidan couldn't say. As always, he thought of Master Sheron,
knowing the teacher was one among the many, absorbed
into what Aidan saw as a collective consciousness. The
knowledge saddened him.

He bowed respectfully. "Elders."

"Tell us more about your Dreamer, Lyssa Bates."

It was a struggle, but he kept his face impassive as he
straightened. Just the sound of her name spoken aloud sent
a shiver of pleasure through him. Despite the darkness of
her dream, he had enjoyed his time with her. He'd felt
secure behind the massive door, comforted by her trust,
inwardly surprised and contented that she would turn to
him for himself, not as a phantasm she had created for her
own relief. And she'd commiserated with him, seen him as
a man, not an automaton who craved nothing so much as
a hearty fight and a willing fuck.

"I've told you everything I know."

"There must be more. Seven sleep cycles have passed
since you gained entry, and she has denied all subsequent
Guardians."

He shrugged. "Leave her alone. She's safe and sane.
When she's ready, she'll let us in. She has no immediate
need for us."

"Perhaps we have need of her."

His posture rigid, Aidan raked his gaze across the sea of
faces, his heart increasing its rhythm. They stared back,
clad in dark gray, cowls raised and shielding the upper

halves of their faces so that they all looked the same. One
entity. "Why?"

"She asked for you."

His breath caught. *She remembered him.* Warmth spread
through him, and he hid his reaction with a dismissive
"So?"

"How is it that she recalls you by your true name?"

"I told it to her when she asked."

"Why does she see through every guise we present to
her?"

"She's a doctor. She's smart."

"Is she the Key?"

Aidan scowled. "No. If you knew her, you would know
how ridiculous that is to even consider. She would never
open the Gateway to the Nightmares. She fears them as
we do. Besides, she has the least amount of dream control
I've ever seen. Turning the lights on is beyond her, so she's
sitting in the damn dark."

"We must send more Guardians to interact with her so
that we may prove you correct, but she will not let us in.
If we cannot gain entry, we will have to assume the worst
and destroy her."

Beginning to pace, Aidan clasped his hands at the small
of his back and tried to find a way to argue reason against
their unfounded paranoia. "What can I do to convince
you?"

"Go to her again and urge her to open the door to us."

As much as he longed to go, he dreaded it. Already this
last week he'd been unable to stop thinking about her.
Was she well?

She was thinking about him . . .

A soft shudder coursed the length of his frame. He'd been in her mind, seen who she was on every level. He knew her as well as she knew herself, and he'd liked what he saw and craved more time in her company.

The conflicting desires to be with her and to avoid her goaded him with equal strength. Like a banquet of desserts set before a hungry man—although he knew an attachment to Lyssa would satisfy, it wasn't good for him and he would only end up hungrier. The turmoil he was experiencing proved that.

"If you will not go, Cross, you will leave us with no choice."

The threat hung heavy in the air. The request to re-visit a Dreamer was not unheard of, but it was very rare and it had never been asked of an Elite Warrior before. He steeled his resolve. He could manage to hold himself aloof, just as he'd done forever. "Of course I'll go."

"You will be assigned to her until she opens to other Guardians."

He couldn't hide his surprise. "But I'm needed elsewhere."

"Yes, your leadership will be missed," the voice conceded. "However, this woman is unique in her ability to bar both Nightmare and Guardian with that door. We must know why she does this, and how. Perhaps it is a skill we can replicate in other Dreamers. Imagine the benefits if they could defend themselves."

"That's not all." He stilled mid-stride and faced them. "If goodwill was your aim, you would assign a Healer or Nurturer to coax her out."

Instead they sent a man known for his aloofness and ability to kill with precision.

There was silence. Then, "If she is the Key, you are best equipped to eliminate her."

His blood ran cold. To think that stupid legend would lead to the death of a woman as sweet and pure as Lyssa Bates made his stomach roil. Every day that passed, Aidan hated his calling more and more. The killing of those who were ruined by madness or inherent evil like the Nightmares was becoming hard enough. If they were now to kill innocents, he didn't know how he would bear it.

"You stayed with her, Cross. You could have withdrawn, allowed another to comfort her. You have only yourself to blame for this mission."

He held his open palms out to them. "What's happened to us that we, the Guardians of the innocents, would now kill simply because we don't understand?"

"The Key must be found and destroyed," the Elders intoned in unison.

"Forget the damn Key!" he yelled, his voice booming through the domed space, causing the Elders to recoil as one body. "You, who are so wise, can't see the truth even though it's staring you in the face. *There is no Key!* It's a dream. A myth. A delusion."

He pointed an accusing finger at them. "You want to live on false hope instead of facing the facts. You want to believe that there is some miraculous thing out there that will absolve you of the guilt you feel in bringing the Nightmares here. But we have nothing more than our will to fight, and we are wasting energy searching for what doesn't exist. The war will never be over! Ever. We can only continue to save whom we can. What'll we become if good is killed along with evil for a lie?

"Unless," his voice lowered ominously, "there's something you're not telling us. Some proof."

The silence that followed his outburst was deafening, but he didn't take it back. He had only spoken the obvious.

Finally, someone spoke. "You did not tell us of your crisis of faith, Captain Cross," came the far too calm rejoinder. "But all things come in good time, and this mission is even more suitable for you now that we are aware of your feelings."

Locking himself away sounded better and better to him, too. "Fine. I'll go to her now. And I'll continue to go to her until you tell me otherwise."

He hoped they would come to their collective senses and realize how fanatic their beliefs had become. In the meantime, he would defend Lyssa from both herself and the Order that was sworn to protect her.

Aidan spun on his heel and left in an angry swirl of black robes.

He didn't see the Elders' collective smile.

And no one saw the one Elder who didn't smile at all.

"What happened to you? You looked so good last weekend."

Lyssa rolled over and pressed her face into the back cushions of her couch. "That one night of rest was a fluke."

Her mother sat on the floor and stroked her hair. "Your whole life you've had trouble sleeping. First it was growing pains, then nightmares, then fevers."

Shivering in memory of ice water baths, Lyssa tucked

her sage green chenille throw closer around her. Jelly Bean hissed at her mom from his customary spot on the armrest.

"That animal is possessed," her mother muttered. "He doesn't like anyone."

"I'm not getting rid of him. He's the only guy who puts up with me being like this."

Cathy sighed. "I wish I knew what to do, baby."

"Yeah, me, too. I'm so sick and tired of being sick and tired."

"You need to have more tests run."

"God, no." Lyssa moaned. "I'm done with being a human pincushion, Mom. No more."

"You can't keep living like this!"

"This is living?" Lyssa muttered. "If it is, I would rather be dead."

"Lyssa Ann Bates, if you ever say such a thing again, I'll . . . I'll . . ." Growling, her mother stood, apparently unable to think of a threat direr than death. "I'm going to the store to get the ingredients for homemade chicken noodle soup. And you're going to eat all of it, young lady. Every drop."

Lyssa groaned, and squeezed her eyes shut. "Mom, just *go away*. Let me sleep."

"I'll be back. I'm not giving up, and you're not either."

She distantly heard her mom gather up keys, then close the front door, leaving her in blissful silence. She sighed wearily and drifted into sleep . . .

And was jarred awake by pounding on the door.

"What do you want?" she cried in exasperation, rolling over in the pitch black darkness. "Go away!"

"Lyssa?"

She paused, the soft brogue sweeping gently through the vast space despite the door between them. Her heart leaped. "Aidan?"

"Can I come in?"

Sitting up, she wrinkled her nose and wrapped her arms around her bent knees. "Where have you been?"

"Working." There was a long silence, and then softly: "I've been worried about you."

"Charmer," she huffed, hiding the pleasure his words gave her. Using her mind, she opened the door with a sigh and wished for the thousandth time that she could see the man who went with that voice. She listened to him step inside, relishing the confident, steady stride that revealed so much about him and made her feel so safe.

"You can close the door now," he said, so she did.

His steps slowed, and she could sense him searching for her. "It's still dark in here."

"You noticed that, did ya?"

As the footsteps drew closer, a warm, deep chuckle filled the air. "We'll work on it."

"I hope you've got a while," she said dryly. "I've been working on it for years."

"I've got all the time you need."

She tried to ignore the little thrill that coursed through her, and ended up laughing at herself. She had a crush on a voice.

And a hard body. And strong arms. And patient tenderness. God, she was lonely. She missed having a social life and a boyfriend.

"Are you going to talk to me so I can find you?"

Her throat was tight with regret and bitterness, so she swallowed hard before speaking. "I'm losing it, Aidan. I'm getting sappy. The lamest shit makes me cry."

He moved closer, his stride never faltering or hesitating despite his inability to see. "I admire people who allow themselves to feel."

"What does that mean?"

"Exactly what I said."

"You can't admire a woman who sits in the dark," she argued, "because she's too stupid to turn the lights on."

Aidan crouched down beside her. "I can. And I do."

"How do you find me like that?" She shivered at his nearness and the intimate tone of his voice. Even without sight, she knew his gaze was hot with sensual intent.

"Your scent."

A moment later his face was in her hair as he breathed deeply. Lyssa froze as goose bumps spread in a wave across her skin. A tiny flutter tickled her belly.

He settled back with her tucked up against him. "You open and close the door by yourself."

Lyssa considered that with a frown.

"So you can control your surroundings if you wish to," he pointed out with an odd note in his voice.

She frowned. *Wow, I did do that, without hardly thinking about it.* "Why can't I wish up a cold beer, then? Or a vacation?"

"And a hot guy?" There was a delicious rumble of laughter in his voice.

I've got the hot guy. She bit her lower lip at the thought. Aidan's voice dripped sensual promise; his hard body and long, powerful legs boasted his stamina. She reached up and touched his hair, finding it short-cropped, thick, and silky. With the darkness robbing her ability to see, lustful images flooded her mind, thoughts of her fingers in that rich hair while his mouth worked magic between her legs.

He hissed through his teeth, and she realized how her altered position pressed her breasts to his chest. Her nipples were hard in response to her thoughts, and she knew he could feel them. Pulling away quickly, Lyssa scrambled to put distance between them.

"Sorry," she muttered, beginning to pace in the darkness she knew so well.

Aidan was silent for a long time, then he cleared his throat and said, "So let's try to figure out how you control the door."

She continued to stride back and forth restlessly, certain she had never felt as awkward in her miserable life.

"Lyssa?" He heaved out his breath. "You know what I think?"

"What?" *That I'm a sex-starved nutcase?*

"I think you're too keyed up to focus on dreaming."

"Don't you mean 'hard up'?" She walked away from temptation, her bare feet padding softly across the warm floor. For the first time in a very long time, she wished she were alone, which made her grumpy along with frustrated.

"You can dream just fine when you're focused," he called after her.

Snorting, she shook her head. "Say it," she grumbled under her breath. "I need to get laid."

She gasped as strong arms caught her about the waist and held her tight to a rock-hard chest. Against the curve of her buttocks she felt his arousal, a hot and substantial presence that burned through her sweats to her skin. Her brain stopped working, unable to process the fact that he might want her, too.

"I'll do more than say it, Hot Stuff," he rumbled in her ear.

Then he spun her to face him and took her mouth with breath-stealing hunger, before lowering her down onto golden sand . . .

Chapter 2

As sunlight flooded his vision, Aidan blinked and stared down at the woman in his arms. His heart stopped, every cell in his body arrested by the flowing golden tresses that tumbled across the sand.

"What . . .?" She gasped, lovely dark eyes widened in surprise as she looked around. "Where are we?"

A soft tropical breeze ruffled his hair, and reggae played in the background, but his eyes never left her face. She was confused, her short nails digging into the skin of his forearms, and he couldn't form one coherent word to re-assure her.

Lyssa Bates was stunningly beautiful, her features both patrician and sensual. Her mouth full and red, kissable. Her eyes tip-tilted seductively, revealing both intelligence and innocence. Why had she pictured herself as worn and tired-looking?

Because that's the way she felt.

"Oh my god," she breathed, her fingertips touching his face reverently. "You're gorgeous."

And then they were plunged into darkness. The music fell silent and the fragrant sea breeze disappeared, leaving only the two of them intertwined, their hearts racing next to each other.

"What happened?" she cried plaintively.

Aidan was immobilized in shock. He had desired her scent, the feel of her body, the blunt way she spoke . . . Regardless of her facial appearance, he'd wanted to take her beneath him and fuck her senseless. Sex as a distraction had always worked for him, and from her response to his embrace, he'd known it would work for her, too.

Then he saw her. And now he wanted something more.

"You got scared," he managed hoarsely. "Lost the dream."

As he struggled with the implications, she resumed caressing his face, learning his features by touch as a sculptor would. He had no idea what she'd seen in the light. Her dream would make him into whatever she desired most. For the first time he resented that, wishing the effect he had on her was genuine and the face she admired so much was his own.

"Aidan?" Her sweet voice was low, tentative. Lonely.

Just as he was.

He rolled, pulling her over him, his arms dropping to the ground. His head fell back and his eyes closed, the weight of his dilemma crushing his chest, making it hard to breathe. An eternity of seducing had given him enough insight to be certain—something fragile had taken root in the brief moment their eyes had met.

It needed to be crushed, and Lyssa forgotten.

"Yes?" His voice was gruff, and he felt the confusion it caused ripple through her. He should let her go, move her off him.

But he couldn't do it.

Then she lowered her mouth to his, her softly fragrant hair surrounding him, encasing them together, until all he was cognizant of was her and how much he wanted her. Her lips touched his, a brief kiss, a gentle pressing. He groaned in painful awareness. Emboldened, her tongue flicked out, wetting his bottom lip before she sucked on it with a rhythmic pull that made his cock swell and ache. Lyssa set her hands on either side of his head, lifting slightly to brush her breasts back and forth across his chest.

Aidan Cross, Elite Warrior and immortal seducer, was being consummately seduced for the first time in his endless memory. And Lyssa Bates was very, very good at it.

He'd wanted to distract her and get laid. Now, mating with Lyssa had become a dangerous tangle. His brain was not analyzing step by step the best way to excite her so he could hurry up and thrust his cock into her. His brain was barely functioning at all, other than registering panic at the depth of his craving. He wanted to hold her close, take his time, arouse her to madness with his mouth and hands before sliding into her and letting her come. Over and over again.

Not to forget himself. But to find himself. To remember what it felt like when he still had hope, to remember when he hadn't been afraid to care about someone.

Opening his mouth to speak, he was instead plundered by her kiss, her tongue sweeping inside, stroking along his, making him shudder. She moved, her thighs straddling his hips, her cunt to his cock, her lithe body gliding sinuously along his in a full-body caress. His chest rose and fell so rapidly, he felt dizzy. Sweating, he reached to push her away, but his muscles refused to comply.

"The sand," he gasped, turning his head, which freed her mouth to nibble along his jaw.

Instantly, sand cushioned his back.

"The sun." If he forced her focus to shift, perhaps her ardor would lessen enough to allow him to resist and save himself. His burgeoning fascination with her couldn't be allowed to deepen. There was nowhere for a relationship between them to go, and even if there was, it was hopeless. He needed to dedicate every bit of energy he had to the fight. He couldn't afford to lose the concentration required to do his job properly.

The air around them lightened slowly, like a sunrise, bathing her in a golden glow that formed a halo through her hair. She was an angel to him, a woman both open and innocent, yet not as fragile as circumstances made her appear.

"Please, don't stop," she breathed in his ear, making him shiver.

"Lyssa." His jaw tightened. "You don't understand."

She ground her hips downward onto him, his cock jerking at the feel of her heat burning through to his most sensitive skin. "You want me," she argued stubbornly.

"Yes, but there are things you don't—"

"And I want you."

Aidan growled as she shimmied again. "Oh, fuck it!" he muttered, rolling to pin her beneath him.

"My thoughts exactly," she said with laughter in her voice and eyes.

Deliberately turning off the part of his brain that was urging him to think twice, Aidan let his body take over.

This was what he knew, what he'd spent centuries doing, and he'd never wanted a woman this badly. He could face off against legions of Nightmares, yet he was afraid to fuck a woman he desired?

"Clear your mind of everything but me," he said roughly. "Give me the lead."

"You've got it."

Concentrating with more focus than he'd ever had to use before, Aidan took over the dream, altering their surroundings, creating a circular room lit by candles and scented with exotic flowers. Spicy incense burned in various holders, releasing thin wisps of fragrant white smoke into the air. Dominating the velvet-draped interior of the space was a massive round bed piled with a profusion of silken scarves in various colors. It was there that he pictured them, lying amid the softness, their skin bared and pressed together. Now that he was decided, he would ensure this was a night neither of them would ever forget. Their time together was limited, and he was determined to burn out their lust before it ran out.

"Wow." Her dark eyes were wide. "How did you do that?"

"Hush." He set his fingers over her lips. "No more talking." Turning onto his side, he caught up her hand and set her palm against his chest. "Feel the rhythm of my breathing."

"Umm . . . I'd rather feel you naked."

He arched a brow. "I've got the lead, remember?" Inhaling deeply, Aidan started out imitating the rapid lift and fall of her chest, then he slowed the pace. "Match me."

Lyssa followed along at Aidan's urging until they were inhaling and exhaling in unison. The concentration required to do as he asked narrowed her focus dramatically. She was inundated with sensory input—the alluring scents of the room, the feel of his hard, powerful frame, and the softness of the material they were sprawled on.

Her wandering gaze noted the profusion of hibiscus flowers adorning water-filled glass jars and the soft violet glow given off by oil-burning lanterns. There were tapers, as well, in jeweled candleholders, and moonlight shining down from an open oculus. Altogether the effect was magical, supremely sensual, and erotically charged.

As her world shrank to encompass only this room and the man with whom she shared it, Lyssa felt her enchantment with Aidan deepen.

"Don't lose the tempo of your breathing." His voice was a low, seductive rumble that flowed through her. Aidan held out his hand, and a small bottle of golden liquid appeared in his palm.

"Will you teach me how to do that?" she whispered, watching as he moved gracefully to a kneeling position beside her, and poured jasmine-scented oil into his hand.

"Someday. Not tonight." His slow smile made her heart leap. "Tonight I'm going to give you what we both want."

Lyssa could hardly believe what was happening. She was about to have sex with a man she barely knew.

But this was a dream, and none of the taboos applied

here. They didn't have to go through the routine dating steps of dinner and a movie, following "the rules" until they could say they knew each other well enough to "go all the way."

So stupid. She already knew everything she needed to know—he was kind and solicitous of her needs, going to great lengths to create lush surroundings in which to take her. If this had been about nothing more than sex, he would have fucked her in the sand and been done with it. Instead, everything about his approach to their lovemaking was geared toward her pleasure.

Keeping her breathing deep and even, Lyssa allowed her gaze to roam all over Aidan's body, admiring his golden skin burnished by the flickering candlelight. It was stretched taut over beautifully defined pectorals and washboard abs, his biceps flexing as he warmed the oil in his hands.

Then she looked lower, taking in the object of her desire. Her mouth watered and her pussy grew wet at the sight of his impressive cock and weighty balls.

"God, you're well-hung." She shivered all over, her mind filling with images of him working her to orgasm with that mouthwatering erection.

Damn. Finally, after all these years, she had the perfect guy. It was enough to make her writhe with desire, her skin burning hot and prickled with awareness.

She licked her lips as he straddled her. His thickly veined cock curved upward to nearly touch his navel. The man was over six feet tall, with shoulders so broad she couldn't see past him, yet she didn't feel overwhelmed by his size. She felt safe and protected, and deeply thrilled to have such a magnificent male in her bed. His torso tapered to a lean waist, trim hips, and powerful thighs. The memory of those thighs between hers made her mouth dry.

Unable to resist, Lyssa lifted her hands and wrapped them around his erection. She slid her fingers upward, judging length, and blinked in awe.

Then again, he was huge everywhere else, why not here, too?

"There is a spiritual philosophy called Tantra," he murmured, cupping her aching breasts and kneading them. "Have you heard of it?"

"Bits and pieces." Her fingertips drifted along the hard length of his cock, learning its shape and texture in minute detail. She heard a slight catch in his inhale, and then he resumed his steady breathing.

His coarse hands squeezed her swollen flesh with expertly gauged pressure. Her gaze grew heavy-lidded as her blood slowed, flowing sluggishly through her veins.

"Tantra teaches believers that the energy of the cosmos exists within our bodies, and that a true tantric sexual union merges these energies into one."

"Aidan." Lyssa whimpered as his fingertips tugged gently on her nipples. They were so hard, nearly painful from the extent of her arousal, and the oil on his hands allowed his touch to glide across her fevered skin. The combination was maddening, both soothing and inciting. "Um . . . I really don't need foreplay now . . ."

Aidan winked, and exuded wicked, erotic, decadent sex from every pore. "That's what I'm trying to tell you. This isn't going to be a fast fuck. In fact, it'll be a while before you'll feel my cock in you."

"You can't be serious."

Her back arched as he pinched the erect points of her breasts.

"Oh yes, I can."

Narrowing her gaze, she wished she had some oil of her own. Instantly her hands felt slick, and a slow smile curved her mouth. She fisted her hands and pumped down the throbbing length of his shaft. He groaned.

"Two can play," she murmured.

"We have to take you down a notch, Hot Stuff." Aidan reached between her legs and parted her so that he could stroke across her clit. He rubbed in softly pressured circles, his other hand still tugging at her nipple. "You're too hungry for it. Too impatient."

"Oh god . . ." she breathed, clasping his cock convulsively as a sharp, quick orgasm took her by storm. Two of Aidan's long, callused fingers slipped inside her, fucking her, his oiled thumb continuing the consummate manipulation of her clit. Her cunt quivered and spasmed, her body tense as a bow. Straining . . . reaching . . .

As she climaxed again, her pussy sucked ravenously at Aidan's pumping fingers.

"So damn hot," he growled, leaning over her, the tight roping of his abdominal muscles supporting the weight of his torso. He took her mouth, his lips drifting across hers, his tongue flickering across the seam in time to the movements of his hand between her thighs. The pendant he wore around his neck swayed with his movements, brushing teasingly across her skin as an added point of sensation.

Lyssa spread her legs with unabashed eagerness, wanting him deeper than his fingers could go. Opening her mouth, she tried to drink him in, her kiss frantic and passionate. He fit his mouth over hers and gave her what she wanted, a deep, drowning kiss. Feeling wild and out of control, she began to jack him off with both fists, squeezing the thick head of his cock on every upward pull.

"Stop," he said hoarsely, as her tight grip squeezed precum out of the tip. "You're going to make me come if you keep that up."

"You said we could take it down a notch," she urged. "We can do it slow next time."

Next time. Aidan had never thought of "next time" with a woman before. There had only ever been *this* time. Of course, he could usually make "this time" last all night. He knew already he'd be lucky to last five minutes inside Lyssa. Thankfully, she was primed and more than ready, her cunt so juicy hot, it was melting around his fingers. And, as she said, they could go slow in the next round.

It aroused him further, the thought of having Lyssa again and again, and his cock swelled painfully. Pulling away, Aidan ordered, "Get on your hands and knees."

Her dark eyes widened as he pulled free of her grasp. She swallowed hard. "I don't know if I can take you that way. You're big."

Aidan grabbed his dick with both hands and coated it with a mixture of her cream and the oil. "Do it. Leave the logistics to me. You just lie there and come."

She rolled over and bared a taut, sweetly curved ass that made his balls draw up tight. The dark gold curls between her legs were trimmed almost to the skin, revealing pale pink folds that glistened with her desire.

His eyes slid closed on a deep breath, every muscle tense

with expectation and deep longing. It wasn't the erotic display that most affected him. It was her trust. His heart was racing, his breathing as erratic and uncontrolled as his mood. As if he were standing on a precipice, knowing he was going to fall, but unable to fight it.

When was the last time he'd been in heat like this? When was the last time he'd wanted a particular woman this badly?

Aidan hoped like hell his emotions were simply set off-kilter by his new assignment. He hadn't had sex since he'd met Lyssa. There just wasn't time with all the work he had, and when he did find a free hour or two, he'd spent it thinking about her. Perhaps he'd shocked his system by going without. That had to be what the problem was. He'd been fucking women for centuries. It shouldn't be any different this time.

"Hurry," she breathed.

He opened his eyes to find Lyssa looking over her shoulder at him. His throat tightened at the sight of the graceful curve of her spine and her slender waist. She was so beautiful, in a way that appealed to him keenly.

Gripping her hip with one hand, he aimed his cock at her slick opening with the other, rubbing the throbbing head across her slit.

"I-I'm nervous," Lyssa admitted, every nerve ending focused on her pussy and the cock ready to slide into it. Perspiration swept across her skin. She quivered as he began his entry, the thick head spreading her wide.

"Don't be," he rumbled. "I've got you."

Aidan entered her slowly, too slowly, working his way inside her, advancing, retreating, making her achingly aware of every inch. His progress was agonizing, teasing, driving her mad until her arms started to shake, forcing her to sink into the scarves. The change in angle tilted her hips upward, allowing him to feed her more of that magnificent cock. She whimpered.

"That's it." His voice was rough, dark velvet. "Let me have that pussy."

"Let me have that cock," she countered, breathless, her eyes closing and her hands fisting into the fragrant silk. She was panting, her hips writhing, but he held her tightly and kept to his leisurely pace. "Ah, god . . . you feel amazing."

Never in her life had Lyssa been more aroused. She was so wet, so hot. She doubted she could take a man of his size if she wasn't.

"Oh, Lyssa," he crooned, one hand stroking the length of her spine, making her arch like a cat. "You've got the tightest, juiciest, hungriest cunt I've ever fucked."

"Aidan." She shuddered violently, his coarse words spoken in that luscious brogue making her cream. The extra lubrication allowed him to slide deeper, making them both gasp. Regulated breaths were out of the question. They were both too far gone, their focus so completely arrested by the place where their bodies joined.

She liked dirty bedroom banter, had fantasized about it, but it took a highly confident man to be so open. Until now, she'd never found one.

Finally, Aidan sank in to the hilt, his tight, heavy balls resting against her clit. He withdrew and pumped forward, the smacking of his sac against her slick flesh forcing a deep moan from her.

Her voice came slurred with pleasure. "You're so deep."

And he was; every crevice of her pussy was stretched to hold him, sheathing him like a custom-made glove. There was no way to ignore how perfectly they fit together.

Aidan paused with one hand at her hip, the other at her shoulder. His chest rose and fell in great bellows against her back, which drew her attention to his quivering thighs. She felt as if she were rattling apart. It appeared he felt the same.

The tantalizing smell of his skin filled the air around her, blending with the incense. Where they touched, they clung, their mingled sweat binding them closer together.

"Maybe if we come fast . . . ?" she suggested shakily, trying to think of a point past this moment of vulnerability.

"Yes."

Reaching beneath her, Aidan rubbed her clit in those maddening circles and began to shaft her cunt with long, measured drives. The sensation was incredible, the feeling of stretching and shrinking, of grasping and sucking, of being pumped with expert precision by a man who knew how to fuck so well, it made her mindless with lust.

Lyssa had no doubt she was in over her head. She didn't have the experience to handle a man like Aidan. It was obvious in the way he mantled her body and rode it with absolute surety that he was in his element. She, on the other hand, could only lie there and take it, her entire body so sensitized that the feel of his pendant brushing across her back made her orgasm.

"So sweet," he groaned, as she shook beneath him with a startled cry. "I'm coming . . ."

She felt his cock jerk inside her as he climaxed hard,

flooding her with pulses of thick, hot semen. Blood roared in her ears, dulling her hearing, but slowly she became aware of his words, softly whispered in a language she didn't comprehend. His tone was reverent, his embrace crushing.

As her knees gave out beneath her, he followed her down, shifting to lie behind her.

Still joined.

Still murmuring those beautiful, mysterious words with his lips pressed to her skin.

Chapter 3

Aidan lay on his back and looked up at the starry night sky through the oculus. Outwardly he was calm and sated. Inside he was shaken to the core. He didn't know how to process the feeling of connection he felt with the woman curled up at his side.

As he'd slid inside Lyssa's lusciously tight body, the connection had been more than a dream, more than sex. He'd tried to make their joining no more than physical pleasure. He had turned her over, faced her away from him, and none of it had worked. The unrestrained anxiousness he felt around her hadn't dissipated with his orgasm. Now it was worse than ever, accompanied as it was by the knowledge that he would have to leave her, and once he did, he would never see her again.

His eyes closed on a ragged breath. She'd made love to *him*, not a fantasy. Not the Captain of the Elite. Not a Guardian with a lascivious reputation. Just Aidan Cross.

In all his life, he was certain she was the only woman to have ever done so.

The effect that knowledge had on him was startling. He'd been as lost to the sex as she was. He, a man who'd fucked literally countless women, had just had a sexual encounter unlike any other.

"So tell me." Her warm breath gusted across his skin. "What are these things you say I don't understand?"

"Lyssa . . ." He heaved out a sigh, and looked down at the top of her head. How could he tell her enough to keep her safe, but not enough to anger the Elders?

"Uh oh." She rose to look at him. "Let me guess. You don't date seriously, you're not looking for a girlfriend, no attachments. It's just sex."

It wasn't, but he could never tell her that. Instead he said, "I'm a Dream Guardian."

Her brows rose. "O-kay . . . That's a new one."

"The beach, this tent, your clothes, even the darkness— they are inventions of your mind."

"'Kay, I got that."

"I'm not."

"You're not what?"

"I'm not a figment of your imagination. You can alter my appearance to suit your desires, but that's the extent of your control over me. You can't make me do anything I don't want to."

"Yeah, I figured that one out already." Lyssa pursed her lips in thought. She offered a shaky smile. "So you're not a tall, dark, and handsome, drop-dead gorgeous sex god?"

Aidan's lips twitched with a withheld smile. "What color is my hair?"

"Black."

"All over?"

Lyssa ran her fingers through his chest hair, then dipped lower to cup his balls. "Yes. All over."

"And my eye color?"

Her eyes narrowed, then she leaned closer. "I'm not sure," she said finally, in a low, hesitant tone. "They look dark. I think the light's not good."

He reached out and caught her hand, then dropped it as if it burned him. That was her first sign that something was wrong. She saw his hands clench into fists and wondered what the hell was going on. "The lighting is fine."

"So I take it, that's not how you look?"

"No."

A shudder moved through her. She'd just made love to a man she couldn't see. It was so bizarre, she didn't know how she was supposed to feel. "What does a Dream Guardian do?"

"It depends," he said, his voice rough. "There are a lot of us, and we're divided into certain specialties. Each Guardian has their strengths. Some are tender and offer comfort to those who grieve or are deeply saddened. Others are playful and fill in dreams of sports heroes or reality television shows."

"I suppose you're one of the tender ones," she guessed, remembering his compassion and caring, and finding peace in that. She didn't know what he looked like, but she knew what type of man he was, and that's what really mattered.

Aidan stiffened beneath her.

Her brows rose. "What?"

"I'm Captain of the Elite Warriors," he said, as if that explained everything.

I keep the bad guys away, he'd told her that first night. But he'd been kind to her. Tender.

"What's an Elite Warrior?"

"I'm assigned to protect Dreamers who have recurring Nightmares."

"Like a bodyguard?"

"More like a military rescue."

"That's why you're so big."

He stared at her intensely. "I'm a large man, yes, but I don't know what you see when you look at me, Lyssa. Your dream is fabricating my appearance. Dreamers can't see Guardians. Your subconscious fills in the gaps."

"Oh." Lyssa sank deeper into the scarves. "Why do I need an Elite Warrior in my dreams? I don't have nightmares."

"The door you built is a formidable one. We had to come in, and I'm the muscle."

Her short laugh held no humor. "That's why you came back tonight? Because I wouldn't open the door to the other . . . Guardians?"

"Yes."

Her stomach knotted. She had totally believed that line about him worrying about her. "Why do they want to come in here so bad? There's nothing to see."

Aidan sat up and rested against a pile of pillows. Aside from the silver chain and stone pendant he wore, he was unabashedly naked. The most luscious masculine *animal* she had ever seen. Even as she applauded her imagination, she mourned that he wasn't real.

His male perfection was all in her head.

"Nightmares are real," he said. "Just not in the way humans have come to see them."

"Huh?" She waited for him to speak, and then listened with damp palms as he explained abbreviated space, space-time, and planes of existence in a voice devoid of inflection.

Since the Nightmares had discovered the human subconscious through the fissure created by the Elders, the battle was never-ending. The dreams created in the human mind had given Nightmares a new power source on which to thrive. Fear, fury, misery—these were easily aroused through dreams, and fed them so well.

"Too many times I've seen the dark circles under human eyes, the slumping shoulders, the weary shuffling stride." Aidan's hands fisted rhythmically in his lap. "Over the years the Elders have tried to close off the tiny crack between the Twilight and your world, but there's no way, Lyssa. We can only do damage control."

And here she'd thought she was an expert on dreams after a lifetime of struggling with hers. How little she knew.

"We fight back as best we can to protect you," he continued. "We've become phantasms, taking on the form and nuances of each individual subconscious."

Lyssa considered everything carefully, and then asked, "Why do I have to know all this? I'm assuming most people don't?"

"Most people don't," he agreed. "But you're stronger than most. You recognize all guises, and you can keep us out if you want to. I've been asked to convince you to open the door. Since you understand that this is a dream, which is rare, but not unheard of, I decided to give it to you straight."

"They just want to come in, look around, and see if there are any Nightmares lurking in here? Isn't that your job?"

Aidan was silent a moment, then, "They're looking for someone, Lyssa. They're not sure who they're looking for, but there are certain traits that raise alarm. You bear some of the traits. I worry that too many years of searching have made them overzealous. I want you to be careful when they visit with you. I would prefer that you reveal as little as possible without appearing suspicious. I'm telling you this because I want you to be prepared."

She nodded. "Okay. We should come up with a secret signal or something. If I start talking too much, you can warn me."

"Lyssa . . ." He inhaled sharply.

Her stomach churned when Aidan didn't say anything further, which said so much.

He wasn't coming back.

"I see." She'd felt his expertise in his touch, had tasted it in his kiss, would have been fucking him blind right now if she hadn't needed a few minutes to recover. The man knew his way around a woman's body. "Is seduction part of your job, too?"

His jaw tightened. "Sometimes."

She winced at the sharp pain she felt in her chest. "A lover and a fighter."

"A warrior," he corrected grimly.

"A man of many talents." Blowing out her breath, Lyssa rolled away from him and crawled to the edge of the bed, hiding her quivering lower lip. "Go ahead and tell them I'll let them in."

She felt him move behind her, and then his large hands were on her shoulders. A moment later his lips were pressed to her skin. She jerked away and left the bed entirely, wishing there was a robe or something to cover herself with. To her surprise, one appeared on the chair by the door, and she caught it up before she stepped outside . . .

. . . where the sun was shining on a sandy beach. Frozen in place with surprise, she was galvanized into movement when she heard Aidan approaching.

She pictured a thatched-roof bar a little ways up the beach and strode toward it rapidly. She needed a drink. Bad. "I think I've got the hang of this dreaming thing. Thanks for your help."

"Perhaps it was fear that held you back," he said behind her, following. "At some point the Nightmares must have really frightened you. You chose the safety of darkness and the door over your dreams."

"Good to know. Guess I'm cured." When he materialized before her, she screamed and jumped back. "Damn it, you scared the shit out of me! Don't do that."

Aidan's dark gaze roiled with powerful emotions she couldn't identify. "Don't turn away from me after what we just did."

The simple statement started a quiver in her belly that expanded into a full-fledged shiver of awareness. All she wanted in the world—this one and her own—was to step into his embrace and feel safe while she sorted this all out in her mind. But she was feeling things she shouldn't be. Longing, possessiveness, desire . . . it would only get worse the longer he stayed. "What do you want me to do, Aidan?"

Something hot flickered in his eyes when she said his name. "Come back inside. We still have time."

"No." Her voice was shakier than she would have wished. Despite the short length of their association, he had been her comfort, her rock to lean on. Losing him was going to be painful. It already hurt. "It would be better if you just left."

"Why?" he asked through gritted teeth.

"I'm not into pity fucks." She actually heard his teeth grind, and she was glad. Her emotions were all out of whack; it was only fair that his should be, too. "I've been protecting myself just fine over the last however-many years. I don't need you to screw me into the Twilight, or whatever the hell it is you do."

His nostrils flared. "You're upset. I sympathize. But you know that's not the reason we had sex."

"I do? Hmm . . ." She turned around and pictured her hut bar in the opposite direction.

"Lyssa—" His grip stopped her so fast, she was yanked to a halt.

"Lyssa! For god's sake, wake up!"

Violent shoving brought her to the awareness of her mother's voice and her taupe-colored living room.

"Okay, okay," she muttered, rubbing her eyes.

Her mother hovered over her. "Christ, Lyssa! You scared me to death."

"Huh?"

"You've been asleep for almost twenty-four hours without moving a muscle. I had to check on you every hour or so just to make sure you were breathing!"

Closing her eyes, Lyssa sighed and stretched, finding every muscle sore from hours of being in the same position.

"I slept in your bed last night because I was afraid to leave you."

Her mother had fussed and poked at her most of her life, searching in vain for a physical cure for what Lyssa had always suspected was a mental ailment.

"I'm okay, Mom." And for the first time in years, she really felt as if that was true. She wasn't sure why she felt that way; she just knew that she did. Like something was settled or resolved. A long-standing question answered. "What time is it?"

"Just after eight."

"Ugh!" Tossing off the chenille throw, Lyssa stood with a grimace. "I'm going to be late for my first patient if I don't get going."

"How the hell can you even think about going to work when you were a vegetable only a minute ago?" The effect of the chastising hands on her mother's hips was ruined by bed-head.

"Work's all I've got left, Mom. I'm not letting that go to hell along with my health and my love life."

"I'm calling your doctor and telling him he needs to run more tests."

Lyssa was already halfway up the stairs. "No way."

"If you don't agree to a checkup, I'm not letting you go to work."

"Mom . . ." She glared down the stairs, but the stubborn set of maternal jaw told her arguing would be pointless. "Fine," she conceded grudgingly, "but you have to make me coffee, too."

A shower and three cups of java later, Lyssa was speeding out of her condo complex on her way to work. It was still a bit foggy and gray in the valley, with a slight chill in the air that invigorated her. She didn't feel rested as she had last week, but she didn't feel as if she was going to fall asleep at the wheel, either. That fact alone started her day off on a lighter foot.

She was whistling when she pulled open the heavy steel door to the back of her clinic, and by the time she entered Exam Room One with its pretty blue and white striped wallpaper, Lyssa was full-on smiling.

"Good morning," she greeted, her eyes widening as her patient's owner turned to face her. "I'm Dr. Bates."

Tall with short-cropped dark hair, he was handsome and well-built, filling a loose pair of jeans and tight black T-shirt to perfection. The writing on the shirt betrayed his occupation as a fireman, a job she admired.

He shook her outstretched hand. "Chad Dawson." He gestured to the beautiful German shepherd who sat elegantly by his feet. "This is Lady."

"Hi, Lady."

Lady held out her paw for a shake.

"What a clever girl you are, Lady," she praised, glancing at the chart in her hand. "Shots, I see. I promise to be gentle."

Never one to torture her patients, Lyssa got straight to it and then offered a treat in reward. The whole time, Mr. Lady hovered nearby, his cologne a gentle presence in the room, his large body absorbing all the space. She was keenly aware of him and his undisguised interest, so when she finished notating the chart and prepared to move on to the next room, she wasn't surprised when he stopped her.

"Dr. Bates?"

"Yes?"

"I appreciate your care for Lady. She hates shots, and shakes like a leaf when we come to the vet."

Lyssa rubbed Lady behind the ears. "You were very brave, Lady. One of my best patients ever." She glanced up. "She's a wonderful dog, Mr. Dawson."

"Call me Chad, please."

She smiled, but her stomach did a little flip that was partly excited and partly panicked.

"I hope you don't mind," he began with a sheepish smile, "but I noticed you're not wearing a wedding band. Are you seeing anyone?"

The urge to say yes was strong and confusing. "Not unless you count grumpy cats."

His returning grin was dazzling. "In that case, I'd like to take you out to dinner sometime, if you're open to dating owners."

"I never have before," she admitted, "but there's always a first time."

She pulled a notepad featuring a pharmaceutical advertisement out of a drawer, and they exchanged numbers and set a date for the weekend.

Lyssa stayed in the room a short while after Chad and Lady left, trying to figure out why a date with a hunky fireman who liked dogs was making her sad.

Hidden beyond the edge of the Twilight, Aidan stared at the woman writhing on the bed. She keened softly, her naked body arching upward as she stroked her clit with one hand while thrusting two fingers deep into the drenched cleft of her sex with the other.

He barely blinked, refusing to look away, his mind urging his errant body to cooperate and become aroused. Around him, he felt and heard the Nightmares moving in, drawn to the energy the Dreamer was exuding into the Twilight. She was as vulnerable as it was possible to be, and it was his job to lead her to safety. But despite his sincere wish to help her, he couldn't find the tiniest bit of desire for the task ahead.

Sighing, Aidan closed his eyes and sent out a silent call for help. As the woman on the bed moaned in the beginnings of a climax, he felt a presence at his side.

"I was coming to find you anyway," said the laughing voice next to him.

"Oh?" Shooting a sidelong glance at Connor, Aidan tried not to look too relieved when his friend began to strip with obvious anticipation.

"I was assigned to your Dreamer tonight, Cross. I figured once you knew, you would want to swap again. You've been giving me all of your sexual assignments for weeks, but I strongly suspected you'd want to have another dream with her. And you need it, man. Bad."

Aidan tensed as emotions he didn't understand flowed through him. "Lyssa Bates?"

Connor nodded, and rubbed his hands together. "Whatever your fascination is with her, I hope it lasts awhile longer. Trading places with you rocks. Now, if you'll excuse me . . ."

The other Guardian stepped into the dream and his outward appearance instantly altered to suit the woman he approached. Aidan turned away and departed swiftly, his thoughts once again fully consumed by the Dreamer he should never see again, but couldn't seem to resist.

A month had passed since he'd last been with her. A month of questioning other Guardians to find out who had spent the evening with her, and then grilling them about what had been said and what she was doing. She was seeing someone now, a man named Chad, and Aidan told himself it was best that her life was now back on track. He had tried to follow her lead and forget her, taking on assignments that would have distracted him in the past.

Nothing worked.

Now he moved through the Twilight with barely suppressed excitement, his heart racing at the prospect of seeing her again. The sweet tone of her voice and softly flowered scent stayed in his mind, as did the deep color of her eyes and the golden strands of her hair. But like a Twilight morning, the details were shrouded in mist and fading. If he gave it a little more time, he could forget.

But he didn't want to forget. For the first time in many, many centuries his blood ran hot, and for the first time ever his heart ached with yearning. He couldn't let her think she was only a job to him. Before he moved on, he needed her to know that he'd made love to her because he wanted to and for no other reason.

Lowering to the ground, Aidan paused before Lyssa's door. He wanted to hold her again, to be the recipient of her passion and seducing caresses. Did Chad benefit from such play? The thought burned, making him sweat.

She hadn't fucked the other man . . . yet. Aidan knew because he inquired every day.

Growling his anger at the thought, he reached for the shiny new handle that hadn't existed the last time he was here. He stepped inside without forewarning, and found the same beach he remembered from before. A short distance away, Lyssa swung in a hammock between swaying palm trees, her long legs revealed by the part in a sarong, her lush breasts barely restrained by the tiny triangle cups of a crocheted bikini top. In her lap, she held a drawing pad, and her lovely features were shielded by the wide brim of a straw hat.

Arrested by the sight of her golden skin and the loose strands of hair the tropical breeze blew across her glossy lips, he stood unmoving.

Why did she affect him this way? He was so eager for her, he could barely walk. A woman had been nude and masturbating before him, eager for a hard cock, and he'd felt nothing. *Nothing.* Just like all the other women he had avoided over the last month.

Steeling himself inwardly, Aidan walked toward her. As she raised her gaze to meet his, the wariness in her dark eyes tightened his chest. The trust she'd given freely when he'd bedded her was gone, and he felt its loss keenly.

Sighing, she moved to a seated position and tossed her notepad to the sand. Kicking her lithe legs, she set the hammock rocking like a swing.

He came to a halt before her. "Hi."

"Hi," she said in a husky whisper, her dark eyes watching him carefully.

"How are you?"

"Fine. And you?"

The meaningless banter made his teeth grind. "Not so well."

"Really?" Her demeanor changed instantly, became more genuine, less stilted. It was her nature to feel concern for others. It was one of the reasons he liked her so much.

"I'm not supposed to be here, and I can't come back after tonight."

"Why?" The hammock slowed to standstill.

"There are laws." He stepped closer. "We are forbidden to form attachments to Dreamers."

"Oh."

"And I can't allow it to happen even if it were permitted. Not with my job being what it is."

Lyssa pushed up the brim of her hat. Her beautiful face so open, so revealing. "Are you speaking hypothetically?"

He shook his head.

"Are you saying it would be possible for you to form an attachment to me?"

"It's not just possible," he admitted gruffly. "It's highly likely."

Frowning, she turned her head to stare at the ocean. Aidan watched the fall of her sunlit hair as it cascaded over her bare shoulder. His mouth went dry and his fists clenched. The desire to rub those golden strands between his fingertips was nearly overwhelming.

"So why did you come then?" she asked, dropping to the sand.

"Because of the way we parted."

She returned her gaze to his.

"I couldn't let you think that what happened between us was part of my job."

Lyssa was so much shorter than he was, she had to tilt her neck back to study his features. "Thank you."

Her quiet dignity was too much for him. Closing the distance between them, he tossed her hat aside. Then he cupped her nape and kissed her. A hard, quick kiss. "I made love to you because I couldn't bear not to. Because I wanted to more than anything. I don't regret it, and I don't want you to regret it, either."

Her small hands circled his wrists. "I don't."

He rested his forehead against hers and breathed in her scent of soft flowers.

"I feel as if I've known you a long time," she whispered. "As if I'm saying good-bye to an old, dear friend."

"I will miss you, too," he admitted, before taking her mouth and kissing her deeply. A kiss that was meant to say farewell, a memento to last him an eternity. Then her taste, sweet and heady like wine, flowed over his tongue and intoxicated him.

"Lyssa." He groaned his misery and need into her mouth.

Her slender arms tried valiantly to encircle his broad shoulders, then gave up and slid down to embrace his straining back. All the while he drank the flavor of her, stroking his tongue between her parted lips as he wanted to do with his cock, sliding his callused hands down the smooth skin of her sides.

His eyes closed, Aidan tilted his head, fitting his lips to her softer ones, swallowing her whimpers with a shudder that wracked the length of his frame. She gave as good as she got, her hands sliding beneath his shirt, caressing his bare skin, her hips arching into him, the invitation blatant and tinged with the same desperation he felt.

When her tongue tangled with his, he pulled away with a curse, every muscle on fire with tension. He nibbled her jaw, licked and bit at her neck, distracted her as he cupped her full breast, kneading it, feeling it grow heavy with her desire. Impatient, he shoved away the fabric that intruded, and caught her nipple with his fingers, rolling it, tugging it, squeezing it with varying pressure.

"Yes . . ." she breathed, urging him to take all that he wanted, failing to see how starved he was for her, starved for the feeling of connection he had found with her.

Lowering his head, he took her in his mouth, her nipple a hard, silken delight. He suckled her with hunger, his cheeks hollowing with every drawing pull, his tempo rhythmic and designed to make her cunt clench for him, to make her ache as he did.

She cupped his ass, squeezed, urged him against her. Through the thin fabrics between them, he felt her heat, and he squeezed his eyes shut, his nose pressed to her skin so that every breath he took was Lyssa, a scent that would forever be imprinted on his memory.

Sadness welled within him, and he lifted his head. How much worse would his attachment be if he took her again? Already all other women had lost their ability to entice him.

Her eyes fluttered open. With her ravished mouth and swollen nipple, she was a picture of wanton abandon. He could lower her to the sand, and free his cock. A quick tug would pull her swimsuit aside, allowing him to sink into her creamy depths. In all his life, he had never wanted anything as much.

"I'm afraid of what will happen," she breathed, her chest rising and falling with her labored breathing, "if we make love again. I want more, Aidan."

Pulling her tight against him, Aidan rested his cheek on the top of her head. "I'm sorry I can't give it to you."

He forced himself to release her, to relinquish her warm, curvy body. Forever.

She righted her swimsuit and looked at him with big, dark eyes. "I'm happy you came, even though you can't stay."

His thumb caressed the curve of her cheekbone. "Good-bye, Lyssa."

"Good-bye."

Turning on his heel, he left her.

He felt her watching him all the way until the door shut and became an impassable barrier between them.

Chapter 4

"You have broken one of our most sacred laws, Captain Cross." The sea of gray-shrouded faces before Aidan nodded as one. "We do not choose the assignments given to Guardians lightly. It is not your place to reassign yourself and others to suit your own needs."

He stood impassive, his hands laced at his back, his stance wide as if prepared for a blow, which he was. He'd known the risks when he went to Lyssa. He had accepted them in return for a few moments with her, and the price was worth being able to hold her as he had.

"You set the example for others," the Elder continued. "Any transgressions on your part can start a chain of disobedience. Because of this, you will spend the next fortnight at the Gateway."

He flinched inwardly. The contrast of his new assignment to the joy of Lyssa's presence was similar to the contrast between hell and heaven.

But perhaps his time at the Gateway would be good for

him. He certainly would not have the luxury of thinking of her there.

"You will begin immediately, Captain."

He bowed before turning on his heel. Having expected some onerous task, he had dressed for battle, and his glaive hung securely in the scabbard that crossed his back. His boots tapped ominously on the marble floor as he left the *haiden* and descended the steps to the open courtyard. Around him, casually robed Guardians stared. Some furtively, others openly. He'd broken a law that had not been broken in centuries, and everyone wanted to know what the punishment would be for so grave an offense.

With a leap, he departed, gliding rapidly through the misty Twilight toward the reddish glow that illuminated the tops of a distant mountain range. As always, he was grateful for the hours-long length of the journey. It allowed him time to sort his thoughts, and then clear them away. At the Gateway, Guardians could think of nothing besides maintaining their grip on their glaives and ignoring the exhausted burning of their muscles. There would be precious little rest and food over the next two weeks. All Guardians who wished to join the ranks of the Elite were required to spend a month at the Gateway. The vast majority failed in that task.

Once every century he returned, as all the Elite did, to remember how vital their task was. The stay was only a few days in duration, just enough to reinforce, but not enough to lose hope.

Two weeks would seem an eternity.

He paused at the top of the range and stared down at the horrors below. The vast door to the Outer Realm bulged with the effort to contain the Nightmares within. A mere crack of red revealed how the portal strained at the hinges and lock. From that tiny opening, black shadows flowed like water, pouring out and infecting the Twilight around the Gateway until lava-spewing pustules formed from the ground. Guardians by the thousands fought an endless battle, their glaives flashing with ruby light as they cut down Nightmares in countless numbers.

Misery and despair was a fetid stench in the air. His stomach roiled, but that, too, was thrust away from his thoughts. Descending the rocky cliff face while cutting a swath through the flood of shadows, Aidan tried to ignore the screams the Nightmares made just before they burst into puffs of foul-smelling ash. Their cries were high-pitched, a near whine that sounded like a child's call for help. It was a horrifying sound that could drive a man mad, and it battered him from all sides.

The Guardians at the bottom noted his approach and began to fight with renewed vigor, taking comfort in his presence. Their regard depleted him, sapped his strength, weighted him down. He could not show fear or hunger or exhaustion in front of the others, and the energy required to maintain the façade had long ago become too draining.

Suddenly the plan to forget Lyssa in this hell was forgotten. Instead her memory floated above all others, a shining beacon of hope and happiness until all he thought of was her, and how he could be himself with her, take comfort in her, as he could with no one else. She was the power behind every swing of his glaive, every gasping breath, every growl that tore from his throat.

She was the hope he had thought long dead, the goal to reach, the dream to work toward. It was no longer the Key.

It was *Lyssa*.

The door pushed open on well-oiled hinges. It was a near soundless whoosh of air, but as had happened every day for the last two weeks, the hairs on Lyssa's nape rose and her muscles tensed. Her entire body was anxiously awaiting the return of the man who stirred it so thoroughly, a man who never came.

She stared down at her drawing pad and forced herself to relax. Against her back, the bark of an oak tree pressed into her skin. Around her, a green meadow with yellow wildflowers swayed gently in a softly fragrant breeze. Nearby, a stream flowed. Though she loved the beach more, she couldn't find it in her heart to imagine herself there again. The beach was Aidan and lust and longing, things she wanted desperately to feel, but refused to allow herself to. He would not return, and hoping for what would never be was a wasted endeavor.

Still, she felt him. The power and strength he'd given to her with his caring had made her surroundings possible. Without him, she would still be sitting in the dark, going crazy.

She sighed and went back to waiting for the night's Guardian to appear, telling herself that she had to move on and be grateful for what she had shared with Aidan, even if she still wanted more.

His people were an odd bunch, approaching her so cautiously, clearly uncomfortable with their inability to integrate themselves seamlessly into her dream world. The Guardians requested that she perform odd exercises, but she remembered Aidan's admonishment to reveal nothing of importance. She never complied or showed them the skills she practiced when she was alone. They, in turn, never revealed very much about themselves. It was a bizarre arrangement, and she couldn't help but wonder how long it would go on.

She also couldn't help but wonder where Aidan was, and what he was doing. Was he fighting with his sword somewhere? Or living out some woman's fantasy?

The last thought made her shiver with a cold chill that swept across her skin in a wave of goose bumps. It was then that she lifted her gaze and saw him.

Aidan.

She blinked to make certain it was he, and when his lusciousness didn't disappear, her heart raced with joy.

He entered her dream with that carelessly arrogant stride she loved, but there was something different about him . . . an invisible mantle of great weight that seemed to hang on his shoulders. His chiseled features—so harshly, blatantly gorgeous—were set in hard, unyielding lines. His eyes cold. His steps relentless as he passed her and went to the stream.

He began to strip off his garments, which were blackened by ash and singed in places. The golden skin of his back was bared to her hungry gaze, and then an ass so perfect it made her want to weep in awe. Still he said nothing. Lyssa struggled to think of something to say.

Instead she made the stream deeper and the water warmer, and put soap on the pebbled bank to assist his bathing.

She widened the blanket she rested on and pictured a picnic basket. Then wine. All the while she watched him, her blood heating and then becoming sluggish with desire. His large hands soaped his chest, gliding over mouthwatering pecs and ridged abs, his biceps flexing and bunching with latent power.

He was a sexual fantasy brought to life. The sight of him did crazy things to her nervous system, but what most affected her was the desolation in his blue eyes. What had he seen? Where had he been? His clothes and demeanor made it seem as if he'd gone to hell and back. What had they done to him to make him so . . . *empty*?

When Aidan sank beneath the surface to rinse his hair and then reemerged, the sunlight caught the droplets on his skin, turning him into some ancient pagan god. Dripping and unabashed, he stepped naked onto the bank and made no effort to retrieve his clothes. She drank him in, every inch of his tawny skin, her gaze lingering on the heavy cock and balls that were impressive even without an erection. He sank to his knees beside her and then caught her close before rolling to his back.

They lay there, his embrace laced with an underlying possessiveness that thrilled her. His breath was hot at her crown, his hands kneading her spine. Inhaling the clean scent of his damp skin, Lyssa stroked his chest in a rhythmic, soothing caress and felt at peace for the first time since he left.

"It was selfish of me to return," he said finally, his soft brogue making her nipples ache.

"If you need something from me, I want to give it to you."

"I'm going to hurt you, but I couldn't stay away."

Lyssa lifted her head and made a soft moue at the torment so evident in his features. "Why?"

Why would he hurt her? Why couldn't he stay away?

"I need you," he whispered hoarsely.

"I'm here." She ran her fingers through his damp hair, then toyed with his pendant. "Tell me what happened."

His large hand slid up to cup the back of her neck, and then pulled her down to his waiting lips. "I ache for you."

He took her mouth with a deep glide of his tongue across hers.

"Aidan . . ." She sighed, her craving for him nearly unbearable.

"Do you love him?"

She blinked in surprise at his question, but didn't misunderstand. "Chad? No. We're just friends, although he would like to be something more, and I'm considering it."

"Then let me have you again, one more time, before he takes you from me."

The raw plea made no effort to hide within the brogue. That he should need her so much . . . that he would come to her despite the rules that said he shouldn't . . . that he would open himself to her so completely, broke open something inside her.

She had heard tales of his prowess from the other Guardians. She knew how fearsome he was, how powerful. He was a near legend among his people, held up as a model for others to emulate. Captain Aidan Cross was said to have no weakness, no qualms, only a single-minded pursuit of the destruction of his enemy.

But that wasn't true. She knew him to be sensitive and kind, in his own brooding way.

His solitary house on the hill, far away from the nearest community, told her how he kept to himself. He was estranged from his family. Reclusive and alone, he was said to be a far different man from the one who had graduated from Elite training with unbeatable scores and boundless optimism for the future.

He leaned on no one, yet he reached out to her.

"What can I do?" she asked, lost. This was not a medical problem with textbook answers. This was a wound to the soul, and she had no clue how to treat it.

"Touch me." As he caught her hand and held it over his heart, his gaze locked with hers. "Seduce me. Like you did that first night on the beach."

For a breathless moment she stared at him. Her fierce warrior retained his humanity, his generosity of spirit, his capacity for kindness. Perhaps it was because of his ability to feel and empathize that his calling wounded him so deeply.

Self-preservation be damned. He needed her, and she would do whatever was required to make him whole again.

She crawled over him, her hips pressed to his, her hands on his chest, her only desire to tend to him and console him. Bending at the waist, Lyssa licked his lips. "Like this?"

"Yes . . ."

Her fingertips found the flat points of his nipples and rubbed. "This, too?"

He shivered, the sensation traveling up her arms and

heating her blood. "Hell, yes . . ." His eyes drifted shut.

Her lips to his ear, she asked, "What's your favorite color?"

There was no hesitation. "The color of your eyes."

She blinked, startled. "They're shit brown."

"They're beautiful," he murmured, stroking her back in a rhythmic caress. "I look into them and forget everything."

Melting inside, she realized his tenderness was the catalyst her dreams had been missing her whole life. Only when she was with him did she feel the peace she needed to rest and recharge.

She imagined away her clothes, leaving behind a chocolate-colored lace bra and thong set. In her waking life, she would never wear such an impractical bit of nothing, but this wasn't her waking life. Aidan was the man of her dreams, in every possible sense.

Wiggling her hips, she let him feel her suddenly bare skin against his rock-hard cock. "How about this?"

When his thick lashes lifted, she found herself staring into fathomless blue of such stark intensity, her heart skipped a beat.

"I'm not leaving this time." His tone was a warning.

"You better not," she retorted. Reaching up, Lyssa cupped her breasts through her bra, kneading them, her thumbs and forefingers pinching her erect nipples.

"Tease," he growled, his eyes half lidded with lust.

"Look who's talking, Mr. Get-Her-Hot-and-Leave."

A smile tugged at the corner of his beautifully sculpted lips. She traced their shape with a fingertip, admiring their perfection. As her mind filled with images of what she

wanted him to do with that mouth, a sharp flare of awareness spread across her skin, making her sweat.

"I'll do all of that," he murmured, cupping her bare buttocks in his hands and squeezing. "And so much more."

"Not fair that you can read my mind, but I can't read
yours."

"You'll enjoy it better if I *show* you what I'm thinking."
His voice was pure sin and sex.

Restless and achy, she wiggled deeper into his touch.
"How much time do we have?"

"Not enough." Aidan rolled and lay beside her, one hand
supporting his head, the other running along her side.

She laughed and pushed his hands away.

"You're ticklish." This time his smile broke free and
transformed his features.

Amazed, she touched his face because she couldn't bear
not to. "Christ, you're gorgeous."

The smile faded, and she remembered—what she saw
was not who he was. He was an alien.

A sudden chill moved through her, making her shiver.
Noting her discomfort, Aidan pulled her closer, sharing his
warmth, and then she didn't care about the fact that they
came from different dimensions.

"It doesn't matter, Aidan." Lyssa parted her lips in blatant invitation for a kiss, which he obliged with a tempered
hunger that made her whimper and grow damp between
her thighs.

"You could look like a troll and have antennae," she
gasped when he allowed her to breathe, "and I'd still want
you."

"Why?" His arched brow refuted her claim.

"Because of the way you hold me, and the way you make me feel." Tossing her leg over his hip, Lyssa pushed him to his back and came over him again. "You really don't have antennae, right?"

He grinned, and her heart stopped. "Right. Guardians are very similar to humans."

She licked the tip of his nose, then his lips, then his nipple, which hardened beneath her tongue. "I wanted you when it was dark in here," she whispered. "Just as much as I want you now."

Sliding lower, she followed the happy trail of silky hair down the rippling muscles of his abdomen. He tensed and arched into her mouth, his hips thrusting in demand, making her feel every silken inch of hard cock between her breasts.

"Want me to go lower?" she asked, knowing damn well he did.

"I want you to make love to me. In whatever way you want."

Make love to me.

Startled at his choice of words, she looked up the length of his torso to meet his gaze. Seeing the austere vulnerability in his handsome features, Lyssa's eyes burned with tears, making his visage blurry. Suddenly their intimacy felt intensely, hauntingly personal.

It would kill her when he left. She didn't know how she would bear it.

But he was worth it. Where he was concerned, she'd take what she could get and be glad of it.

"I've come to realize that I feel the same," he murmured in that deep rumble she loved.

Aidan looked up at the blond beauty who lay atop him and was content for the first time in centuries. He felt the depth of Lyssa's affection in every glance, every touch, every word she spoke, and he hungered for it. Needed it.

"Hurry," she said urgently, as impatient as he was to be connected in every way possible.

He reversed their positions and ripped away the tiny scrap of lace that held her thong to her hip. Taking her mouth with fervent intensity, he reached between her legs and found her slick and hot. His cock jerked in eagerness to be inside her, to be one with her so that nothing could keep them apart.

With reverent fingers he parted her, finding her clit and stroking it with cream-coated fingers, coaxing it from its hood. She moaned into his kiss, her legs falling open, her body undulating in rhythm with his touch.

Leaning his weight on one arm, Aidan settled his hips between hers, his fingers leaving her swollen sex to take his cock in hand. He used the head of his dick to tease her, to arouse her, rubbing it through the liquid evidence of her desire. All the while his tongue fucked her mouth in a deliberate imitation of what was to come. What he longed for more than his next breath.

And he wasn't alone in his rampant hunger. Lyssa gave as good as she got.

His thoughts were filled with the lewd and lascivious dialogue she was having in her mind, cravings so raw they drenched his skin with sweat. He'd discovered that facet of her sexual desire the first time they made love. Lyssa thought of sex in language so carnal, his balls drew up, aching to be emptied inside her. Her hands clenched and unclenched convulsively at his sides. He snatched one of her wrists and made her grip his cock.

Tearing his mouth from hers, he bit her earlobe and growled, "Feel how hard you make me? I'd have to ride you for days to get my fill. Nonstop, deep, hard fucking."

Lyssa's chest heaved with labored breaths and her skin became as hot as his, then hotter, so that it burned him. She was his oasis, his angel, but when it came to sex with him, she liked it just the way he did—no holds barred. No barriers. Just pure, raw carnality binding them together.

"And you're so tiny," he taunted, feeling her desire swell as mental images acted out the words he spoke. "Your cunt so deliciously tight. I can't wait to feel that again . . . The way your pussy grips my cock as I work it into you . . ."

She turned her head and bit his neck with no gentleness, just before she lifted her hips and sucked the pulsing head of his dick just barely inside.

"Start working, then, tough guy," she challenged, breathless.

Aidan shuddered violently as her drenched, hungry pussy closed tight as a fist around him. The control he'd felt just a moment ago fled, replaced by unadulterated lust. He gritted his teeth and began to pump his hips slowly, feeling her soft-as-velvet walls struggle to expand and take his cock.

Her head fell back and she moaned. "Ah god . . . you feel amazing."

He wanted to reply, but couldn't speak. So many women, so many years . . . None of them had ever taken *him*. His duty was to fill in dreams about other men. He was never himself, only a phantasm of someone else. Even when he'd lain with other Guardians, it wasn't Aidan they wanted, but Captain Cross. The legend, not the man.

No one knew how he'd come to hate that disconnection, how empty his life seemed to him now, how satisfaction with a job well done eluded him. Because it was never done. It was endless.

I wanted you when it was dark in here, Lyssa had said.

He believed her.

She was the only one who knew him. She was the only lover who wanted *him*. The woman who used adoring fingertips to stroke *his* skin, who shifted her hips to make *him* more comfortable, who whispered her encouragement with no shame or insecurity.

"Yes . . ." she breathed. "Give it to me."

He swiveled his hips and worked his cock deeper into her, his entire frame tensed against the pleasure that threatened to unman him.

All the agony of the last two weeks fell away, the hard knots in his shoulders and back loosening from the sensual heat. There was only this moment. The moment when he sank balls-deep into a juicy cunt that belonged to a woman he admired and longed for. A woman who made him smile, and touched him with such reverence.

Gratitude and affection closed his throat.

Feeling the shaking of Aidan's arms, Lyssa stared up into his flushed face and felt tears well. Deep inside her, he pulsed, every beat of his heart echoed in the throbbing of the hard flesh that filled her.

"I've missed you," she admitted, needing him to know that he was important to her.

His jaw tightened, and he nodded. She knew he had missed her, too. Not just because he was here again, but because she felt it radiating from him. His need and longing were tangible.

"Give me the top," she murmured, gripping his shoulders as he complied.

For a moment she stared, taking the time to absorb the feel of him beneath her and inside her. It was because of him that she couldn't move forward with Chad. Chad couldn't make her feel like this. Chad wasn't the voice that had found her in the darkness, or the strong arms that held her in sleep, or the quiet strength that made her feel safe. Aidan was her anchor.

"You were right," she said softly, lifting onto her knees, her eyelids growing heavy at the feel of his cock caressing her as it withdrew.

"About what?" His large body shuddered as she lowered again.

"About making love." Her hands stroked over the tops of his shoulders.

"Lyssa . . ." He laced his fingers with hers, supporting her as she began to ride him with greater urgency. She whimpered in pleasure.

"That's it," he crooned, watching her with intense blue eyes. "Take me any way you want."

Sweat beaded on his forehead as she began a steady rhythm of lifting and falling, stroking the thick length of his cock with the adoring clasp of her body. He was too big for her, his hips spreading her thighs wide enough that the lips of her cunt kissed the root of his erection with every deep lunge. A moan escaped, and then another, as she struggled to rub the spot inside that ached for him.

"I—I can't . . ."

Knowing what she needed, Aidan took over, releasing her hands to hold her hips as he pumped upward in steady drives. It was perfect, the way he moved, the variations in the depths of his thrusts, the circling of his hips. She could barely breathe, barely think, her body helplessly lost to his skill.

Leaning forward on all fours, she let him have his way, let him kill her with feeling and sensation, let him take her where he would. The sound of his luscious voice, husky with lust and purring heated sex words, made her cunt flutter along his cock, then clutch tightly in orgasm.

"Ah god . . .!" The cry that left her throat was not her own. She didn't know where it came from; it poured up from the same place as her pleasure, from deep within.

"Sweet Lyssa," he growled, his mouth to her ear as her arms collapsed, leaving her hips suspended by his strength alone. Now he took what he needed, using her body to satisfy his own, his face buried between her breasts, wallowing in her scent, as he drove upward into her spasming depths with long, deep plunges.

His entire frame convulsed when he came, the words he groaned were in some ancient language she couldn't understand. Except for her name. She heard it, heard the possessiveness in it, and she held him, rocked him, soothed him as he emptied himself inside her in hot, pulsing streams. Giving her all that he was. All that she wanted to keep.

But would be forced to lose when the night was over.

* * *

Aidan held Lyssa's damp body tightly to his, hearing the rasping of his own labored breathing, feeling her raging heartbeat against his chest.

Around them, the soft summer breeze blew, cooling their burning skin. How long had it been since sex had truly satisfied him? He couldn't remember. He knew only that it had never left him feeling like this.

"Aidan," she breathed in her soft, innocent voice, a sound filled with wonder and satiety.

"Hmm?"

She sighed and attempted to move off him. Unwilling to be separated, he turned carefully, keeping his cock buried deep inside her. Side by side they faced each other. He lifted a hand to brush the damp hair from her face, then pressed a kiss to her forehead. One of gratitude and joy.

This morning, death had been almost welcome. Exhausted and disheartened, the flow of shadows from the Gateway endless, he'd wondered why he should keep fighting. What good did it do?

Now it seemed so simple. His battle kept Lyssa safe, kept her alive and well. That was enough reason to go on.

It was then that the rustling sounds of papers in her drawing pad caught his attention. He reached over her, his intent to tuck it beneath the blanket, when a soft gust of wind flipped the page. His heart stopped at what he saw, his chest tightening in the viselike grip of pure fear. Everything faded away, even Lyssa, as he stared at her drawings with horror such as he'd never known.

Nightmares, the Gateway, endless years of death and war . . . None had struck terror in him like the sight of *his own face* staring back at him.

"Lyssa." His voice was low and gravelly, forcing him to clear his throat before he could go on. "Have you shown these to anyone else?"

"What?" She nuzzled into his throat, her lips brushing against his skin. Golden hair flowed across the arm he used to hold her close, hair that smelled of flowers and hard sex, a potent combination that stirred him deep inside.

"These pictures, have you shared them with other Guardians?"

"No." She pulled back, her dark eyes capped with a frown. "Why?"

"We must destroy them." His hands shook. *What can I do?*

"Why?" She lifted her head to look at the image with a soft, adoring smile. "I told you the lighting was bad. I couldn't make out your eye color in the candlelight. Your irises are such a deep blue, they looked dark. And your hair. The silver is so faint." She glanced at him. "But I like it. In fact, it turns me on."

He inhaled sharply. All this time it had been *his* appearance she enjoyed so much. Even as masculine satisfaction spread warmth through his veins, the ramifications of her unique cognizance spread goose bumps across his skin.

She winced. "Am I that far off from how you really look? I'm sorry. We'll tear them up and throw them away."

Everything he knew, all the work of his friends and the Elders, all his training . . . For one thing . . .

To kill the Key. A prophecy whose traits Lyssa displayed in abundance—she controlled the dream, she called him by name, she could see him. It was the last that was the most damning. That she could see into the Twilight. It was rare enough to find those Dreamers who recognized that they were dreaming and took control of the events. Never had they found a Dreamer who could see clearly into their world and comprehended that they were interacting with a real being. If the Elders learned of her abilities, they would kill her. Aidan himself didn't know what to make of the revelation.

But he'd think about it later. Right now he needed to find a way to keep Lyssa safe. Every time she fell asleep, she was in danger. Time was running out. If the Elders didn't know what she was capable of yet, they soon would.

"When the Guardians come to you, do they ask you to describe them? To draw them? Anything like that?"

"Yes. Weirdos." She wrinkled her nose. "I told them this isn't a dog show. I'm not jumping hoops."

Aidan hugged her tightly to him. He couldn't do a damn thing for her in the Twilight. By the time sleep brought her here, she was vulnerable. He had to protect her before she arrived. Before she fell asleep.

What the hell am I going to do?

If only there were more Guardians who harbored the same doubts he did, he could ask for their help. If enough of them approached the Elders as one voice, perhaps they would be heard. But if there were others like him, they guarded their thoughts as zealously as he had. As far as he knew, he was the only one to question the wisdom of the Elders.

She could lock herself in again . . .

But who knew how long it would take him to build support. She had been on the verge of losing her mind when he found her, a recollection that led him to a darker thought.

Perhaps she hadn't been hiding from the Nightmares. Perhaps all this time she had been hiding from him. From his kind. She'd been a child when she first erected the door. With her ability to see into the Twilight, she might have been frightened of the Guardians who came to see her.

What the fuck was he going to do? He couldn't take on both the Guardians and the Nightmares alone. If he couldn't alter the Elders' reasoning, there would be only one recourse.

He would have to leave the Twilight. He would have to protect Lyssa from the Outside.

There had to be a way to journey into her world. The Elders had created the fissure in abbreviated space that led them to this conduit. Surely they could do it again.

He was about to find out.

Despite the certainty he felt in his decision, he was aware of the ramifications. In addition to all the inherent risks, it would be only a temporary measure, a desperate tactic to buy Lyssa some time until he could figure out what to do. Figure out a way to convince the Elders of their grave error.

"You're thinking so hard, I can hear your brain ticking," she said dryly, nipping at his jaw with her teeth. "Are you really upset about my pictures? I'm sorry. I—"

"Lyssa, no." He cupped the back of her head and pressed a hard kiss to her forehead. "Don't be sorry. The drawings are wonderful. I'm flattered."

"Then what's wrong?"

"Everything, except you." He met her frown with earnest intensity. "When I leave, you're going to lock the door behind me, and you're not going to let anyone in. Not even me."

"Huh?"

His tone lowered, became more urgent. Even now, his skin crawled with the realization that Guardians were out there, hunting her with precision. "They'll come. They'll try to trick you into thinking it's me at the door, but it won't be."

"Aidan, you're scaring me." Her embrace tightened, saying without words that she trusted him to protect her.

He would die trying. For him, the legend of the Key was in doubt, but it was woven into the very tapestry of their lives. Guardians risked their lives in pursuit of the Key. There was no alternative to them or the Elders. The Key must be destroyed. No questions asked. By joining with Lyssa, he, too, would be hunted.

"Promise me you won't open the door to anyone."

"All right, I promise." She chewed her lower lip, her eyes shiny with unspent tears. "You're telling me I won't see you again, aren't you?"

"You'll see me again, Hot Stuff." He caught her face in his hands and kissed her with all the hunger she aroused in him. "But you won't know who I am."

Chapter 5

For an age now, the simulated lightening of the sky had filled Aidan with relief. It meant his shift was over. Another day had passed. He could travel up the hill to his home and try to forget that the endless days before him would be just like the last.

But today the incremental passing of time set his heart pumping in unsteady measure. He paced his covered porch like a caged animal.

Tick tock, tick tock. Like the clocks he had seen in the remembrances of Dreamers. In a matter of hours, Lyssa would fall asleep again, and someone would be sent to her. When she denied them entry, it would force the collective hand of the Elders and they would go after her en masse.

He had to find a portal between his world and Lyssa's, and he had to find it *now*.

The possible risks were no deterrent. Aidan was decided. There were no options, no choices. If he didn't go, Lyssa would die.

Where to begin? Aidan's curiosity had led to months of researching data in the Hall of Knowledge, and he'd found only vague references to fissure creation in a few of them.

Aidan didn't have months.

"You've got that look on your face," muttered a voice behind him.

Glancing aside, Aidan found Connor ascending the short steps to the porch. "I think I've found what some might consider to be the Key."

Connor reached the deck and shook off the dewy blades of grass that clung to his robe's hem. "I thought you said the Key doesn't exist."

"She doesn't." Aidan shook his head. "*It* doesn't. Or if it does, it sure as hell isn't Lyssa."

"Okay . . . ?"

"Lyssa can see me," Aidan explained.

Connor's eyes narrowed. "You're certain?"

"She drew a picture of me."

The low whistle that rent the still morning was filled with things that did not need to be said aloud—surprise, worry, and a heavy dose of chastisement. "I hope you're planning to step back and let the Elders take over. You should leave this task to someone else."

Aidan paused mid-step, his robes falling to rest around his ankles. "She is *not* going to die."

"Cross," Connor warned in a low tone, "stop thinking with your dick."

"You know she's not the Key," Aidan growled. "There's no way in hell Lyssa would open the Gateway. No way for her to even get there. Why should she die to perpetuate a myth?"

"Can you say with absolute certainty that it's a myth?" Connor ran his hand over his jaw. "You thought we'd never find a person with the traits, so of course it was all bullshit. But now you have found someone. If she's real, maybe the prophecy is, too. Are you willing to risk everything and everyone we know for a piece of ass?"

Clenching his fists, Aidan stared at his friend and felt the true weight of his convictions settle on his shoulders. If he didn't have Connor's support, he was completely on his own.

"She's not just a piece of ass. Say that again and see what happens."

"Awww, man." Connor flinched and shook his head. "You've never given any other woman a chance. This is the first time you've spent more than a few hours with one. Trust me. They're all great. If you want a steady fuck, any one of the single Guardians would volunteer. Shit, most of the partnered ones would, too."

"I'm sick of fucking."

Connor stilled, staring at him in obvious stupefaction. "Who are you, and what have you done with my best friend?"

Aidan's laugh was harsh. "You *know* me, Bruce. Would I put anyone at risk without a damn good reason?"

"Men aren't the same when they're pussy-whipped. You know that. You've seen it."

Walking to the end of the porch, Aidan set his hands on the wooden rail and watched as the sky grew lighter. *Tick tock.* He hadn't yet bathed, and the scent of hard sex clung to his skin. It riled everything primitive within him, while thrusting home how unique Lyssa's appeal to him was. Their time together was not something to be washed away and forgotten.

"Look around," Aidan said, his gaze moving over the rolling mountain view. "None of this is real. It's all an illusion to keep us sane in this conduit."

"And you think what you have with this Dreamer is 'real'?" Connor snorted. "It's a *dream*, Cross. It's all in your head. You've never touched her, kissed her, fucked her. You're living in two different worlds. *This*, at least, is filled with people you know are 'real.'"

How could he explain? How could he put into words how Lyssa's dream touch was so much more alive to him than another Guardian's?

"She's a veterinarian." Aidan faced his friend. "She has a way with animals and wounded souls. She loves pasta, especially when it's served with cream sauce and sun-dried tomatoes. She drives too fast and gets a lot of tickets, but she doesn't mind. 'You only live once.' That's her motto. She loves the beach and margaritas, and looks sexy as hell in a bikini. She's dating a guy named Chad and she likes him, but it's me she wants." The last made him smile.

Connor sank to sit on the top step and dropped his blond head in his hands. "Why are you telling me this?"

"Because she's not just a Dreamer, she's real. And when I'm with her, *I* feel real."

Blowing out a frustrated breath, Connor asked, "What will you do? It's not as if you can pull her from her slipstream and hide her."

Aidan rested his hip against the rail and crossed his arms. "I have to keep Lyssa from entering the Twilight."

"How the fuck . . .?" Scowling, Connor shot to his feet.

"No way! No way in hell. You don't even know how the Elders created the fissure the first time."

"They know. It's not as if I have a choice. I don't have enough time to do anything productive here. On the Outside, I can—"

"You can what? The answers you need are in here, not out there."

"Yes," Aidan said quietly. "That's true."

Connor's eyes widened. "You want to drag me into this?"

"I'm not asking you for anything. Except your discretion. But if you're feeling altruistic and decide to help me, I won't refuse."

"Cut the crap." Connor shot him a scathing sidelong glance. "I've always been your second. Damned if I'll stop now. Then it would be *my* fuckup instead of yours. And *this* . . . This, my friend, is all you."

Aidan's mouth curved with a grateful smile.

Descending the three short steps to the front lawn, Connor began prowling in obvious frustration. He moved with a warrior's grace, despite his massive size, the weight of which compressed the grass beneath his feet and left a trail in his wake. "What do you need me to do?"

"After I leave, find a way into the Temple of the Elders and access the database. See if you can find a way to bring me back. I've got an idea that will allow me to work on this while I'm gone, but you're right. Most of what I'll need will be here."

"What's your plan for how you're going to reach your Dreamer?"

"It's a poor plan, but it's the only one I've got."

"Are you going to tell me what it is?"

"Well, I imagine I'll just grab an Elder and hold him hostage until he tells me what I need to do."

Connor jerked to a halt and gaped. "*That's* your plan? Man . . . she really fucked your brains out."

"Got a better idea, smart ass?"

"No." Connor kicked at the grass. "But it's a stupid plan. You have no idea if the Elders know what you're after or not."

"Well"—Aidan shrugged—"I'm about to find out."

Dressed for battle in loose trousers and tunic, Aidan slipped into the Temple of the Elders on silent feet. He moved within the shadows, ever conscious of the vids that recorded every visitor.

His chest rose and fell in steady rhythm, his heart slow and sure. He'd watched as the majority of Elders had departed, leaving behind the lone sentinel whose day it was to remain in secluded meditation. The single guard at the door was easily distracted by suspicious noises created by Connor, and Aidan slipped behind him and entered the cool, dark *haiden*.

Tick tock. In the deathly silence of the stone edifice, the relentless dwindling of time was inescapable.

Aidan traversed the long hallway that led to the *honden*— a separate part of the Temple complex he doubted had ever felt the feet of a Guardian. The floor beneath him began to waver, growing translucent, revealing a swirling kaleidoscope of colors. The part of him that questioned and researched everything wanted to linger and look, but his heart urged him forward.

He paused a moment on the threshold of an arched entryway, the hairs on his neck rising with acute awareness. The warning was clear, and he never doubted his instincts. When he leaped into the round room, he was prepared for the glaive that thrust toward him, knocking it aside with a perfectly aimed parry.

He had only a split second to note the walls lined with bound volumes and a large console that dominated the center of the vast space before the gray-robed figure lunged at him again.

"You trespass, Captain," hissed the voice from the shadowed depths of the cowl. Lunging forward, wide sleeves falling back to reveal pale but brawny arms, the Elder fought with surprising ferocity.

Which did not deter Aidan at all. Focused and determined, he was coldly calculated. He had no idea what fueled the Elder, but *he* was fueled by desperation. Since failure was not an option, he had nothing to lose.

Forward and back, spinning and arching away from gleaming glaives in a macabre dance, neither took the advantage. Aidan wondered at this, his chest heaving only slightly from his exertions, his body too fit to feel even a hint of fatigue. He needed the Elder alive, but the Elder had no discernible reason for returning the favor.

Soon the Elder, though skilled, began to tire. He was simply no match for an opponent who held a blade most hours and days of his life. He tripped on the hem of his robe and fell backward. As his arms flailed, his glaive flew from his hand and went skidding across the stone. Fighting for balance, he slapped his hand palm down on the surface of the center console, setting it ablaze in flashing lights.

Aidan froze in mid-swing as he saw the face revealed when the gray hood was dislodged.

"Master Sheron," he breathed, his sword arm falling.

Then he quickly raised it again, pressing the deadly point against the Elder's rapidly pumping carotid when he reached for the touchpad. "Don't."

"You must let me."

"No." Aidan studied his old teacher with wide eyes.

Pale skin, pure white hair, and pupils so wide and dark they swallowed the whites of his eyes altogether made the mentor he'd known look like a corpse of the vital man he once was.

"If you don't allow me to fix what I've done," Sheron rasped, "We will all die, including your precious Dreamer."

Aidan stilled, his gaze narrowing as a low rumble of sound permeated the soles of his feet and spread upward through his bones. "What the hell . . . ?"

"If you let me proceed"—Sheron lifted his chin in silent challenge—"I will tell you what you came here to learn."

Growling out a low breath and knowing he didn't have time to argue, Aidan nodded and stepped back, withdrawing his blade. The Elder immediately spun about and worked furiously at the console, eventually entering a combination of keystrokes that turned the flashing lights solid, then blue, and finally off.

Resting his palms on the edge, Sheron visibly collapsed with relief. "You don't have much time."

"Time for what?"

"Time to make it to the lake before your absence is noted."

"Explain," Aidan ordered curtly.

"You want to cross over." Sheron reached back and lifted his hood, once again hiding behind the veil of shadows. "Your increasing dissatisfaction has been obvious to us for the last few decades, and your infatuation with the Dreamer has been whispered about for weeks. Your actions today can mean only one thing—you want to be with her rather than do your duty here."

Lifting his arm, Aidan slipped his glaive into the scabbard that crossed his back. He released a deep breath, wondering if Sheron suspected the true reason he wished to leave. Without the benefit of reading the Elder's facial expressions, there was no way for him to know. The toneless, emotionless voice revealed nothing. "What do I have to do?"

"Search your conscience. You are our best warrior. Your loss will change the balance between Guardians and Nightmares considerably. Morale will plummet. A selfish choice, wouldn't you say?"

"Fuck you." Aidan crossed his arms. "I have given more than enough. I refuse to feel guilt for wanting something for myself. You hold no hesitation in sucking me dry, yet I'm selfish?"

The quick rise and fall of Sheron's chest was the only sign that he'd struck a chord.

"You will have to travel past the Gateway," the Elder rasped. "Beyond the rise you'll find a lake."

"Yes, I've seen it." Aidan felt his mentor's smile.

"Why am I not surprised? You were always overly curious."

"Go on. I don't have time to reminisce."

"When you get to the lake, dive beneath the surface.

You'll see light emanating from a cave. There is a grotto there, tended by two Elders."

"What are they doing down there?"

Sheron held out both hands, palms parallel. "In the space between waking and dreaming, there is the place where some humans come by force. They hover here, more awake than asleep, but not cognizant enough to comprehend. Once we thought the Key would come to us this way. Now we simply guard them from coming too far into this conduit. Nightmares are predators. They would use that tenuous tie if they could."

Aidan frowned, and then his eyes widened. "Hypnosis!"

"Yes." Sheron nodded his approval. "That is what the Dreamers call it."

"Is that how we entered here to begin with?"

"No."

Something in the Elder's tone gave him pause. "There is more than one way to make the journey?"

"There is only one way that will allow a lone Guardian to make the journey," came the evasive reply.

"How can I trust you to tell me the truth?"

"How can I trust you not to kill me now that you know?"

There had been occasions when he'd had to act based on faulty or suspect intel, but Aidan never liked it. This time he hated it. If he was sent in the wrong direction . . .

He caught the Elder by the elbow. "You're coming with me."

"You can't—"

"Yes. I can." He dragged him out of the room and down

the hall, making a quick stop at the private Elder library.

"What are you doing?" Sheron snapped, when Aidan went straight to the historical volumes that were omitted from the entirely electronic public Hall of Knowledge.

"Taking answers with me." His fingertips drifted over the spines until he reached the spot where he should have found the text chronicling the two years preceding and directly following their discovery of this conduit. "Where is it?"

"It was lost."

"Bullshit."

"It is lost to me," Sheron said dryly. "I have no idea where it is."

Aidan reached up, gripped the hilt of his sword, and withdrew it with quiet deliberation. "I need you alive, but I don't need you healthy."

"You throw aside centuries of living with Guardians who admire and respect you for a few hours spent with a Dreamer?"

"You allowed my discontent to fester with your secrets." Aidan pressed the tip of his blade into Sheron's chest. "Now tell me, Master, where did the Elders hide the volume I seek?"

"Never. You may have abandoned your people, but I will not."

"As you wish." Aidan grabbed Sheron, and dragged him out into the hall and back toward the control room.

"What are you doing?"

"We're going to bang on the console a bit, get those lights flashing and alarms ringing. Then we'll head toward the lake."

"You cannot do that!" Sheron began to struggle, his eyes wide. "You will destroy everything."

"Hey, you're the one who said I abandoned my people. What do I care if you all blow up like a supernova or whatever the hell it is that's going to happen? I'll be on Earth with my Dreamer."

"Damn you."

Aidan's brows rose. "What'll it be?"

Sheron inhaled harshly, then he gestured back at the library with an impatient jerk of his hand. Once returned to the vast room, the Elder moved to a case of ancient medical texts and withdrew several, exposing a small door behind them, which, when opened, revealed the volume Aidan sought.

Collecting it from Sheron's outstretched hand, Aidan slipped it into the pouch strapped to his thigh and sealed it. "Right. Let's go."

Together they walked out to the *haiden*, where he sent out a low whistle that rose and fell in deliberate rhythm. A moment later, the same sound was returned to him. Connor would follow at a discreet distance.

"There are more than one of you," Sheron said flatly.

"Nope. Just me." Aidan reached the outer courtyard and leaped into the upper Twilight, pulling the struggling Sheron behind him. Gliding rapidly through the mist, he put every ounce of power he had into achieving the fastest possible speed.

The sky was beginning to darken when they reached the lake. Aidan dived straight down, into the icy water that didn't heat even though he wished it to. Beside him, Sheron stilled, allowing them to slice through like a blade. It took a moment to find the grotto, and then they emerged, gasping.

Aidan's first impression was of moss-covered black rock, but a closer inspection showed there was no subterfuge here. As he crawled up over a shallow ledge, he pulled Sheron out of the water after him, his gaze moving swiftly over the circular console manned by one very startled Elder-in-training. At a nearby desk, another trainee leaped to his feet. Above their heads, scenes flashed like movies, glimpses into the open minds of thousands of hypnotized people.

He stood, his hostage dripping, and moved to the other men with rapid, near running strides. Aidan shoved Sheron into the man at the desk, effectively knocking them out of the way, freeing his arm to swing forward with punishing force.

The sickening crack of his fist to the jaw of the trainee at the console was loud and echoed, causing the other to cry out and lunge at him. A quick crouch and upward thrust of his body threw the man back and into the rock wall, where he was rendered as unconscious as his partner.

Rolling his shoulders, Aidan straightened his tunic and caught Sheron with a steely glare. "Get to work."

Unfazed, the Elder moved to the console and sat in a metallic swiveling chair that was anchored to the stone floor. "We have to catch a Medium when they are at their deepest state. You will attach yourself to their subconscious, and ride the slipstream into their plane of existence. Once there, the temporal disturbance created by your appearance should cause a . . . hiccup in time. A brief pause that will allow you to leave the area undetected. That is the theory, anyway."

"The *theory*?" Aidan arched a brow. "That's the best you can do?"

"It is not as if I have done it myself," Sheron pointed out.

Nodding grimly, Aidan asked, "Is there any way to choose a Medium who is near to her?" If he arrived on the other side of her world, it could be days before he reached her. He would not get to her before she fell asleep again. The thought of Lyssa dealing with the banging at the door and sinister-minded cajoling infuriated him and aroused possessive feelings he never knew he was capable of.

"Where is your lauded patience, Captain?"

"Running out," Aidan warned.

Sheron shook his head in silent chastisement. "Lucky for you, the Dreamer you want lives in an area of eccentrics. There is a high concentration of Mediums in California. Understand: once you go, there is no known way to return."

"Quit talking, and do it."

Aidan began to pace, his hands clasped at his lower back, his gaze wandering. Scattered across the nearby desktop were loose-leaf papers and open-faced books. He was about to turn away when an odd glare caught his eye. Wedged beneath the corner was a slim volume boasting a jeweled cover that betrayed its position. A quick glance at Sheron showed the Elder occupied and unaware.

Summoning the book, Aidan flipped through it silently,

recognizing the handwritten language of the Ancients. He was rusty, but was able to make out enough words to know the book was one he wanted to take with him. One page in particular gave him pause, the reference to "pausing abbreviated space" one of vast interest. Collecting a makeshift bookmark from the desk, Aidan saved the page and slipped the volume into his waistband where his tunic could hide it from view.

"Here," Sheron murmured. "You can catch this stream." He swiveled and set both hands on his knees. With his cowl thrown back, and his white hair wet and sticking out in all directions, he was an odd sight. But his facial features were familiar, despite their lack of coloring. The sight of them reminded Aidan of the time when they had been mentor and student, and he had been an idealistic youth with great hope for the future. That boy could never have foreseen this event.

"I beg you to reconsider, Captain. You are not the first Guardian to grow an unnatural attachment to a Dreamer. It can be resolved with time."

For a moment Aidan paused, giving his heart and mind a last chance to object.

In the end, he knew he was making the right decision. He hoped he had in his possession the secrets he'd been searching for. Either he would discover that the Elders were correct and he could resume his fight with renewed determination, or he would find out they weren't, in which case he could enlighten the others. He would be helping his people however he looked at it. He wanted to believe in the Elders, he truly did, but Aidan saw no reason for them to hide information that wasn't incriminating in some way.

And then there was Lyssa, a sweet, wonderful woman who didn't deserve to be dragged into this struggle. A woman who'd already suffered a lifetime of sickness and discomfort because of her dreams.

But what would he find in her plane? A world he knew only from dreams and a lover who would not remember him.

But the possibilities . . . the chance to be with Lyssa and explore the tentative bond they shared . . . to touch her, kiss her, make love to her for real. Skin to skin. The thought was an oasis in an endless existence that had long been as barren as the desert.

"You do not have to do something so drastic," Sheron said in a low, urgent tone.

"Yes," Aidan said with a wry smile. "I do."

Sheron watched Captain Cross move beyond the console to the various slipstreams that formed pillars of lights connecting the floor to the cavern roof. Without hesitation, Cross stepped into the stream he'd been directed to and vanished, gliding into the semidream state of the chosen Medium with an expertise born of eons of practice.

When Sheron was alone, he entered a series of keystrokes and reported, "Cross is gone."

"You did well, Sheron," echoed the collective voice of the other Elders. *"Perfectly executed."*

Tilting his head in acknowledgment of the praise, he moved to assist the fallen trainees. As he lowered to a crouch, his gaze moved to the nearby desk. "He took the book."

The feeling of satisfaction was tangible.

"Excellent."

He kept the knowledge about the other volume to himself.

Chapter 6

Aidan pushed himself up from the coarse carpet where he sprawled, groaning in pain. Every part of his body ached something fierce, even the roots of his hair. As he lifted his head, his gaze searched the room, taking in the pale yellow walls and the two people who sat just a few feet away. They were frozen in place, trapped in a single moment of time.

There was a portly man with one ankle resting on the opposite knee and a notepad in his lap, and another lying on a chaise, eyes closed, his stream of consciousness the vehicle Aidan had used to arrive.

Wincing with every movement, Aidan couldn't remember ever feeling this dreadful in his life. Lurching to his feet, he reached out and caught the edge of the nearby desk, sucking in deep breaths as the small room spun violently.

A slow, soft click sounded loudly in the room.

Aidan looked at the clock on the wall, understanding

that one second had passed since he'd arrived. Time was beginning to recover, which meant he didn't have long. He knew a guy with a sword wasn't going to go over well here.

Shoving his physical discomfort aside, he moved to the nearby closet, which was distinguished by its smaller door compared to the two that flanked it. Inside, he found several garments covered in dry-cleaning bags.

A quick glance over his shoulder confirmed that the hypnotist was about the same height, but while the man—at rough guess—weighed similarly, his body was mostly fat. Still, the extra large clothes looked as if they might fit, so Aidan grabbed a pale blue shirt, dark blue pants, and belt, then quickly left the room.

In the reception area, a young woman was paused in the process of stuffing envelopes. Looking over her shoulder, Aidan noted the return address—San Diego, California—and smiled. Sheron had done remarkably well considering how short a time the Elder had been given.

Reaching beneath the desk, Aidan caught up the burgundy leather purse there and rifled through it, withdrawing a hundred dollars' worth of various denomination bills and a set of car keys. He wrote a simple "Thank you" on a piece of paper, slipped it into her wallet, and set the bag back where he'd found it.

Outside the office, in the nondescript hallway that led to the elevators, Aidan found a restroom, where he changed clothes. The overly large pants necessitated some alteration of the belt to secure them around his lean hips, but this took only a moment, and he was quickly on the move. He kept everything with him, refusing to be in a strange world without his accoutrements of battle. The subsequent long trip down the stairs in his weakened state nearly did him in. He stopped often, holding the rail and gasping, while willing his uncooperative body to function properly.

Tick tock. Time was still passing for him, despite what the clocks said, and he needed to reach Lyssa before nightfall.

By the time Aidan reached the lobby, time was advancing full speed ahead. The elevators were once again functional, and humans scurried industriously through the foyer that led to the outside. He wondered if anyone would stop him and question the scabbard he held at his side, but aside from blatantly appreciative female glances, no one paid any attention to his glaive. Clinging to the weapon with white-knuckled force, Aidan longed for the comfort the feel of the hilt normally imparted. While he wasn't afraid, he felt very much alone.

Lyssa.

He was assaulted by a variety of smells, some pleasant, some not. In dreams, this plethora of sensory input was muted or overlooked. Not so in actuality. The sounds of this world were many, a cacophony of voices and machinery that increased his nausea. He stumbled out the front glass doors with a desperate need for circulating air.

Using trial-and-error in tandem with the alarm remote on the key chain, Aidan located the early-model white Toyota Corolla, the interior of which smelled like something stale and burnt. Once he realized the hideous odor came from the ashtray, Aidan tossed the entire thing out the window. He'd shared postcoital cigarettes in dreams, but never had the true rankness of the habit been revealed to him.

Altogether, his first impression of the new world was not a positive one, which only made him long for Lyssa with a biting hunger.

A torn map, endless one-way streets, and drivers who couldn't stay in their lanes made getting to the freeway beyond frustrating, but Aidan was determined, and he used every bit of memory Dreamers had given him over the years to get on his way.

Toward the woman of his dreams.

"That sounds wonderful, Chad," Lyssa murmured into the phone while absently drawing doodles on her puppy-shaped notepad. "Really. But I'm not up for it tonight. I'm wiped out." Glancing up at the clock on the kitchen wall, she noted the time—six o'clock.

"Okay, forget the movie. I'll cook."

Sighing, Lyssa rolled her tense shoulders and dropped the pencil to rub the back of her neck. "Dinner sounds great, it really does, but it's been such a long day, and—"

The ring of the doorbell interrupted her.

"You work too hard, babe," Chad chastised softly. "You need to learn to say, 'Come back tomorrow. I've got a man who wants to be with me.'"

She smiled. He was so patient with her, never pushing her to give more than she was ready for. There were a couple of times she had been really close to inviting him to spend the night, but she couldn't shake the feeling that something was . . . *off*.

Had she now developed a fear of intimacy? Did the certainty that she wouldn't live to a ripe old age make her wary and standoffish?

"The mailman's at the door." Sliding off the stool at her breakfast bar, Lyssa stretched weary muscles. She *was* going to let Chad get close to her. No matter what. "Tomorrow's Friday. Wanna take a rain check for Saturday?"

Chad's frustrated exhale sounded across the lines that connected them. "Yes. Saturday. For sure."

"For sure. I promise. See you then." She set the receiver back into the cradle and crossed her small living room to the front door. Jelly Bean fell into step beside her while rumbling a low warning.

"Kick back, attack cat," Lyssa scolded, knowing that JB would ignore her and hiss with his usual grumpy fervor.

The bell buzzed again, and she jogged the last couple of steps. "I'm coming." Lyssa turned the knob and pulled the door open. "Do you need me to sign or some . . . th-thing . . . ?"

Her voice stuttered into silence as her gaze lifted and met eyes of deeply intense sapphire brilliance. Well over six feet of pure, unadulterated, gorgeous male stood on her porch step.

She gaped.

He was so tall, so broad of shoulder, so overwhelming that he filled every inch of her doorway. The scent of his skin, something exotic and spicy and scrumptious, hit her at the same moment as the wickedly provocative curving of his sensual lips.

JB's grumbling came to an abrupt halt.

"Holy shit." Her hand clutched the doorknob with white-knuckled strength. She had to force herself to breathe. In and out.

His gaze slid along the length of her body as a hot, tangible caress. Her knees went weak. She stumbled, and he stepped into her personal space, catching her elbow and anchoring her upright.

"Lyssa."

She blinked, the shock of that low-timbered voice with its soft brogue flaring across her skin. She'd heard that voice before, had heard her name spoken by it, and the heated awareness of his touch was near painful in its acuteness.

The man on her doorstep was delicious. Impossibly so. Dark hair with silver-streaked temples, winged brows over eyes that devoured her, a firm jaw, and masterfully etched lips. A pale blue dress shirt was parted at the neck, revealing a light dusting of hair on a bronzed chest, and an opal-like stone hanging from a silver chain. Strong arms were revealed by rolled-up cuffs, arms that pulled her closer to that mesmerizing, erotically charged stare.

I've kissed him before.

No. She shook her head. She hadn't. There was no way she could forget a man who looked as he did. He was almost otherworldly handsome, a man who was too hard, too chiseled, too dangerously male to be truly beautiful. But he was damn close.

Swallowing hard, she parted her lips to speak. Instead, he bent his head and took her mouth. Her legs gave out beneath her, causing her to sink a few inches before he caught her close and lifted her feet from the tiled entryway.

A deep, hungry growl rumbled up from the man's chest, vibrating softly against her breasts, making her nipples ache. Dizzy and confused, she lifted her hands to push him away, but the scent of his skin intoxicated her. *I know him.* Her fingers slipped into the silky hair at his nape.

The expert slanting of his lips across hers made her shiver. He hummed a soothing sound and stroked the length of her spine, gentling his kiss. The soft glide of his tongue, the deep licks, the gentle urging of his hips that rocked his erection against her . . . She moaned into his mouth, *"Aidan."*

His name came out of nowhere, filled with yearning and heated demands.

"I'm here, Hot Stuff." As if he knew her. As if he had come here for her. And that endearment . . . She felt as if she'd heard it before. In *his* voice.

Her chest heaving with panting breaths, Lyssa closed her eyes and rested her cheek on his shoulder. Her breath gusted across his exposed throat, making him shudder and hug her tighter.

"I—I don't remember you," she whispered, inwardly certain they must have met—no, been *intimate*—at some point in her life.

He nuzzled his cheek against the top of her head and breathed deeply. "Don't you?"

"I don't . . ." The last time she had felt this disoriented was when she'd polished off a bottle of Captain Morgan with her best friend.

"I'll make the introductions, then." His voice was a rough caress. "You're Lyssa Bates. I'm Aidan Cross."

"You're Aidan . . . I'm crazy."

His chuckle rumbled upward and made her toes curl. Then he stepped into her house as if he had every right to, and kicked the door closed behind him.

Strangely secure in his embrace, Lyssa leaned back to look at him, which was a mistake. The look he gave her was richly sexual and warmly amused. It was affectionate and appreciative—a lover's look. He wrapped his fist in her hair and tugged her head back to lick and nibble at her throat. Overpowering her with the pure erotic heat he exuded.

She was not as surprised by his actions as she should have been. The gesture was deeply comforting, the touch of his lips to her skin as natural as breathing. He was so arrogantly assured, so confident of his right to touch her as he desired.

"I've lost my mind," she said with a sigh of defeat. "Finally."

"Hmm?" He nipped her earlobe.

"Or maybe I fell asleep and this is my dream? It would be totally okay to make out with hot strangers in dreams."

Aidan paused. "Totally okay to make out with *this* stranger."

"I've been reading too many romance novels with alpha males," she muttered. Then her tummy growled. Loudly. At first she thought it was JB, but no, he was rubbing up against Aidan Cross's legs and purring like a kitten. Which Jelly Bean had *never* done even when he *was* a kitten. The darn cat had been born grumpy.

They'd both gone crazy, which was oddly comforting.

"You didn't eat all day again?" Aidan chastised, scowling down at her.

"Uh, dream guys don't scold." As he set her away from him, Lyssa clung to his rock-hard forearms for balance. "I get enough of that from my mother."

"You need scolding to get you to eat regularly. You're

going to need your strength." He stepped back and then teetered. "Whoa!"

"Are you okay?" She steadied his significant weight with great difficulty.

"I've got jet lag. I think."

She sighed loudly. Fantasies weren't supposed to get jet lag, so either this was real and she had just made out with a stranger, or this was the oddest dream ever. Of course, she'd only recently started remembering vague pieces of dreams, so maybe all the ones she couldn't recall had been a bit wacky, too. How depressing.

Pushing him toward the sofa, she went along with the weirdness and asked, "Where are you from?"

Aidan smiled, and her heart did a little flip. "San Diego."

"Right. You flew up from San Diego."

"No. I *drove* up from San Diego." He sat, settling into the down cushions with an appreciative sigh. "It's less than an hour's drive, you know. When there aren't so many cars in the way."

"Traffic. Yes, I know. So how'd you get the jet lag?"

"On the way to San Diego."

"Okay." Lyssa stepped back and crossed her arms. "Where did you come from *before* San Diego? Ireland? I admit I suck at pinning down accents. And yours is unusually luscious."

Struck by sudden déjà vu at her own words, Lyssa stared, arrested, as Aidan's smile widened, making him even more gorgeous. *Why do I feel as if I know him so well? As if we've had this conversation before?*

It was surreal to be hovering over a stranger who'd just kissed her senseless. But no matter what she told herself, she couldn't convince herself that she had done something wrong.

"You're very sexy when you're grumpy," he said.

"Yeah? Well, you're very sexy when you're grinning like an idiot. And I'm *not* grumpy. Now, where did you come from?"

"Your dreams."

"Okay. Now I know I'm asleep. Real-life hot guys don't say corny shit like that." It hadn't really sounded corny, though. It had sounded sweet, kind of breathless, as if he was really happy to see her.

He caught her hand and tugged her into his lap. She considered a token protest, then thought, *Screw it.* He was hot and nice, and she was insane.

"Did we date in kindergarten or something?" she asked, studying his features with a frown.

"Or something," he replied evasively. "As a doctor, you're trained to look for specific signs and then, based on those, you narrow it down to a diagnosis."

Lyssa arched a brow at her dream guy. "Something like that."

"But sometimes you just have to go with your gut, right? Like now. You don't remember me, but you're pretty sure about me anyway."

"No. The only thing I'm sure about is that I'm certifiable."

Aidan closed his eyes and shook his head. Released from the snare of that intense gaze, Lyssa was able to look at the rest of his features more closely. His cheeks were flushed, his lips red. She touched his forehead with her inner wrist and detected fever.

"You're burning up."

"It's not contagious," he assured her, his eyes opening and his arms tightening when she tried to stand. "I'm just adjusting, I think."

"To what? Let me up." Wiggling, she broke free. "You should be in bed. We can reminisce about where we know each other from some other time."

"I could really use a bed. I haven't slept in two days."

Lyssa stared at Aidan's upturned face with wide eyes. "Long flight, huh? Do you need help finding a hotel?"

"The only thing I need is to be with you." He sank into the sofa back and groaned. "I ache all over."

"Shit." What the hell was she supposed to do with him? "This is where I call the police, right?"

Hello? 911? The hottest man I've ever seen (also the best kisser and best-smelling guy ever) just accosted me and is now passed out on my—

She watched with mouth agape as JB crawled into Aidan's lap and settled comfortably, nuzzling his gray and black head into her dream guy's abdomen. Aidan lifted his hand and rubbed her cat behind the ears, even though he was obviously sick as a dog. The tender gesture made her feel all mushy inside.

"Please don't," he breathed, his head falling back. "You know me. You . . . me . . . you and I . . ." He yawned, and looked adorable. "I'm sorry. I don't mean to fall asleep like this. I've never felt this crappy in my life. And your couch is comfortable."

"Yeah, well . . . Don't mention it," she said lamely. "But you should take something for that fever." Before she knew what she was doing, Lyssa walked into the kitchen and fetched a bottle of Tylenol. Her hands shook as she opened it.

Aidan.

She had known his name. Surely that meant she knew *him*. Why the hell couldn't she remember?

The ringing of the phone caused her to jump and drop the bottle on the floor. Lucky for her, the childproof cap hung in there. She leaned over the sink and grabbed the receiver, glancing aside to see her guest fast asleep on her couch. The sight of him, so large and formidable, now sprawled and relaxed, made her sigh. Even wearing ill-fitting clothes, Aidan Cross made her mouth water.

"Dr. Bates," she said in muted tones as she set the phone to her ear.

"Hey, Doc." Stacey's cheerful voice was like a lifeline thrown to a drowning woman. "I'm just reminding you that we're opening late tomorrow, because of Justin's birthday thing at school."

"Gotcha. Thanks. I forgot. Again." Lyssa rounded the breakfast bar and slid onto her customary stool so she could drink in Aidan's dark good looks while he slept. "Stace?"

"Yeah?"

"Something weird is going on over here."

"Hot monkey sex?"

Lyssa snorted. "Since when is hot monkey sex weird?"

"True."

"Weird to me is when the doorbell rings and the most delicious man you've ever seen walks in, kisses you senseless, and then camps out on your couch."

"Oh my god!" Stacey squealed, forcing Lyssa to hold the

phone away from her ear. "Chad finally got you to let him spend the night?! Go, you! Or go, Chad!"

"Uh . . . no. It's not Chad," she whispered furiously, cupping her hand over her mouth and receiver.

The stunned silence on the other end made Lyssa wince.

"Wow . . ." Stacey gave a surprised little laugh. "No judgment here, but you know I'm dying of curiosity. Who's the hunk on the couch?"

"Well . . . you see . . . That's the thing. I'm not sure."

"You're not sure? Some unknown, good-looking guy came to your door, kissed you, and now he's sitting on your couch? Yeah, that's weird all right. I'm jealous. Shit like that never happens to me. Where's my hunk delivery?"

Sighing, Lyssa looked at her notepad and froze, shocked to her toes to see Aidan's smiling face staring back at her. *My god . . .*

"All kidding aside, Doc," Stacey whispered conspiratorially, as if Aidan might hear her. "Do you want me to call the cops? Or are you pulling my leg?"

Lyssa traced the drawn shape of the blatantly sensual lips she'd managed to capture so well. A childhood therapist had encouraged her to take art classes, saying the ability to commit her thoughts to paper might help her to remember her dreams and share them with her mother. It hadn't worked for the purposes intended, but drawing was soothing to her, and she fell into the habit often.

"Lyssa? Is everything okay?"

"I feel like it is," she said absently, her heart racing, making her feel dizzier than she already was. "I mean, common sense says no, but . . ."

"But *what*? You're killing me!"

Sliding off the bar stool again, Lyssa straightened her shoulders. "Everything else says 'yes.' "

"Okay, listen. You take a picture of this guy and then hide your camera in your car. Stick a note in the bag with his name— Oh! Can you get his wallet?"

"Stacey!" Lyssa laughed. "I think he's okay. Jelly Bean loves him." She stared at the sofa, where JB slept in Aidan's lap like an angel . . .

Are you an angel?

No, darling. I'm not.

"No way," Stacey scoffed. "JB doesn't like anyone, not even Justin, and everyone loves my kid."

"He's a great kid." Suddenly Lyssa's smile was genuine. Something inside her knew the man in her living room— and liked him. A lot. "I'm going to get off here, Stace. See you at ten?"

"I better. If you don't show up to work, I'm coming over with the National Guard. What's this guy's name anyway?"

"Aidan Cross."

"I like it! Sounds edible."

"He is." Lyssa rounded the counter and bent to pick up the Tylenol. "I'll talk to you tomorrow."

"I'll expect to hear everything, Doc."

"Yeah, yeah. Bye." Hitting the off button, Lyssa set the handset on the granite top and filled a glass with chilled water dispensed through the fridge door. Then she moved to the living room and knelt on the floor next to the couch.

Leaning forward, she touched Aidan, unable to help

herself. She ran a hand through the short lock of hair that hung over his forehead, and his eyes fluttered open.

A soft smile curved his lips. "I'm glad to be here with you."

"Charmer." She swallowed down the lump in her throat. If it weren't for the fierce intelligence in those dark sapphire eyes, she would think he might be a little touched in the head. Hot guys weren't usually so sweet. "I bet you say that to all the ladies you barge in on."

"I've never said that to anyone in my life, Hot Stuff."

"Stop it. You're making me sappy."

The feeling of déjà vu struck her again.

"Promise me . . ." Aidan yawned while reaching for her hand. "Promise me you'll eat something while I nap. And don't fall asleep."

Her brows arched. "No?"

He shook his head, his gaze intent on her face. "No. Stay awake until I get up."

"Okay." She cupped his cheek and felt his high temperature, just before he shivered violently. "But you have to promise to take these."

Shaking two tablets out of the bottle and into her hand, Lyssa made him swallow them, despite his wince of displeasure, then she arranged him on the couch and covered him with her throw. JB moved up to his standard spot on the armrest with an irritated flick of his tail.

"Eat," Aidan ordered. "No sleep."

"I got it."

Lyssa watched him fall into a fitful slumber, and studied his features for a long time after that. Then she made herself a sandwich and sat at the dining table with her book about dreams and reincarnation.

And thought about love at first sight.

Burning.

As awareness took over, that was first thing that registered in Aidan's mind. A scorching breeze moved over him, blistering his skin, drying his nostrils, cracking his lips. The air was fetid, filled with the stench of death and despair.

Opening his eyes, he found himself facing the Gateway, tied to a pole with his arms behind him. Nightmares poured out in endless, unchecked numbers. Around him, hundreds of voices shouted, casting blame at his feet for actions he couldn't remember. He was alone except for the slender, golden-haired figure who reached for the door . . .

No!

Aidan jerked awake, startling JB, who screeched in alarm. His heart racing, it took him a moment to realize where he was. He ran both hands through his hair, wincing at the damp roots and his sticky skin.

Nightmares.

The bastards. He was no longer safe from them in his sleep. They dug deep into his mind, finding his fears and feeding on them. He felt drained and on edge at the same time.

Never having met his foe unguarded before, he felt violated. Wretched. His stomach heaved.

Seeking the only true solace he had ever known, Aidan turned his head toward the low drone of the TV and saw Lyssa at his side, seated on the floor. It was dark, the blinds drawn, the only illumination coming from the flickering light of the television and the aquarium in the dining room. He reached for her, running his hand through the loose golden strands he loved. She moved, sliding slowly away, toward the floor . . .

. . . a dead weight.

The panic he'd recently retreated from flared anew, pounding through his blood until his heart was ready to explode. He leaped from the couch, barely catching her slumping body before it hit the floor.

"Lyssa!" He shook her violently. "Damn it, I told you to stay awake!"

Her eyelids fluttered, but her subconscious was already connected to the deadly Twilight.

The cry that tore from him was both desperate and inhuman. His nightmare wasn't over.

It had only just begun.

Chapter 7

As icy shards tore into her flesh, Lyssa flailed in agony, her subconscious pulling free of the mechanical banging and insidious whispers that were tearing her mind apart. She gulped down a massive breath into tight lungs and opened her throat to scream. Instead, her mouth was covered, increasing her terror.

Struggling to breathe and desperate to evade the needles that struck her everywhere, she clawed at the unyielding arms that trapped and held her immobile.

Sucking in air through her nose, she smelled a scent that caused her eyes to fly open . . .

. . . and met darkly determined sapphire blue ones.

Panicked, she clung to the wet, hard body that held hers so rigidly. She gasped for breath, inhaling Aidan's exhale as he swallowed her cries with the heat of his mouth.

Suddenly her surroundings became clear—the stone tile of her bathroom, the freezing spray from the showerhead behind her, the fully dressed form pressed so tightly to hers.

She ceased her struggles, sagging into him, so relieved to be in safe arms after the horror of only a moment before.

He tore his mouth away, breathing harshly, his embrace so tight that no water slipped between them. The feel of his chest was warm, a stark contrast to the river of melted ice water that coursed down her back.

"I-it's c-cold," she complained, circling his powerful upper back with her arms.

Turning, he took the brunt of the water from her, the tensing of his jaw the only sign of his discomfort. Lyssa attempted to step away, to free her arms to adjust the temperature, but he held fast.

"L-let me t-turn up the h-heat."

It took him a long moment to do as she asked, as if he was reluctant to release her. Reaching around him, Lyssa turned the knob. The water began to heat, and steam rose around them. Then she chanced another look up. A tic in his jaw matched his formidable scowl.

"I told you not to fall asleep," he bit out.

"I didn't mean to."

Her arms wrapped his waist in a vain effort to warm up. Aidan moved then, his hands catching the hem of her shirt and tugging upward. If he hadn't looked so formidable, she might have protested his forwardness. Or she might not have . . .

"You scared the crap out of me," he muttered, intensely focused on stripping her bare.

She moved with him, taking his silent commands, understanding by his forcefulness that he was a man who bore the weight of power and responsibility with unusual finesse. Despite how her wet clothes clung to her skin, he

had her undressed in no time at all. An expert. The absolute certainty that he undressed women often added to her
sense of unrest.

"Yeah, well," she began grumpily, "I got the crap scared
out of me, too, so . . . mmpph—" She grunted as he tugged
her into him and crushed her close. Her stiffened frame
relaxed immediately, and she sank into his strength and
the comfort he offered.

"I'll take care of you," he promised gruffly. "Don't be
scared."

She almost cried. Unlike everyone else in her life who
told her what *she* had to do to make herself feel better—see
the doctor, take more meds, eat healthier—Aidan took the
burden completely from her. She gave it to him gladly.

"I had the worst nightmare," she confided. "There was
pounding and banging against metal, grinding and scratching, and this god-awful wailing sound."

"You can't just drift into sleep." He gave her a little
shake to emphasize his words. "You've got to fall hard and
fast into it."

Tilting her head back, she caught the torment in his
gaze, amazed to realize he cared about her. More than casually. "*You* scare me, too."

"No." Aidan shook his head. "You trust me. You need
me."

"That's what's scary." She felt safe with him, her fear
unable to affect her when he was in her arms. That de-
pendence on something so new was frightening. Could she
trust something she didn't comprehend?

His lips brushed across hers, firm and delicious, the taste
of him lingering, teasing her already heightened senses.

Her tongue traced the curve of his lower lip, seeking more of it. The quiver of fear in her belly intensified, and then turned into something else.

He exhaled harshly and pulled away, resting his forehead against hers, his hair dripping water down her cheek. The mood around them altered, the anxiety she felt turning into a very different kind of desperation.

His eyes slid closed, then he began to free the buttons of his shirt. She stepped backward and gaped as a deep, strangely familiar heat spread through her chilled limbs.

Stacey kept a Chippendales' calendar on the wall at the clinic. Not one of the men displayed on those pages could hold a candle to Aidan Cross. He was solid rippling muscle. Every line, curve, and plane flexing with latent power and pure masculine grace. He was more lean than bulk. More sinew than bulging mass.

"Gorgeous," she breathed, before she could turn her brain on enough to keep her mouth shut. Chad had never once made her feel this hunger. She hadn't even known it was *possible* to crave someone like this.

The look Aidan gave her in response to her praise was scorching, needy. And unmistakable.

She wasn't a slouch in the figure department, but Aidan was perfection in a way that unsettled her. There was something about him, a foreign quality that called to her, a sense of being . . . *more*. More beautiful, more intense, more sexually charged. More than a mere man, though she couldn't see where that thought came from. *A god.*

Suddenly shy, Lyssa turned slightly to the side.

When he caught her by the elbow and tugged her back around, she blinked in surprise.

"I'm looking at you," he rumbled arrogantly.

She raised her brows. "Yeah, I'm looking at you, too."

"Stop trying to hide."

"Stop being so bossy."

His gaze narrowed. Then he released her and reached for his belt. Thoughts of anything else were impossible when her brain was fully focused on him and the fact that he was about to be naked.

The end of the belt slapped against the wall when Aidan yanked it free. Despite the closed fly, the pants fell from his lean hips into a soggy puddle at his feet. Part of her brain wondered why his clothes were so damn big. The other part could care less, far more interested in the cock that curved upward to almost touch his belly button.

Her mouth went dry. Long, thick, and pulsing with veins, it was a wet dream come to life.

Where did you come from?

Your dreams.

And he was dripping wet and getting wetter. She giggled.

He leaned back and arched a brow, his mouth slightly raised in a half smile that urged her to cup his cheek. He was too arrogant and self-assured to take her momentary amusement as anything to do with the size of that impressive cock, and she loved him for it.

"Let's get cleaned up," he said, tugging her closer again. Then he reached for the liquid soap, squirted some into his palm, and went to work. On *her* body.

She jerked in surprise when his slick hands cupped her breasts. He tried to look innocent, but with the mischievous gleam in his eyes, it didn't work. Never one to back down from a challenge, Lyssa scooped up a trail of bubbles from her tummy and grabbed his cock.

He arched a brow and washed between her legs.

She arched her own and tugged at his balls. Her chest rose and fell rapidly in response to how intimately and possessively he touched her. Aidan took note, adjusting his movements with unparalleled skill. There was none of the hesitation or silent query that other men displayed with a new partner. And she showed none with him, washing his cock and balls as if it was her right to do so.

Aidan laughed, the severity of his expression softening with obvious affection. "You're a handful, Hot Stuff."

"So are you." She shot a pointed glance at her overflowing hands. "More than a handful."

Leaning forward, he pressed a kiss to her forehead, the tender gesture so at odds with the sinful way he stoked her desire. As he moved around her, running his hands all over her, her eyes slid closed on a sigh. Her blood was hot and sluggish, her mind lost in the sensual spell he wove so well. Low and deep within her, she ached, clenching in emptiness and expectation of what she knew was coming.

If this was a dream, she didn't want to wake up. Never in her life had she known wanting like this, a need so intense she was panting with it, her knees weakening until he was forced to hold her upright with easy strength.

"Was it spring break in Cabo?" she asked breathlessly.

"Huh?" He pulled back to look down at her, revealing half-lidded eyes that couldn't hide the burning lust within.

"When we met. Cabo San Lucas. That's the last time I remember that I can't remember."

"Ah . . . I get it. No." Catching her shoulders, he spun her away from him, and a moment later, his strong fingers were rubbing shampoo into her scalp.

She turned into a boneless puddle. He knew just how to touch her, kneading the tense muscles of her shoulders and stroking the length of her spine until all the anxiety of her nightmare washed down the drain. She felt the calluses on his palms and the strength he wielded with such care. When he wrapped his arms around her and pulled her backward into the spray with him, she leaned against him with a trust she shouldn't feel, but did.

"But we've had sex," she persisted, shivering at the thought of what it must have been like. He was in no rush, taking his time, as if he had an eternity, as if time didn't exist for him. If he took the same care when making love . . .

He licked the wet shell of her ear. "Something like that."

Turning in his arms, Lyssa leaned her head back and met blue eyes fringed with thick, wet lashes. "Something like sex?"

"Yep. Wash me." He thrust the bottle into her hands. "I want to feel your hands on me."

She shook her head as she reached for the soap. She almost told him no, just to curb his arrogance, but she wanted to touch him. So much that her palms itched with the need.

With soap-slicked fingertips, she slid her palms across his chest, marveling at the feel of his skin stretched taut over muscles that were hard as stone. His eyes closed on a low groan, his hands cupping her hips, his head falling back in a gesture of supplication that took her by surprise. Aidan was wallowing in her caresses, absorbing them, relishing every time she lingered in an especially susceptible spot.

It was riveting, the sight of so large and dangerous a man turned to putty in her hands. And he was dangerous, she knew. There was something in his eyes. They were ancient, wizened, jaded beyond his years. And something in the way he watched her, the way he moved, the note of command in every casual phrase. This man was never without his guard. Yet here he was. Bared to her in more than his appearance.

So she indulged, taking her time, washing his front from his head to his toes, then turning him and paying the same attention to his rear, which was just as magnificent.

When he faced her again, Lyssa positioned him beneath the spray and shifted her fingers through his hair, making sure every bit of shampoo was gone. She was so much shorter than he was, she had to lift onto her tippytoes to reach him. The loss of balance forced her to lean against him, her breasts to his chest. The hard, heavy length of his erect cock pressed into her stomach, but he made no move to take things further.

"I think I'm clean." He stilled her roving hands with his own before pushing her gently away.

Lyssa bit her lower lip in embarrassment. Nodding her agreement, she pushed open the floating glass door and reached for the towel closest to her. She didn't bother to dry herself. Instead she wrapped the towel beneath her arms and moved to the linen closet, taking out a fresh towel, which she thrust backward without turning her head.

She heard the knobs turn and the water stop.

"Now you don't want to look at me?" he asked softly, his fingers curling around hers, sending sharp awareness up her arm.

She tugged free and moved toward the door, restless and edgy with confusion and unsatisfied arousal. She didn't know what to make of the fact that he had touched her so intimately, then pulled back. The hardness of his cock betrayed him, as did the dark hunger in his gaze, but he'd put on the brakes.

So why was he here at her house, driving her crazy, if he didn't want to get laid?

"I'll give you some privacy," she muttered.

Her hand was reaching for the knob when Aidan caught her in a full-body embrace—his arms pinning hers, his bare chest behind her, his erection an unmistakable pressure against her lower back.

"Talk to me." His lips were hot against her neck.

She shuddered with the force of her craving, her heart leaping into a mad rhythm.

"What's the matter, Lyssa?" One arm crossed upward between her breasts, his biceps bulging beneath her gripping palms, his fingers angling her jaw toward his waiting mouth. He kissed her at the same moment he rolled his hips with practiced grace, inundating her from all sides with the feel of him.

"I was trying to save my sanity," he whispered into her mouth, "not discourage you."

Moaning, she spent the space of one breath resisting him, and then she gave in, her tongue meeting his, then chasing his, as he advanced and retreated with deep licks.

"More," she demanded, her nails in his flesh.

His hand at her throat shook. "Not in here. Take me to your bed."

"I'm not sure I can make it." She writhed against him, stroking that thick, hard cock with the upper curve of her buttocks.

"It's on the other side of the door."

"Too far."

He bent his knees, notching himself between the cheeks of her ass, and began to rub against her. His free hand touched her thigh, then slid up beneath her towel. A hungry sound vibrated against her back when he cupped her wet pussy.

"You're so slick and hot," he purred. "I could slide into your cunt from behind. Ride you hard, right here, just the way you like it. Just the way *I* like it." His fingers mimicked the actions he described, slipping into her, pumping knuckle-deep and fast.

"Yes . . ." Her head lolled against his shoulder, her lips parted, wanting more of him. She licked at him desperately, her tongue flickering, trying to taste him. "Do it."

"I could bend you over the counter, facing our reflections. You could watch me take you." The growl that rumbled up from his chest was pure sexual hunger. His coarse words made her nipples hard, made her pussy quiver around his fingers, made her cry out softly.

"Aidan."

"But I won't, Lyssa. Not this time. This time I want you naked and spread out on a bed for my pleasure."

As his skin heated with his desire, the scent of him, spicy and rich, filled her nostrils. It was achingly familiar, making her womb clench tight in recognition. His hand slid from her neck and cupped her breast, squeezing it, making it swell. Her knees gave out, but he held her tightly. All the while he fucked her mouth with those delicious thrusts of his tongue, and urged his hips against her in a wicked imitation of what she really wanted.

"I'm going to make you come in a thousand different ways," he promised. "Around my fingers, against my lips, around my cock. I'm going to wear you out, exhaust you. You'll sleep like the dead . . . When I let you sleep."

She whimpered. She had never in her life been this hot for sex.

"I can't wait." His words were a dark threat that excited her. "And I won't. Take me to your bed so we can get started. I want you comfortable so we can take our time."

"I—I can't walk."

Aidan's fingers left her, then he bent and lifted her. "Open the door."

She stretched her arm out behind her, reaching blindly for the knob, her mouth pressing feverish kisses to his throat.

"It might go faster if you looked," he said with warm amusement.

"Then I'd have to stop nibbling on you."

"But there are so many other parts of me to nibble on."

Lyssa turned her head just long enough to open the door. Aidan stepped back as it swung inward, the sound of his laughter spilling out into the bedroom along with puffs of steam. He closed the distance between the bathroom and the bed in just a few long-legged strides. When he set her down, she scrambled to her knees and threw herself into him. He didn't budge an inch with the impact.

"Hot Stuff," he said, his smiling lips moving against her temple. "You're always hard-charging." With one steely arm supporting her back, he reached between her legs again. "Time to take you down a notch."

She moaned, her eyes clenched shut against the heat that spread all over her body, first in a wave of goose bumps and then in a mist of sweat. The nearly overwhelming sensation she had of deep, intimate familiarity combined with the here and now of a gorgeous man making love to her was too much. When Aidan slid a long, callused finger inside her, she panted for air and dug her nails into his forearms.

He muttered something in a foreign language and then withdrew, hushing her protest with his mouth. His fingertip, slick with her cream, circled her clit, then rubbed it with perfectly gauged pressure. Primed for orgasm by the things he'd done to her in the shower, Lyssa came with a cry, and Aidan held her reverently, stroking her with such tenderness, drawing out her climax until she settled limply into his embrace.

As Aidan laid her gently across her bed, Lyssa found she couldn't think, could barely catch her breath. Her chest rose and fell rapidly, her heart thumped desperately in her chest. She could only watch with heavy-lidded eyes as he positioned her with her hips at the edge of the bed and then dropped to his knees.

"Please," she breathed, her hunger flaring to renewed life. His large hands cupped her inner thighs and spread them wide. The color of his skin, so dark compared to her own, sent a shiver through her. The heat of his breath, gusting through her wet curls, made her muscles tense.

"Christ." A rough, edgy sound escaped him as his thumbs held her lips open so nothing was hidden. "You're melting."

Lyssa's back arched upward as he licked her in a slow, deliberate glide, then pulled back to look at her again.

He pointed his tongue and flicked it rapidly over the tiny slitted entrance to her body, licking up the liquid result of her recent orgasm. Then he tilted his head and thrust his tongue inside her.

She moaned, and her hands fisted in her pale blue comforter. Aidan draped her legs over his shoulders, so he could get closer. Wet, smacking sounds rose up as he ate at her as if she were a dessert he couldn't get enough of, his tongue fucking in and out of her pussy with rapid, shallow strokes.

Aching, sweating, Lyssa cupped her breasts and pinched at her nipples, pulling them, trying to relieve their desperate hardness.

Growling his pleasure, Aidan reached up and brushed her hands away, his much larger ones surrounding her breasts and squeezing them with expertly gauged pressure. All the while he licked at her, sucked her, teased her.

"Yes," she whispered, rocking her hips upward to match the lashing rhythm of his tongue. She reached down, her fingers sliding into his hair, massaging his scalp. "Make me come."

Circling her clit with his firm lips, he tugged on it with soft suction, the tip of his tongue rubbing against the tiny bundle of nerves.

Lyssa climaxed with a breathless cry, arching upward as

he continued the delicious torment until she begged him to stop, her flesh swollen and oversensitive.

Aidan smiled wickedly as he pulled away, licking his lips. "Now you're relaxed enough to fit me," he purred.

She couldn't move a single muscle when he shrugged out from under her and rose to stand between her spread legs. The sight of him taking his long, thick cock in hand and tilting it down to breach her pussy was the most erotic thing she'd ever seen. He was so deliberate in his movements, so focused, his gaze riveted to where the warm, silky smooth head of his cock was pressing into her.

The sound that came out of her throat was the embodiment of lust and longing. That beautiful cock was pushing into her, caressing slick, pulsing tissues, forcing them to part for him.

She writhed, struggling to take all that he had. "Protection?" she gasped.

"Trust me," he urged. "It's okay."

Lyssa almost argued, but then found she couldn't. Despite everything she didn't know about Aidan, she believed he would never hurt her or put her in jeopardy. It was a bone-deep certainty that was unshakable. She felt comforted by his presence and his touch, as if she'd been waiting for him, longing for him to return. Even though she hadn't known that *he* was the missing part of her life.

"Promise me you'll remember this." His voice was sandpaper-rough, his hands shaking where he held down her hips. "How it feels—you and me, connected—when we talk later about why I'm here."

She remembered it already. The feeling that they had

been together this way before was so strong, it was beyond mere déjà vu.

God, he was big.

She whimpered.

He rolled his hips and slid deeper, filling her in a way she knew only he ever had, or ever could.

Aidan felt wonderful inside her, truly divine, and when he leaned over her, Lyssa hugged him closer and tried to take more of him.

"Don't rush." He nipped her earlobe, the brief spot of pain causing her to jerk in surprise. "I'll be inside you more times than I'm not. Waking, sleeping. I don't want you sore."

"I need you." Her nails dug into his shoulders as he stroked deeper, massaging the broad head of his cock across the spot inside her that ached for him. She reached for his lean hips and tugged at the same time she lifted, forcing him in to the root, his heavy balls slapping against the seam of her ass.

"Lyssa," he breathed roughly, shuddering. He stared at her with dark, fathomless eyes, his handsome features passion flushed and his chest heaving with labored breaths. "Christ. It's . . . even better . . . when it's real."

She had no idea what that meant, but it didn't matter. The only thing that mattered was Aidan, who laced his fingers with hers and pulled her arms over her head. He took her mouth with heartbreaking tenderness, his lips brushing across hers.

"Lyssa." Her name was filled with aching longing when spoken in that luscious brogue. It made her eyes teary.

"Please," she begged, kissing him back with desperation. Her body was on fire beneath his, her cunt spasming around the big cock that throbbed inside it.

Echoes of past encounters flowed through her—his chest against her back as he took her from behind, his hands kneading her thighs as she rode him hard toward a searing climax.

"Please," she said again, rubbing her painfully tightened nipples against his furred chest.

"Hush. I've got you."

She knew he'd said that to her before in a similar moment.

Aidan began to move, withdrawing, then returning on a perfect downstroke, thrusting slow and easy, measured in his passion.

Locking her ankles at the small of his back, Lyssa urged him to ride her harder, faster, but he was too controlled. She licked the straining column of his throat, and he groaned loudly but maintained his rhythm. His hips swiveled and thrust, in and out. Beneath her calves she felt his taut ass clench and release as he pumped his cock into her.

His mouth to her ear, Aidan whispered, "You're hot. Tight as a fist. But wet, Hot Stuff. Soaked inside. Your cunt was made for me."

She shivered.

"Later"—his tone was a sensual threat—"you'll be on your hands and knees, and I'm going to fuck you like that for hours. Long, deep thrusts into this sweet pussy."

Her cunt rippled along his length, on the verge of another orgasm. He knew her so well. As if he was a longtime lover who cared deeply about her pleasure.

He released her hands and set his elbows into the mattress so he could cup her breasts. "I'm going to suck on your nipples until you come. You'll scream my name until you're hoarse."

Lyssa's back arched, her entire body tense and expectant. "Yes . . . I want . . ."

Straightening, Aidan hooked his arms beneath her legs and lifted her hips from the mattress. In her raised position, he could stroke deeper, his weighty testicles slapping rhythmically against the curve of her ass, the sound so erotic, it made her clench tightly around him.

She watched him with heavy-lidded eyes, taking in his clenched jaw and the lock of black hair that fell over his brow. His biceps and pectorals were defined by the effortless hold he had on her. His abdomen flexed as he fucked her, the golden skin glistening with sweat.

"You're beautiful," he gritted out, his rough tone betraying how tightly he restrained himself.

His praise was all she could take, pushing her that last little bit she needed to orgasm again. Lyssa gasped for air as the climax tightened her entire body.

Aidan grunted and fucked through her spasms, flesh slapping against flesh, increasing his pace until she couldn't breathe for the pleasure. She felt him swell, grow impossibly harder, and then he plunged to the hilt and groaned, "Lyssa . . ."

He ground the root of his cock hard against her pelvis, spurting his cum as deep inside her as he could. He came hard, but silently. His entire body shaking, his jaw locked, his blue eyes burning into her. She felt it, all of it—the jerking of his cock; the hot, thick rush of his semen; the pulse beat of his heart deep inside her. Her eyes grew wet, her vision blurry. As he emptied himself into her, his with-held breath hissed out between his teeth.

"Fuck," he gasped, folding over her. He cupped her face, his thumbs brushing aside her tears, kisses moving across her cheeks. His beloved voice whispering a combination of foreign words and her name. Over and over again.

Aidan gathered her up, tucked her head under his chin, and rolled to drape her limp body over his. Still connected.

His lips pressed ardently against her damp scalp. "I can't believe I'm here, that I'm with you, inside you for real."

"Maybe we're dreaming," she slurred, thinking she must have died and gone to heaven.

"No way," he argued, his arms tightening around her. "Trust me, no dream could ever be as wonderful as this."

Chapter 8

Aidan's growling stomach broke the silence that wrapped them in a comforting blanket.

"Your turn to be hungry," she teased, her chest pressed to his chest, one arm and leg tossed over his body.

"Did you eat earlier like you promised?" he asked.

"Yep. Sure did. I had a sandwich."

"That's not enough. We both need to eat."

She lifted her head to stare down at him. "I don't eat at this time of night."

"You do when I'm around," he retorted with the arrogant note of command that was innate to him.

She wondered if anyone had every said no to him, and doubted it. She rose from the bed and went to fetch her robe, which hung from a hook on the back of the door. Shrugging into it as she turned around, she paused in mid-rotation, arrested by the sight of Aidan rolling out of her bed. Despite her recent series of toe-curling orgasms, her dry mouth watered.

She'd never in her life seen such golden masculine perfection. She could stare at him for hours, she loved the sight of him so much.

Lyssa grinned like an idiot; she couldn't help it. "You didn't bring a bag with you?"

"For what?"

"Clothes, toothbrush, razor?"

He shook his head. "Things were a bit . . . crazy."

"Yeah, the airlines lose my sister's luggage all the time. That's why I only take carry-on bags." She shrugged. "I suppose there are worse things than having naked yumminess wandering around."

"Why don't you stay naked, too?" he suggested with a wink.

"Oh no, don't look at me like that."

"Like what?" he purred, stepping closer.

"Like I'm dinner, and you're hungry."

"I'm starving," he breathed softly, looming over her, the tip of his finger following the line of her collarbone.

"You're dangerous," she whispered, staring at his throat.

His touch burned where it coursed over her skin. "Not to you."

"Oh yeah?" She set her hands on his hips. "Is this where you tell me why you're here?"

"Almost." He kissed the tip of her nose. "Food first."

Lyssa blew out her breath. "All right. Food first." She thought of him wandering around her house naked, and shivered. Oh man, she'd go crazy. "I might have something you can wear."

"If you insist."

Sylvia Day

She narrowed her eyes, and Aidan stepped back with a laugh, allowing her room to move to the dresser. She felt him watching her, his gaze steady and hot.

Rummaging through her lower drawer, Lyssa searched for the pair of sweatpants her last boyfriend had left behind. They didn't have much in the way of sentimental value and they were way too big, but they made great slob gear, which was why she kept them around.

She straightened and turned, taking a moment to study the man who stood waiting at the foot of her bed. In her room with its dark blue walls and baby blue comforter, the color intended to soothe her to sleep, Aidan looked both very much at home and very, very attractive. "Here you go."

Lyssa swallowed hard, her gaze riveted while he tugged the gray sweats up and over the delicious package between his legs.

"You're tempting me to forgo food and just snack on you," he drawled, glancing at her with a wicked smile.

She wrinkled her nose. "Sorry. Why don't you head on down to the kitchen? I need to use the bathroom."

"Okay. I'll see what I can dig up." He cupped her cheek with a large hand and stared at her with heartrending tenderness before heading down the stairs.

When she stepped into the bathroom, her eyes went straight to the soggy puddle of clothes on the floor of her shower and her mind flooded with memories of what they'd done there. How long had she been hoping for a man like him to come into her life?

Her eyes squeezed shut against the sudden flare of white-hot guilt. She did have someone—*Chad*—a guy who had been more than patient and understanding while she kept a large gulf between them. Lyssa flinched and reached out to grab the lip of her pedestal sink. Christ, how could she have forgotten about Chad?

Curling her hands around the cool porcelain, she looked at herself in the mirror and winced. Kiss-swollen lips, sex-mussed hair, and an overall dazed appearance told her what she hadn't wanted to admit. There had always been a disconnect with Chad. He was a great guy, and he was fun to spend time with. She was comfortable with him and enjoyed his company, but after a month of casual dating she still hadn't slept with him. Was in fact trying to *convince* herself to have sex with him, when all Aidan had to do was walk in the door and she was ready to go. Not just with lust, but with deep tenderness and longing.

She should have handled things differently, but in the end, it wasn't Aidan who had wedged between her and Chad. The gap had always been there.

When Lyssa came out of the bathroom, the smell of cooking food was wafting up to the second floor. She padded barefoot down the hardwood stairs and found Aidan in the kitchen heating up SpaghettiOs, which he then poured into two bowls and served with bread taken right out of the bag.

They sat at her dining table with plastic bowls and over-sized metal spoons, and he offered her a soft smile before beginning to eat.

"You know," he said, around a mouthful of food, "this stuff is better than I thought."

"Yeah? Been a while since you had a meal in a can?"

"It doesn't taste like this where I come from."

"Oh?" She set her elbows on the table. "And where's that?"

"You got any sleeping pills left?" he asked, ignoring her.

"Who says I have sleeping pills?"

He snorted. "Get used to me knowing a lot about you. I don't mean to freak you out, and I promise I'll explain everything this weekend when we have the time to really get into it. Two o'clock in the morning is too late when you've got work in a few hours."

"It's also too late to take a sleeping pill. They make me nonfunctional the next day. That's why I stopped taking them."

Gesturing toward her bowl, Aidan ordered, "Eat. Then pill. No arguing."

She stuck her tongue out at him.

"I've got one of those," he drawled softly. "And if you're a good girl, I'll show you more of the things I can do with it."

Shivering, Lyssa grabbed her spoon and ate faster than she had in a long time. He laughed at her, the sound rich and warm, filled with something she couldn't define. Part joy, part freedom, part something else. She was teasing, playing along, enjoying the moment, because tomorrow she would either wake up from the weirdest dream she could ever remember, or this would be all too real and she had some serious things to consider.

"Trust me," he urged softly, setting his hand atop the one she had resting on the table. "You're thinking too hard. Trust your instincts."

He met her gaze squarely, hiding nothing from her. The circumstances themselves led to intimacy. She in her silk robe. He dressed only in low-slung sweats. They ate a casual meal. Had made love with unrestrained passion. Had held each other tenderly in the aftermath. As if they were a long-established couple.

Promise me you won't open the door to anyone.

"Lyssa? Did you hear me?"

She blinked. "Huh?"

Aidan's thumb stroked over her knuckles. "Promise me that you'll come to me with any doubts or concerns. Don't let your imagination run away from you. I know how weird this is, but you have to believe that I only want to keep you safe."

"No one wants to hurt me."

He sighed, and lifted her hand to kiss the back. "Let's go back to bed. We both need to rest up for tomorrow."

I keep the bad guys away.

"You're a soldier," she breathed, surprised at how certain she was about that. It was faint, that connection she felt to him, but it was enough for her to go on. For now.

"I'm tired," he countered, rising to his feet and pulling her up with him. "Where are those pills?"

"Why should I take them?"

"Remember. Hard and fast into sleep. No tossing and turning. I want your mind far away from Nightmares." He paused. "And other nasty things."

Feeling a transient flash of the terror from her earlier dream, Lyssa nodded and went to the cabinet in the kitchen where she kept all her meds and did as he asked. He held her hand as she turned off the lights, leaving the mess from dinner in the sink when he told her he would take care of it in the morning.

They took the stairs side by side, his longer stride shortened to match hers. He pulled back the crisp white sheets and then slid into them, his back upright against the padded headboard of her contemporary bed. She curled into his open arms, settling into his side as if it were custom-made for her.

You're almost hard enough to be uncomfortable.

"Aidan?"

"Hmm?" He buried his nose in her hair and breathed deeply.

Are you an angel?

With her eyes closed, she frowned, confused by the bits and pieces of memories that surfaced randomly. Too randomly to make any sense. "Does it bother you that I don't remember our time together?"

Lyssa felt the press of his lips against the top of her head.

"I wish you did," he admitted, hugging her closer. "But we'll make new memories."

Burying her face in his chest, Lyssa felt the unnaturally intense pull of sleep brought on by the powerful drug.

Just before she lost consciousness, she remembered what she had forgotten and felt a brief flash of panic. *She'd promised this weekend to Chad.*

Then she felt nothing at all.

Rising up from the depths of drug-induced sleep was always a bitch, but today wasn't as bad as usual. At least that's what Lyssa told herself as JB's persistent grumbling woke her. Eyes closed, she snuggled further into the warmth of the blanket and realized she was cuddling chenille. Which could only mean one thing—she had slept on the couch again. The only place she kept a chenille throw.

To wake up on the sofa meant . . . It had all been a dream.

Aidan.

She heaved out a breath that was both relieved and sad. She finally remembered a dream in vivid detail, which was great, but so was Aidan. At least he seemed as if he was. And he wasn't real.

JB continued his impatient kneading of her thigh. She took the hint and opened her eyes. The ceiling was lit with mid-morning sunlight. She sighed again, and her nostrils filled with the smell of fresh coffee. Turning her head, Lyssa looked for her mother, then froze in place, her breath seizing in her lungs.

Just a few feet away was a sight that filled her with awe. In the center of her living room, Aidan stood with legs spread wide, his powerful back glistening with a fine sheen of sweat as he arched his body sinuously through a series of movements that looked like Tai Chi. With one major difference—Aidan was holding a massive sword that looked something like Excalibur. Her coffee table had been pushed aside to make room for his lunges and his wielding of the glinting blade.

She watched him with mouth agape, amazed at the beauty of his rippling muscles and the easy strength with which he held that impossibly heavy-looking sword. He tossed it easily to his other hand, working that side, displaying the same proficiency with that arm as he had shown with his dominant one. He moved silently, making no sound. Not even the rapid swing of the blade disturbed the peaceful morning silence.

As she admired him with ever heightening arousal, Lyssa wondered why the sight of a stranger with a wicked sword didn't scare the shit out of her. Instead she was getting turned on. *Seriously* turned on.

Aidan turned at that moment, his blue eyes meeting hers, the intense concentration on his features melting into a devastatingly wicked smile. He winked, burning out every brain cell she had, and continued his routine.

"Morning, Hot Stuff," he murmured, his voice not even breathless.

"Hi," she whispered back, enthralled by the beauty of his honed warrior's body and the feeling of contentment she felt at his endearment. He was pure, sexually charged male, and his blatant sensuality reminded her that she was female, with needs that had long been suppressed by exhaustion. Her nipples peaked hard and tight, aching. Her skin flushed, making her hot, reminding her of his fever. "How are you feeling this morning?"

He arched a brow. "Great. And if you keep looking at me like that, I'll show you just how great."

A tremor shifted through her. "Promises, promises," she teased, her voice husky.

"Don't tempt me more than you already are. After spending the night with you wrapped around me, I'm more than willing to make you late for work."

Wrapped around him. Damn, that's why she hated taking drugs. She wished she could remember that.

"How did I end up on the couch?"

"I carried you. I wanted to be the first thing you saw when you woke up. We have to talk."

Pushing up from the sofa, she ran a hand over her mussed hair and wrinkled her nose. She didn't look tempting in the morning. She looked like shit. A quick glance at the clock revealed that it was nine in the morning. "I have to take a shower. I have work in an hour."

"Go get ready," he said, his words tossed over his shoulder as he turned away from her again. "I'll have coffee waiting for you when you come down."

She stood and stretched. "Thanks. There's vanilla creamer in the fridge."

"Got it. And you like two sweetener packets, too."

"Uh, yeah . . ." She frowned at how much he remembered about her, then took the stairs.

It felt a little strange, the settled domesticity they were sharing, especially when the man she was being domestic with was half naked and waving a sword in her living room. But it was only slightly strange. Mostly it fit, soothed her, gave her a spring to her step and a higher lift to her chin.

She took her time in the shower, even though she knew she was going to be late. Stacey wouldn't admit it, but she had been scheduling the first appointment a bit later than she let on, giving Lyssa time to get it together in the morning. Today Lyssa made the most of it, shaving her legs with extra care and then rubbing her favorite country-apple-scented body oil into her wet skin. As the pelting spray washed away the last of her grogginess, Lyssa started thinking about Aidan.

Aidan, the mystery man, who acted as if they had been dating forever and said next to nothing about himself.

He was right. They needed to talk, because she needed answers.

Dried and dressed, her mouth watering at the thought of hot fresh coffee, Lyssa found her living room restored to its former furniture arrangement and Aidan leaning like a sex god against the counter, laughing into the phone.

She paused, arrested by the sound, one that was both deep and light, and endlessly seductive. It was the kind of rumbling laughter that made a woman think of passionate play in bed, rolling and laughing amid warm tumbled sheets, lost in the moment.

His mouth curved on one side as he stared at her, his gaze dipping to cruise the length of her body, heating her blood. "Here she is, Cathy," he murmured, straightening. "All in one piece, and looking amazing."

Lyssa's eyes widened. She'd thought he was talking to a friend. Maybe letting someone know he had arrived without trouble. She never would have guessed her mother.

She stepped closer, and he covered the receiver with his hand. "Sorry," he whispered. "I was going to ignore it. Then she threatened to call the police if you didn't pick up."

Shaking her head, Lyssa collected the phone, trying to ignore the thrill she felt when their fingers touched. She turned away from him to hide her reaction. "Hi, Mom."

"What the hell is going on?"

"Nothing." She jumped as strong hands clasped her waist. Then firm, warm lips pressed against the side of her neck. She leaned backward, soaking up his attention.

"I'm sweaty," he whispered, stepping back. But his touch didn't leave her. "We really need to talk, Lyssa."

She nodded her understanding.

"Don't tell me 'nothing,'" her mother chastised with unmistakable eagerness. "Who is Aidan?"

Lyssa thought about that a moment, and then, feeling impish, she thrust her hips back and brushed against Aidan's cock. His breath hissed out between his teeth, and he released her.

"Cold shower for me," he muttered, heading for the stairs. "You're paying for that later."

Laughing, Lyssa said into the phone, "He's an old friend."

"From where? He sounds Irish."

"Delicious, isn't it? I've always loved men with accents."

"Why haven't I met him before?" Cathy asked in an accusatory tone.

"Long-distance. Besides, I'm old enough to have friends you don't vet first."

"I want to meet him."

"I'm sure you do." Lyssa glanced at the clock. "Oh crap! It's ten. I'm due at the clinic. I gotta go."

"Lyssa Ann Bates! You can't—"

Dropping the receiver in the cradle, Lyssa turned too quickly and knocked her purse to floor. She retrieved it and was about to toss it onto the counter when a twinkle of colored light drew her eye. It was then she noted the slim, jewel-encrusted volume on the counter below the bar. For a moment, Lyssa could only stare at it in awe. Then she gripped her purse tighter with one hand, while reaching out tentatively for the book with the other. Lifting it, she revealed another beneath that one, though the second volume lacked ornamentation and had only a worn, leatherlike cover.

She wasn't a jeweler, didn't even own that many pieces of jewelry, but she knew, just *knew*, that she was staring at something priceless. Guessing the age of the odd, almost-material-feeling paper and seeing the foreign text, Lyssa couldn't help but wonder what these books were doing outside a museum. She examined every page of the jeweled volume, ran her fingertips over every illustration, and understood nothing. But the worth of both books was firmly established in her mind, which left a troubling question—what was Aidan doing with them?

Suddenly the oddness of his unannounced appearance at her door, feverish and without luggage, wearing clothes far too big and telling her far too little, struck home with enough force to make her gasp and lean against the breakfast bar.

Who the hell was the sword-wielding man in her shower, and what the fuck did he want with her?

Chapter 9

Determined to tackle her gorgeous problem head on, Lyssa took the stairs two at a time. She sprinted into her room just in time to catch a still wet Aidan stepping naked from the bathroom, his arms lifted to towel-dry his hair, his pectorals and abs flexing in a way that made her mouth water. She skidded to a halt. "I . . . you . . . you're . . . Oh man . . . yum . . ."

She sputtered into silence as he grew hard right before her eyes.

He heaved out a sigh, and his arms fell to his sides. "I just got rid of that."

She swallowed hard, images flooding her mind of how he might have done that. Water beating down, soap-slick hands stroking the throbbing length of him, pumping with a primitive rhythm until he spurted his lust down the drain. She knew how that beautiful cock felt in her hands, how thick and hard it was when erect. Shit, it looked great pre–hard-on. How many men could say that?

He has a freckle on his right hip.

Her gaze flew to the spot, and her mouth fell open at the sight of the tiny little brown circle. Then she pulled herself together. She could have taken note of it in the shower. Remembering it didn't mean anything.

"Don't worry." His voice, low and husky, slipped into her musings. "There's more than enough left for you."

God, she loved the way he talked, how open he was about his sexuality and his desire for her. Had he approached her this way before? In a club, perhaps, when she'd been younger? She had been wild in college, skating through her school day and partying hard at night. She imagined the scene—dressed in shorts and backless tank, leaning against the bar, shouting her drink order at the bartender so she could be heard over the pulsing music. Then Aidan's hands at her hips, his erection at her lower back, his mouth to her throat as he had done downstairs. Before he led her away . . .

Was that how it had happened? She tried so hard to recall. Regardless, her body remembered his, even if her mind didn't.

He moved toward her with silent grace, one arm circling her waist, his other hand thrusting through her wet hair, angling her head to better fit her lips to his. He took her mouth with lush, deep licks of his tongue, making her shudder and clutch at his wet back.

"What are you thinking about when you look at me like that?" he asked in a voice dripping sin.

"Huh . . .?" She wasn't thinking about anything; he'd fried her brain with that kiss.

"How dirty was the sex?" He tugged her hips into his,

making certain she felt every hot, throbbing inch of him. His large hand cupped the back of her head; his mouth brushed against her ear. "Was I fucking you yet? Or just about to?"

"Aidan . . ." she moaned, tormented by her lustful body and his raw, heated seduction. "It's so good between us, I can't stop thinking about it."

Her eyes squeezed shut, her fingertips kneading restlessly into the hard muscles of his back.

"The best," he said hoarsely.

She nodded. "Is that why you came? To see if it's as good as you remembered? Is this just a booty call sort of thing?"

Will there be more? Or just this? Already the thought of his leaving made her chest tight.

He tucked her flushed face in the crook of his neck. "No, no, and no. Do you have time to talk?"

Sighing, she shook her head. "I have to go to work. I'm late."

"Can I come with you?"

For a moment she paused. What was she supposed to do with him? She needed some distance so she could think. Maybe do some investigating. Call some old friends. See if anyone else remembered Aidan. "It would be better if I went alone. I'll be busy, and I'm sure there are things you have to do while you're in town."

"There are things you need to know."

You don't date seriously, you're not looking for a girlfriend, no attachments. It's just sex.

"Please, Lyssa."

The strength of her déjà vu was overwhelming. And

painful. A one-night stand. That's what they'd had. That's all Aidan wanted.

He leaned back. "Don't shut me out. Listen to what I have to tell you."

She looked up at him, saw the brief flare of longing that he quickly hid with a crooked smile, and knew she had no choice. "Yeah, get dressed and . . . Crap. You don't have anything to wear." Lyssa wrinkled her nose. "Any idea when the airline is going to deliver your stuff?"

Then she thought about their situation, and her eyes narrowed suspiciously. "How did you know where I lived?"

"You told me," he said simply, his hands stroking down her back.

"You should have called before you showed up."

He nuzzled his nose against hers, rubbing his body all over her. "I know."

"How long are you planning to stay?"

"I haven't thought that far ahead," he murmured, his mouth brushing back and forth across hers.

She sighed, too tired to fight the feeling that she belonged in his arms. "We have to go. I'm going to be so late."

Aidan nodded, pulling back to retrieve the sweats from where he'd tossed them across the unmade bed. He tugged them on first, then a wicked-looking pair of combat boots that self-sealed with a simple tap of his fingertips.

When he stood, she crossed her arms and shook her head. "Neat boots, but you can't go out like that."

"Oh?" He arched a brow. "Why not?"

"It's cold outside."

"I'll be fine."

He was already damn fine with his luscious torso bared for all the world to see. A thick lock of dark hair hung over his brow, drawing attention to those beautiful eyes and sexy-as-hell lips. If they went outside with him looking like that, they would be mobbed by a pack of infatuated women.

Her lips pursed. "I'm not taking you around like that."

Aidan frowned. "What do you want me to do?" Then his eyes widened and he crossed his arms, mimicking her pose. "Is this your way of saying you don't want me to go with you?"

"No! Well . . . yes." She tossed up her hands. "Maybe I can come back at lunchtime with something for you to wear? Then you can spend the rest of the day with me."

"Remember what we talked about?" he asked grimly. "You be open with me. I do the same with you."

Snorting out a laugh, Lyssa said, "Funny how that's led to you knowing everything about me and me knowing jackshit about you."

"I'm ready to talk anytime. Now would be good. You're the one who's got to fit me into her schedule."

"You're the one who invited himself over without a common courtesy call first!"

Aidan opened his mouth to retort, then blew out an exasperated breath. "You want to tell me why we're arguing?"

"We're not—" Lyssa stopped when he arched that brow at her again. She shrugged lamely. "I've got a problem with you being seen half naked, okay?"

He blinked. Then a slow, sinful grin spread across his

features. "Are you feeling possessive, Hot Stuff?" he asked with laughter in his voice.

"No," she lied, turning away and moving quickly toward the door. "I've got to go. I'll be back around—"

He caught her with both arms around her middle, lifted her feet from the floor, and carried her out. Down the stairs they went, with him chuckling the whole way.

"What are you doing?" she asked in the sternest voice she could manage while grinning like an idiot. He was a big, brawny bully with an adorable smile and far too much arrogance.

She liked him. A lot.

"Coming with you. I'll wear one of Mike's lab coats, if that makes you feel better."

She stiffened. "You know what? The stalkerlike amount of information you have about me is freaking me out."

"I'm sure it is." He stopped in front of the breakfast bar. "Grab your stuff." She caught up her purse and keys. "And the two books right there."

"Yeah, about these books. What the hell are they, Aidan, and why are they in my house?"

"They're homework to keep me busy."

She bit back a retort, and then found herself fighting to stay mad, which wasn't easy while being carried around like a sack of potatoes. Aidan nipping at her neck didn't help, either.

"Stop that! Watch where we're going."

He didn't need the admonishment. He moved with unerring precision, clutching her with one arm while using the other hand to turn off the lights and coffeemaker, and open the door to the garage.

"We're putting the top up," she muttered as she dropped into the driver's seat, imagining stopping at a red light and the stares Aidan would elicit.

"You're being silly." He stilled her hand when she reached to engage the automatic soft top.

His mouth was a breath away from hers. He paused there, caging her in, making her wait. She could lean forward just that little bit and press her lips to his, but the need for answers and her growing unease were strong enough to hold her back.

Aidan hid his mounting frustration as Lyssa held out, her tongue darting out to wet her lips, but otherwise making no move to close the gap between them. He caught the seat belt, pulling it across her lap and snapping it into place. Then he gave her a quick buss on the lips, walked around the front end, and slid into the passenger seat.

She waited a moment, staring at him with those dark eyes that told him everything she was thinking. It was one of the many things he adored about her—the lack of guile. With her, he could just *be*. There was no mask to wear, no rigidity to maintain.

The relief of that was like a deep sigh after holding one's breath too long, but the new wariness he felt in her made his entire body tense. Needing to hold her to him, Aidan reached out and laced his fingers with hers.

"You're trouble with a capital T," she murmured with a sigh.

"Wait until I've got you back in bed."

He felt her shiver through their handclasp. Sweet Lyssa with the open-book smile did have some secrets, like her hidden desire to be ridden hard and put away wet. He couldn't help but wonder if any other man had taken the time to learn that about her. He would have eventually, even had he not been privy to her thoughts in her dreams. He was grateful, however, that he didn't need to wait to find out. Their strongest tie was the desire her body remembered. He wouldn't let her forget it.

In the meantime, they had to make it through the day, which so far had worked against him every step of the way. But he *would* get Lyssa alone, and he *would* tell her everything, just as soon as she slowed down long enough to listen. Needing his explanation to be both clear and believable, Aidan leaned his head back and closed his eyes, absorbing the feel of the morning air rushing over him.

It was a bit chilly, as she'd warned, but the warmth he felt inside from Lyssa's repeated heated glances kept him comfortable. Beneath his left hand, he felt the books he'd brought from the Twilight. He hoped they would give him the answers he needed to keep Lyssa safe. Something, anything that could prove without a doubt either that there was no Key or, if the Elders were correct about its existence, that Lyssa wasn't it.

Aidan cursed the fact that he hadn't paid more attention during history lessons, but he had been young and randy. Ready to fight and fuck to his heart's content. He hadn't been mature enough to consider the future in all its many facets. He certainly hadn't known that one day he would find someone who would remind him that he had deeper needs than carnal ones.

Lyssa kept her silence, making him wish he could read her thoughts as he had been able to do in the Twilight. Her conscious mind was understandably confused, but her subconscious remembered him. He could only hope that would be enough to carry them through his explanations. He was going to sound like a madman.

"Talk to me," he said in a low voice, just loud enough to be heard over the wind.

"Why don't you do the talking?" she retorted. "Tell me how you know so much about me."

He sighed. So that's what she was thinking about.

Where to begin? Did he start with the part explaining he was an alien? Or did he begin with her being the prophesied destruction of two worlds?

Either way, she had to understand who he was and what he was doing, before common sense overrode her gut instincts and urged her to kick him out. He didn't want to kidnap her or force her to do anything against her will. But he would, if doing so saved her life.

The Roadster pulled to an abrupt stop, ending that train of thought. Lifting his head and opening his eyes, Aidan saw the back door to the clinic just a few feet away. When Lyssa hopped out of the car, he leaned over and grabbed her wrist. "Can you get out of here early?"

She pursed her lush lips a moment and then nodded. "I'm going to try."

"Hey. What's going on?" a voice called out.

Aidan kept his gaze trained on the woman of his dreams as guilt and confusion clouded her lovely features.

"Shit," she breathed. "It's Chad."

Lyssa stared down at the half-naked wet dream in her passenger seat and told herself, *Wake up wake up wake up . . .*

Talk about a nightmare in broad daylight. How the hell

was she going to explain this, when she had no idea what was going on herself? She had damp hair. Aidan did, too, *and* he was bare-chested. They looked guilty of everything they'd done.

"Uh . . . hate to interrupt, but Mrs. Yamamoto is starting to get pissy." The sound of Stacey's voice coming from the rear door of the clinic was such a relief, Lyssa decided to give her a raise. "She and her cat have been waiting almost twenty minutes."

"I'm coming in now." Taking a deep breath of courage, Lyssa tugged free of Aidan's grip and faced a scowling Chad.

"What's going on?" he asked, his gaze looking over her shoulder and then rising above her head as she heard the passenger door open and shut behind her.

"Chad, this is Aidan. He's a . . . friend of my mom." She adjusted her stance to see both men at once, and then cringed when she saw their aggressive postures. "Aidan, this is Chad."

"Hi." Chad thrust out his hand. "I'm Lyssa's boyfriend. Nice to meet you."

The tensing of Aidan's jaw was audible, but he reciprocated the gesture.

When Chad pulled his hand away he was flexing it, and Lyssa could only imagine how crushing Aidan's grip had been.

"Well . . ." She cleared her throat nervously and caught up her purse. "I've got to get to work. Chad, did you need something?"

His gaze narrowed on her face. "I was in the neighborhood and wanted to see if you're free for lunch."

She nodded violently. "Yes. One o'clock, okay? I'll need to catch up before I can leave."

"Yeah." Chad looked at Aidan again. "I'll see you at one." Then he dipped his knees and kissed her. Full on the mouth. With a soft swipe of his tongue across her lips for good measure.

Lyssa couldn't look at Aidan as Chad walked back to his Jeep. Like a coward, she slammed her door shut, hit the alarm, and nearly ran to where Stacey waited with wide eyes.

"Holy shit!" Stacey hissed, as she passed her. "You are so fucked."

"Noticed that, did ya?"

Unable to help it, Lyssa looked over her shoulder and saw Aidan coming after her, his long-legged stride even and rhythmic, almost a stalk. *Hunter after prey.* When she saw the flaring nostrils and smoldering eyes, she knew if she waited for him to get to her, she was going to be in big trouble.

"Which room is Mrs. Yamamoto in?" she asked quickly.

"Exam Two." Stacey whistled, her gaze riveted and filled with a wholly feminine appreciation that made Lyssa's teeth grind. "Would you look at the abs on that guy? Talk about sin on a stick. He's delish."

"Damn it. Get a lab coat for him. And bring me one, too."

She went straight to Exam Two, purse and keys in hand, and got to work. Sometimes avoidance had its usefulness.

It took until a quarter to one to get caught up on her patients. The first few times she'd been forced to run past her office, Aidan had been waiting with wide-legged stance, crossed arms, and intimidating scowl. She had tried to look cool and collected, but she couldn't forget that he was commando under those sweats. It did strange things to her nervous system just to think of it. Later he'd been seated at her desk, studiously poring over his books. And now that she needed to clean up for lunch with Chad, the door was closed.

All morning long she'd debated what to do about her predicament and had finally come to have some confidence in her decision. Regardless of what happened with Aidan, Chad wasn't the guy for her. She'd always known it. She just hadn't wanted to admit it. Breaking it off was the obvious answer, but guilt weighed on her heavily. In a perfect world, she would have ended things with Chad before hooking up with Aidan. But life wasn't perfect, and she'd have to make amends as best she could. She hoped, in the end, they could remain friends.

But she hadn't yet decided what to do with Aidan. All she knew was that every time she had caught sight of him today, her pulse rate picked up. Even with that grumpy, scowling face of his, he still drove her nuts in the best possible way.

So she would take care of Chad, wrap up the workday, and then listen to whatever Aidan had to say. She hoped like hell it would fill in the gaps of her memory and remove all the doubts she had.

Resolved, Lyssa caught the handle of her office door, and velocity took her to the center of the room before she realized it was empty.

Oh god, had he left?

Her heart racing, she turned to yell for Stacey . . .

. . . and found Aidan leaning casually against the closed door. The lab coat was hung on the rack beside him, leaving him once again bare from the waist up. Her gaze lifted to meet his, and she found a gleam in his eyes that told her he knew what the sight of his bare chest would do to her.

"Jesus!" she cried, her hand lifting to her chest. "You scared the shit out of me. What are you doing hiding behind the door?"

"I wasn't hiding," he said dryly. "I was about to hunt you down when you barged in. I barely got out of the way in time."

"Oh." She moved the short distance to her antique reproduction desk and leaned her butt against it. "Chad's going to be here in a few minutes."

"I know." He crossed the room with a sultry stride that made her mouth water. It wasn't blatant, like a swagger. It was simply predatory and sexually charged. Setting his hands on either side of her hips, Aidan caged her to the desk and nuzzled his lips against her neck. "I'm going to miss you."

Beneath her palms she felt warm, silken skin stretched over hard, flexing muscle, and she melted inside. She groaned inwardly when his teeth nipped her earlobe.

"Tell me I have no reason to feel jealous," he ordered gruffly.

Leaning back, Lyssa met his gaze. It was impassive except for the muscle in his jaw that ticced. "There's no reason," she assured him softly, appreciating him more for his honesty about his feelings.

He caught her close so that his big, hard body was literally wrapped around hers, his large hands holding her so sweetly. She knew how strong he was, yet he held her with such tenderness.

"Aidan," she whispered, her nostrils filling with his scent. There was no other scent in the world like his. It was spicy and exotic. Foreign. She loved it, craved it. "I won't be gone long."

"A minute is too long." His voice was dark as sin, his accent thick and delicious, a vocal caress.

Then Aidan kissed her with tightly restrained passion, his tongue gliding along hers expertly, reminding her of how good it was with him. The best. A rough, edgy growl rumbled in his chest as she melted into him. Just from a kiss.

She hugged him back with all the strength she had in her. There was so much she wanted to say, to ask, to know. But there wasn't time, and she hated that. Over his shoulder, she could see the clock. It was five minutes to one.

"I need to go." She pressed her face into his shoulder, feeling guilty as sin.

Aidan couldn't figure out what to do with his desire to snatch Lyssa up and take her far away.

A knock came to the door just as Lyssa slid to her feet.

"Yeah?" she called out, her voice husky.

"Chad's here." Stacey's voice through the door was more serious than any Aidan had heard from her today.

Lyssa breathed in sharply. "How do I explain to him," she asked plaintively, "when I don't know what's going on myself?"

He caught her chin and urged her gaze to meet his. His

chest ached at the sight of her. She was pale, her dark eyes tormented, her lower lip worried between her teeth. "Tell him the truth. An old flame showed up and you have to reevaluate."

She nodded, but looked shamed enough to set him on edge.

Her hand came to rest on his bare shoulder, and his eyes closed a moment in pleasure at her touch. She moved then, her fingers sifting through his hair.

"Are you okay?" Lyssa asked, her voice filled with concern.

Aidan nodded. Inside him, something vibrated anxiously, making his stomach clench tight. "I hate this. I don't want you to go."

"You're awfully possessive for a guy who walked out of my life at some point," she said dryly.

He stilled, conveying the truth of his words with a steely stare. "I've looked for you my whole life."

All these years he couldn't figure out what he was missing. He'd searched for answers in an attempt to calm his restlessness, and he still wanted them. But what he'd needed was Lyssa and the connection he found with her.

She shook her head, her lush lips drawn tight. "You say the corniest shit, but it never sounds corny coming from you. You could give lessons on how to make the worst pickup lines in history work."

Reaching for her purse, Lyssa set her keys and some money on the desktop. "Get some clothes. I don't carry much cash—I'm a debit card girl—but there should be enough here for some jeans, shirt, and boxers. Talk to Stacey, she'll tell you where to go."

Aidan caught her wrist before she turned away. She lifted her gaze to meet his. They stared at each other, questions and confusion filling the air.

"I have to go," she said finally.

He caught her then, his hands fisting in her hair, tugging her head back, his mouth taking hers. *Taking* it, completely, his tongue gliding deep and thrusting. Drinking in the taste of her, leaving his flavor in return. Her hands clutched at his back, her knees weakened, her body sagged with the weight of her desire. Only when she was whimpering into his mouth did he release her.

His nostrils flared. "Make it quick, or I'll hunt you down. You won't like what happens if I do."

She swallowed hard and nodded, backing away slowly. Dazed.

As the door closed with a click of finality behind her, Lyssa released her pent-up breath. There was no denying it. She was head over heels.

But she still had to deal with Chad.

"Shit."

The last time she had felt this torn was when she'd made Jenna Lee cry in college because of a thoughtless comment. Chad deserved someone who was really crazy about him. That bit of knowledge was the only thing that kept her from hating herself completely.

Lyssa lifted her chin and moved down the hallway to the rear clinic door. She could do this. She could.

Then she stepped outside, saw the handsome man leaning against his Jeep, and began to cry.

It wasn't that she regretted what she had done with Aidan last night; she didn't. But she should have handled this entire situation better. Add in the events of the last twenty or so hours and her overwhelming feelings for Aidan, and she was reduced to an emotional wreck.

"Hey," Chad said softly, coming up to her and holding her close. "It's not the end of the world. I'm a big boy. I can handle it."

Lyssa leaned into him, grateful that he was letting her off the hook. After years of hoping for a great guy to come along, she somehow ended up with two at the same time.

She was letting go of one. She prayed like hell she didn't lose the other.

Chapter 10

"Who the hell are you?"

Aidan glanced at Stacey, who stood in the doorway of Lyssa's office, and raised his brows. "Excuse me?"

"You heard me. What do you want with Lyssa?"

He settled back against the desk and crossed his arms. He knew Lyssa cared a lot about her friend Stacey, and it appeared Stacey felt the same in return. "I don't think that's any of your business."

"Sure it is." Her gaze narrowed. "Chad's a nice guy. He's good to her."

"I'm a nice guy. I'm good to her."

"I don't call what you're doing good for her. You left her before, and you don't look like you're planning on sticking around this time, either."

There was nothing he could say to that. He didn't know what his next move would be. In the last forty-eight hours, he hadn't had much time to think about it. Even when Lyssa had been busy with her patients, his thoughts had been more on the rift between them than it had been about the days ahead. He needed to focus. "My work keeps me away."

"What is it you do? Lyssa said you're Special Forces or something."

Clever. "Or something."

Her foot tapped. "Don't you think it's a little selfish to just drop in when you feel like it, especially when she's got someone steady?"

"I tried to stay away, Stacey," he said softly. "I really did."

She studied him for a long moment, then said, "I'm withholding judgment for now."

"Thank you." And he meant it. If Stacey took sides against him, it would make an already uphill battle worse.

"In the meantime, we need to get you some clothes."

"That would nice," he agreed. Looking "normal" was one way to soothe Lyssa's nerves.

Taking a second to put the precious books away in the top desk drawer, Aidan snatched up the keys and cash, and gestured for Stacey to precede him out to the parking lot. He was having a hard time feeling so helpless. It was a state of being he'd never experienced before, and it definitely didn't suit him. He needed to get Lyssa settled, then he could concentrate on the ancient texts in earnest. The day was half over. The evening would be upon them soon. Then sleep, when Lyssa would be most vulnerable.

Time, something he was used to having in endless quantities, was running out.

* * *

"For a man who was just promoted to Captain of the Elite, you're awfully quiet."

Connor shot a sidelong glance at the curvaceous Guardian sprawled across his bed. Flushed from their recent fucking, Morgan was lovely, tempting him to abandon the polishing of his glaive to take her again. "Cross is captain."

"He's gone." Morgan pouted.

"He'll find a way back. I'll make sure of it." Aidan was a warrior to the core. He couldn't live without a sword in his hand. "Can you see him driving a mini-van?"

"No." She laughed and rolled over, baring her body in a sinuous stretch. "But then I can't see him so attached to one woman, either."

Snorting, Connor returned his attention to his task. "Temporary insanity. The Elders screwed with him. First they sent him to the Dreamer twice. Then they sent him to the Gateway."

"Is it as horrible as they say?"

"Worse. He's not thinking with the right head, trust me. He'll find the Dreamer and they'll fuck like rabbits. Then he'll get over her and do his job."

"Do you think she's the Key?"

He paused. "I don't know. But you're going to try and find out."

"What?" Morgan sat straight up in bed.

"I checked the roster. Philip Wager is set to lead the team tonight." The team that would make a second attempt to enter the mind of Aidan's Dreamer. He was kicking himself now for switching places with his friend that one night. Now he wished he'd both kept Aidan away from her and checked her out himself. He simply couldn't picture a woman alluring enough to swear off bachelorhood.

"Philip's mad at me. He's not going to tell me anything." She tossed her dark hair over her shoulder. "And I don't particularly want to talk to him anyway."

Connor's mouth curved. "Yes, you do. You're curious about the Dreamer. You had a thing for Cross for a long time."

"I had a thing for you, too."

His grin widened. "You still do." He set aside his glaive with barely enough time to catch the tasseled pillow Morgan threw at him. Standing, he moved to the bed, noting the way her dark eyes dipped to his rapidly swelling cock before lifting to meet his gaze.

"Oh no," she murmured dryly. "I recognize that look. You want something. Unfortunately for you, I'm feeling pretty good from the orgasms I've had already, so I'm not likely to agree."

"I can make you feel even better," he rumbled, setting one knee on the edge of the bed before crawling over her.

Her smile faded. "Seriously, Connor, you're asking too much. The Elders would punish me for going around them like that."

"I'll protect you."

"No one can be protected from the Elders."

"Try me."

When her jaw set stubbornly, he cursed inwardly and changed tactics. "I just want you to talk to Wager," he cajoled. "Find out what their orders are. What methods he's using. What resistance he's facing."

"What excuse would I have for wanting to know all that?"

He kissed her breathless, his mouth slanting across hers in a blatant promise of reward, one he hoped hid his desperation. "I'll make it worth your while, Morgan love."

"That would take a lot." She inhaled sharply as his chest touched hers. She paused a moment, then her arms came around him.

"I've got a lot to give." Adjusting his hips, he thrust smoothly into her tight, slick cunt. Then he withdrew completely. "If you want it, that is."

She growled softly, a sound that made his heart beat faster with a combination of arousal and anxiety. "You're cheating," she complained.

Yes, he was, but he would do whatever was necessary to help Aidan. He would not leave his commanding officer and best friend out there alone.

Stonehenge.

As memories flooded Aidan's mind, his fingertips drifted over the recently deciphered text in the jeweled book. He had been to Stonehenge once. A Dreamer had a fantasy there—passionate sex under the stars in the center of the stones. The formation had been whole then, complete, not decimated by time as he now knew it to be.

That woman and the acts he'd committed with her were so distant and foggy as to be rendered meaningless. From the moment he first slid inside Lyssa's mind, every woman in his past had faded to insignificance. He hadn't thought such a loss of memory was possible, had even considered the possibility that the journey from the Twilight had altered his brain in some way. But he remembered every other thing in his immortal life. It was only when it came to his sexual past that things got fuzzy. Only Lyssa shone with golden vibrancy in his thoughts, warming his blood, making his heart beat faster.

Lyssa.

His hand closed into a fist and a growl rumbled up from deep in his chest. He was in bad shape. She had been gone nearly two hours now, and he was slowly going insane. Concentrating on the ancient text helped a tiny bit, but not a whole hell of a lot. Even when he managed to decipher a section, it didn't lead to comprehension. Stonehenge, petroglyphs, and astronomy would be fascinating if Lyssa were beside him, believing in him. Safe. But that wasn't the case. He feared he was losing her. He, a man who had never feared anything.

He forced his thoughts back to the book. He needed more information. Since a trip to England would leave Lyssa vulnerable, it was immediately ruled out. Somehow he needed to learn what was necessary from thousands of miles away.

The unmistakable sound of the heavy rear door opening brought his head up. He stood, his mouth dry, and waited for her to appear. When she did, he held the edge of the desk with damp palms and searched her features for some hint of her thoughts.

"Hi," she said wearily.

He came around the desk, but didn't go to her, afraid that if he kept pushing, he would push her completely away. "Hi."

"Everything go okay while I was gone?"

"I missed you." *The* understatement of his entire life. She made him feel alive, her proximity bringing a tangible wave of awareness across the space that separated them. How different this was, their physical bodies existing and touching on the same plane. Sex with her had been amazing in the Twilight. In real time it was phenomenal. Altering.

She heaved out her breath, dropped her purse to the floor, and walked into his embrace. His arms went around her; his eyes squeezed shut against the painful ache in his chest. He buried his nose in her hair and breathed her in. Her tiny hands stroked up and down his back, soothing him, once again offering him the comfort he hadn't known he needed until he met her.

"I missed you, too." She rubbed her face into his new white cotton T-shirt and clung to him. "You look great in jeans."

Recognizing an olive branch when it was presented to him, he managed a smile and kissed her forehead. "I'm glad you approve."

"Stacey wasn't too hard on you, was she?"

"Nah, she's all right. It's you I'm worried about. How are you holding up?" There was such sadness in her eyes, and she carried herself as if burdened by a great weight. The distance between them was painful, crushing.

Lyssa tilted her head back and stared up at him. "I'm okay. I'm glad there are only a few more hours left before we can leave."

"Me, too. Anything I can do to help speed things along?"

She gave a wry laugh. "Keep my office door closed. Every time I walk by and see you, I get flustered. Slows me down."

As warmth suffused his blood, Aidan's mouth curved. He half sat on the edge of the desk and pulled her between his legs. "Flustered? Or hot and horny?"

"All of the above." Her hands stroked across the soft cotton that covered his chest, then she caught the chain that peeped out above his neckline and pulled it into view. "What kind of stone is this?"

It looked like an opal but appeared to glow from inside. She turned it over, but found that the mounting was solid silver in the back, leaving no place for light to pass through.

"I have no idea. It was a gift."

"From a woman?"

He took the space of one breath to relish the jealousy evident in her tone, then shook his head. "No. A favorite teacher."

"Good." Lyssa dropped it back beneath his shirt and wrapped her arms around his neck. She pressed her lips to his, making him groan. "Back to work I go. Stay out of trouble."

His hands cupped her ass and held her to him when she tried to step back. "Not so fast."

Lyssa arched a brow at him.

"Did you eat?" When she wrinkled her nose, he had his answer. "You didn't have breakfast, either. You need to take better care of yourself."

Twisting at the waist, he caught up the bag that rested on the corner of the desk. He tucked his ankles behind her calves to keep her close, and reached inside for the Styrofoam container and spoon. He caught the handle of the plastic utensil between his teeth and used both hands to pry the lid open. Instantly the delicious scent of potato-cheese soup filled the air between them. He retrieved the spoon and grinned when her tummy growled in response to the mouthwatering smell.

"That's my favorite soup," she murmured, licking her lips in a way that goaded him to mimic her, his tongue following the lush lower curve of her mouth.

"I know." He scooped up a spoonful. "Open wide."

He alternated between feeding her and kissing her. It was as intimate as sex and just as moving. She laughed, her dark eyes bright with pleasure, and he wanted her. Wanted her this way, open and warm. He couldn't wait to go home with her, to take her again. And again. And again. Indulging his every desire, every sexual whim, listening to the little whimpers she made when she was desperate for orgasm, wallowing in the lust that grew from the inside and worked its way out, not the other way around. Not for physical release, but for physical closeness, a connection as real as the one he felt inside him.

Then, when she was exhausted, her mind plunging straight through the Twilight into deep unconsciousness, he would be able to study the Stonehenge clue without distractions.

"No more," she protested, when the contents were two-thirds gone. "I'm going to burst."

"Just a little more," he coaxed, encouraged by the healthy pink flush that had replaced her previous paleness. He winked. "You'll need your strength later."

She shivered in that delightful way that made his cock twitch, then opened her mouth, finishing every drop.

When she went back to work, she closed the door, and

Aidan returned his attention to the books he'd stolen from the Elders. The jeweled volume read as if it was part of a collection, referencing information he suspected was located elsewhere. The text he'd stolen from the Temple of the Elders was even more difficult, filled with words that no longer existed and were not the roots of the language they used today. But it was all he had, and he would make the best of it.

He pushed back from the desk and stood, rolling his shoulders to alleviate the stiffness brought on by too many hours of unaccustomed inactivity. Then he opened the door and took the hallway to the front desk.

Stacey arched her brows at him, the silent toughness belying the cute image her cartoon tropical fish scrubs portrayed. "What's up?"

"Where's the nearest library?"

"Hell if I know." She opened a drawer, pulled out the phone book, and slapped it onto the counter. "Here ya go. Knock yourself out."

Shit. Aidan caught up the book and turned, almost knocking over the elderly woman who had come up behind him.

"Excuse me, young man." Stooped at the shoulders and wearing hot pink sweats with a matching headband in her gray curls, she gifted him with a bright smile.

He grinned at her use of the appellation "young man," considering he was easily several centuries older than she was. "Entirely my fault," he said, steadying her with a hand at her elbow.

"Well, aren't you a looker?" she murmured with a wink. "Would you help me carry out my Mathilda? She's been sick lately and when I move her carrier, I jostle her too much."

Aidan bent and slipped his hand though the handle of the cat cage at their feet. "It would be my pleasure."

"You should keep this one around," the woman said to Stacey.

"Yeah? Tell him that," Stacey retorted. Then she smiled warmly. "I'll be calling you Monday morning, Mrs. Laughin, to see how you and Mathilda are doing."

"Talk to you then, honey."

Aidan held the glass front door to the clinic open and gestured for Mrs. Laughin to precede him out, but once they stepped outside, she urged him ahead of her.

"Don't wait for me," she said. "I'm so slow it'll cramp those long legs of yours. That's my car over there, the yellow Hummer." The horn sounded once and the taillights flashed as she disengaged the alarm. "You can just set her on the floor."

Following instructions, he had Mathilda settled securely on the passenger floorboard in no time, then he returned to Mrs. Laughin and offered his arm.

"Dr. Bates is a pretty thing, isn't she?" she asked, shooting him a not-so-innocent sidelong glance.

"Yes, she is."

"I think she's single. Hardworking. Smart. Got great taste in decorating, too. Best-looking vet clinic in town. And Mathilda loves her."

Aidan's grin widened. "Mathilda has great taste."

"Yes, she does. I can always tell when a solicitor is at the door, because she piddles on the entryway tile."

Choking back a laugh, he opened the driver's side door

and watched as a custom step lowered from the undercarriage, enabling her to get up into the vehicle without his help. She surprised him by holding out a hundred-dollar bill.

"I don't want that," he said.

"Take it. I got plenty. My dear Charles, bless his heart, made us rich."

"I still don't want it."

"I ogled your ass." She shook the bill at him. "Take the damn money or I'll feel guilty for doing it. You don't want to make an old woman feel guilty, do you?"

Laughing, Aidan took the money, determined to give it to Stacey as a credit to Mrs. Laughin's account.

"Dr. Bates has a nice heinie, too," she said.

"Yes, she does," he agreed.

She beamed at him as she pushed sunglasses onto her face. "I knew I liked you. Now, go buy yourself something nice or something for Dr. Bates. Women like gifts. It was money well spent for me. Haven't seen an ass as fine as yours in a very long time."

"Thank you." He waved as she pulled out of the parking lot, then turned in a circle, carrying the ridiculous hope that he would spot a library nearby. He didn't, of course, but he did spot a mass transit bus roll by with a Discovery Channel advertisement emblazoned on the side.

He was willing to bet he could purchase the items he wanted, rather than borrow them. After all, he knew where the stores were, which was more than he could say for the library. Whatever his next move, he needed to make it quickly. Everything seemed to be working against him today, but he wasn't giving up without a fight. He'd be damned if the night came and he had nothing to show for his efforts.

Returning to the clinic, he stopped by the desk. "Where's Lyssa?"

"With a patient."

He set his elbows on the counter. "Can you give me an inch? Please."

She stared at him for a long moment, then sighed. "Exam One."

"Thank you."

Reaching the paneled door with a gilt-framed sign that said "Exam One" attached to it, Aidan knocked lightly and waited.

It swung open a moment later, and just like the first time he'd seen Lyssa sprawled upon golden sand beneath him, he felt as if he had been sucker punched in the stomach. Blond, curvy perfection with dark eyes that went from professional coolness to melted desire just from the sight of him. He caught the door frame for balance and breathed in harshly.

"Oh shit," she hissed, her fingers white where she gripped the knob. She stepped out into the hall to afford them some privacy. "You should have warned me it was you before I opened the door."

"I knew it was you and it didn't help."

She stared up at him with liquid, seductive eyes. He didn't have to read her thoughts to know she was thinking the same things he was—hot sex, naked sweaty bodies straining together, the fierce, aching pleasure that was almost too much to handle. It had been this way from the beginning, the depth of desire between them that wiped out every other thought but the need to be as close as possible.

Unable to stop himself, Aidan reached out and cupped her breast beneath the open flap of her lab coat, his thumb stroking across her nipple and finding it already peaked hard.

Lyssa smacked his hand away. "Stop that. I need my brain cells."

His jaw clenched against the urges it wasn't time to indulge in. Focus. On. The. Books. "I need to borrow your car again. Do you mind?"

"No, go ahead." Her pause was nearly imperceptible, but he caught it. "I'll be done in an hour, though."

"I'll be back long before then." He dipped his head and pressed his lips to hers, physically crossing the distance he sensed growing between them. Two steps forward and one back. "I won't delay our talk for even a minute."

She sighed. "My brain is fried now."

When she turned away from him, he reached out and pinched her ass, making her jump and glare at him. He made a kissing gesture with his lips and then went back to her office.

When Stacey had gone out with him earlier, she'd taken him to a large mall complex that housed a couple of bookstores as well as clothing and other merchants. That's where he intended to go in search of information about Stonehenge's relationship to astronomy. He suspected a connection between the purpose of the stone alignment and the world his people had abandoned when the Nightmares had taken over. If he eventually linked fissure creation to the ancient monument in England, he wanted to make sure he understood as much as possible.

He hoped like hell he was on the right track. A dead end could cost Lyssa her life.

Chapter 11

"So you're keeping Chad on a leash while you figure out what's up with your hunk delivery?"

Lyssa glared. "No, Stace. I'm not keeping Chad on a leash. We've just agreed to stay in touch, as friends."

"And you still can't remember meeting Aidan, only shagging him." Stacey leaned back in one of the little settees that graced the waiting room and shook her head. "Maybe he slipped you a roofie or something."

"Stacey! Christ. Look at him! He doesn't need to drug women to get them in bed."

Setting her forearms on her knees, Lyssa closed her eyes. "You know, I opened the door to Exam One and saw him standing there, and my toes curled? The only time my fucking toes curl is when I'm having an orgasm."

"You had an orgasm just looking at him?"

"Damn near." Even now, the memory of him leaning against the doorjamb in loose-legged jeans and white

T-shirt made her breasts ache. Aidan Cross looked, smelled, walked, talked sex. Period.

"Wish I had a hair trigger like that." Stacey snorted. "'Kay, here are my thoughts. Maybe this is one of those deals like when a juror marries a serial murderer after the trial. The whole dangerous-bad boy-I'm-gonna-tame-him thing."

Lyssa stared.

"I'm just saying," Stacey said, holding up both hands defensively.

"Aidan is not a serial murderer."

"He might be if he's Special Forces."

"That would be different!"

"Yeah." Stacey slumped back into the chair. "I guess so. Maybe you're just crazy, or maybe he is. I hope it all works out and you're happy, but man, I have my doubts. There's something weird going on here."

Lyssa sighed loudly. "I think so, too."

"Here, take this." Stacey dug into her purse next to her and pulled out a pen. Then she tugged off the top and revealed an atomizer top.

"What is that? Mace?"

"Pepper spray. This shit's nasty stuff. Justin messed with a tube once and damn near killed us both. Your eyes water, your nose runs, and your skin burns like hell."

Staring down at the innocuous-looking tube, Lyssa felt like crying. Could she be more scattered and confused? "You think I might have to use this?"

"Better safe than sorry. This guy is a stranger to you. Who knows what his deal is? No clothes, no money. It's just bizarre. If he starts talking about religious sacrifices or says he's an alien, you'll be grateful for that spray."

"Fuck."

Stacey leaned over and squeezed her wrist. "Call me often over the weekend, or else I'm sending the cops over. And bring him to dinner at my place tomorrow. I want to see you in person."

"You're freaking me out." Lyssa stood and began to pace. When she was with Aidan, she felt safe. Cherished. But when they were apart she was flooded with doubts.

"Put Aidan up in a hotel until everything is worked out and explained."

"Fine."

"Fine, you'll do it? Or fine, shut the hell up?"

"Fine, I'll find him a hotel."

When the rear door to the clinic slammed shut, they both turned their heads. Aidan appeared a moment later, his hair windblown and tousled in a super-sexy way, a bookstore bag in his hand. He'd bought sunglasses, which he pushed up as he approached, revealing blue eyes filled with pleasure and lust at the sight of her. He was walking his signature walk, the one that screamed, *Hot sex*. Beneath the thin cotton of his shirt, she could just make out the shape of his washboard abs and strong chest.

Her toes curled.

"Ready to go?" he asked in that deep voice with its luscious accent. That tone struck a chord deep inside her, once again creating a sense of familiarity that was soul deep.

Clutching the pepper pen tightly, she nodded. "Yes. I'm ready."

* * *

Lyssa wasn't sure how they ended up at her house. Her thoughts were on Chad and Stacey's valid concerns, and her driving had been on autopilot. Still, as she pulled to a stop in her garage, she didn't feel panic that she hadn't dropped Aidan off at a hotel. In fact, as the garage door lowered, she felt relief.

Holding the steering wheel with both hands, she stared straight ahead and blew out her breath.

"You want to tell me what's on your mind?" Aidan asked, his left hand sliding over to rest on her thigh. "You haven't said a word since we left the clinic."

Beneath his palm, her skin burned. The heat spread, warming her blood, making her shift in her seat. He stroked softly, slowly, and her body responded by melting for him. Her knuckles went white.

A rough sound rumbled in his chest.

"If you'd like a bed beneath your back when I fuck you again," he murmured darkly, "you better get out of the car."

She scrambled out and slammed the door. He rounded the trunk so swiftly, they reached the kitchen entry at the same time. His hand curved around hers where it gripped the knob, his chest pressed against her back, his thighs touching hers. The hard length of his erection was an unmistakable shape against the upper curve of her buttocks. He dipped his knees and stroked it against her.

Closing her eyes, Lyssa pressed her hot forehead against the cool door and moaned softly. Aidan's lips touched the side of her neck, and his tongue stroked leisurely over her rapidly beating pulse.

She heard a thud, but it wasn't until his left hand cupped

her hip that she realized he'd dropped the bag of books.

"What are you doing?" she breathed, so in lust with him, her lungs were tight.

"You're tense. I'm relaxing you."

Aidan's accent was divine when he was plain speaking. When he was aroused, it was pure seduction.

She reached back and cupped his ass, mimicking his movements, stroking the length of his cock with her body. He growled and bit into the tender spot between her neck and shoulder. It pinned her in place, subduing her writhing, telling her without words that she was at his mercy.

"No fair." She pouted.

He licked his teeth marks in her skin. "Is that a complaint?" His large hand slid lower, between her legs. "Can't have that."

Her breath hissed out as he rubbed her lightly through her trousers, the barely-there pressure enough to make her wet, but not enough to satisfy. "Oh, Aidan . . ."

His grip became fierce, pulling her body taut against his, as if the sound of his name impassioned him.

"Next time," he muttered.

His fingers freed the button at her waist, lowered her zipper, and then he shoved her pants down roughly.

"Wh-what . . . ?"

"The bed. We won't make it."

He thrust his hand into the juncture between her legs.

"Oh shit." She clung to the knob for balance.

Aidan crowded her, his fingers parting her and then thrusting into her. His mouth to her ear, he whispered, "I'm going to take you, Lyssa. Right here. No holds barred."

Her knees buckled. If not for his fingers deep inside

her, she would have sunk to the floor. "Do it."

She leaned heavily into the door as he began to fuck her with his fingers, fast and hard and not deep enough. His desire goaded hers, making it wild and out of control.

And he knew it.

"Spread your legs." His rough command made her shiver with anticipation, and when his hand left hers on the knob and rose to pinch her nipple through her shirt and bra, her moan was loud and pleading.

Bending her knee, she kicked free of one pants leg and set her foot on the threshold, which was raised a few inches higher than the garage floor. She spread herself shamelessly.

"Yes." She shivered violently when his two fingers withdrew and then he returned with three woven tightly together. He was fervent, but beneath that impatience was underlying reverence. All her doubts faded to insignificance. No man could touch a woman like this without caring for her, without *knowing* her and wanting to please her. The driving force was lust and base craving, but there was also desperation and neediness that came from a far more intimate place.

She could hear cars driving past her garage and distant voices—her neighbors talking, parents yelling, children playing. The active community she lived in was just a few feet away. She didn't care. She just wanted Aidan. *Needed* him.

"You're melting in my hand." His words were spoken against her skin, his lips nuzzling into her neck.

"I . . ." She nuzzled back. "Hurry."

Before she understood what was happening, he stepped

back and spun her to face him. He stared down at her, blue eyes intensely searching. Then he caught her face in his hands and kissed her passionately.

No holds barred.

She was startled by this new side of him, unable to shake the feeling that Aidan did everything with iron-fisted control, even sex. But his actions now were far from controlled. He was ready to ride her to the finish, she could tell. And she wanted him to. Wanted him to lose himself in her.

Then he surprised her again by dropping to his knees.

Hooking her leg over his shoulder with shaking hands, he bared her to his gaze.

"So pretty," he said, his thumbs parting her. She knew what was coming before he licked her, but it still rocked her world.

"Oh!" She thrust her fingers through the dark silk of his hair and held on as his warm lips surrounded her clit. The rough pad of his tongue stroked back and forth across the sensitive bundle of nerves. His mouth was hot, the texture perfect, his skill evident. When he groaned against her and increased his rhythm, she bit her lower lip to keep silent. Then he tilted his head and thrust his tongue into her, and she gave up and cried out.

Aidan hummed his encouragement.

Lost to the pleasure, she rode his mouth, her hips undulating into the gentle, shallow stroking inside her that was driving her crazy. "Please," she begged, her hands dropping to his shoulders.

His every exhale burned her skin, the kneading of his fingertips on her hips made her tingle all over, the steady fucking of his tongue into her pussy made her mindless.

Clutching his arm for support, she moaned, "Please . . ."

He kissed upward to her clit, and her muscles tensed, preparing for the coming orgasm she wanted more than her next breath. When it came, the force of her climax nearly took her to her knees, but Aidan held her upright, his shoulders bulging beneath her palms, supporting her, not just physically but deep inside, his attention to her needs both reassuring and welcome.

When she slumped backward, Aidan stood and lifted her with amazing ease. She wrapped her legs around his hips and then shivered as their gazes locked together. There was no satisfied smile in his eyes or on his lips. There was only desire and a deep intensity, as if he was looking for something within her features.

"Take me," she whispered.

Holding her effortlessly with one hand beneath her buttocks, Aidan yanked his button fly free and shoved his garments low on his hips.

He gritted his teeth and pulled her down at the same time he surged upward. She twisted in his arms, the slick, swollen tissues inside her aching with the penetration. He was hard as a rock, thick and long.

His nostrils flared as he slid slowly from her in a heavy glide, only to thrust into her harshly, pinning her to the door.

Her toes curled. "Ah god, your cock . . ."

Wrapping her arms around his broad shoulders, she felt the dampness of the cotton that separated his steamy skin from hers. Beneath her fingertips, the muscles of his upper back were trembling. His knees bent again on a torturous withdrawal, then his ass clenched beneath her calves as he pumped back into her, filling her so full she gasped for breath.

She held on with what strength she had left. Aidan took her like a man possessed, riding her high and hard and deep. He growled on every plunge, his breath hissed on every retreat. Her lower back banged repeatedly into the door, the rhythmic sound unmistakable. *Hard sex.* She loved it, craved it, craved *him.* Just as he claimed to crave her.

Blood roared through her veins, muting her hearing, but gradually she recognized his voice, though the words were foreign and breathless. It was hot in the garage. Airless. Creating a sauna effect that heightened her arousal. She felt drugged, languid, though every cell in her body was finely attuned to the man who fucked her so well.

"Aidan." Her lips pressed his name against the sweat-slick skin of his neck, her fingertips slipping through the wet strands of his hair.

In response, he hugged her tightly, the tender embrace so at odds with his lower body, which battered her hips with the force of his lust, his cock shafting her cunt over and over again.

"Can't . . . I'm sorry," he bit out, just before he pressed her into the door and shuddered in orgasm, his thighs quaking beneath hers, his cock jerking inside her, his cum scalding with its heat.

Lyssa ground downward onto him, rubbing her clit against his pelvic bone, pushing herself into climax with him. They clung together, shuddered together, her nose

pressed to his skin, breathing in the scent that was uniquely Aidan.

His heart pounded against her breast, his chest rose and
fell as laboriously as hers, the sweat on his forehead mingled with hers.

Connected.

Aidan stepped out of the downstairs shower stall before
Lyssa finished in the bath upstairs. He wrapped a towel
around his waist and swiped a hand across the foggy mirror. The man who looked back at him—with a touch of
fear in his eyes to go along with the determined set of his
jaw—was not someone he knew.

He heaved out his breath and stepped into the hall. Tossing the towel in the laundry basket, Aidan tugged on the
pajama bottoms he'd bought and then went to the kitchen
to search for something to feed his Dreamer.

He'd discovered last night that Lyssa had the shopping
sense of a bachelor. Beer, soda, leftovers, and sandwich
stuff were the extent of her refrigerated stores. Iced rum,
boxed meals, and ice cream made up her frozen items.
Knowing better than to look in the fridge, he went straight
to the pantry, where he knew pasta and various canned
goods waited.

He was momentarily tempted to make SpaghettiOs
again, but then decided to try his hand at something different. He pulled out a few things and set to work.

"Smells good," Lyssa said a little while later.

Aidan looked over his shoulder and smiled with contentment. Lyssa sat at the breakfast bar with her wet hair
combed back into a ponytail and a thin-strapped satin top

he suspected had matching bottoms. "Let's hope it tastes good, too."

Her lush mouth curved on one side in a half smile. Her bare shoulders were so pale and slight, reminding him of how tiny she was compared to him. He should have been more gentle with her earlier; he should have followed her into the house, let her bathe, then leisurely seduced her senses so that he could win her trust. Instead he'd sensed the distance and worry in her. Fear had goaded him to touch her, to remind her of how good they were together. Then she'd whimpered his name, *his* name, not a fantasy, not a warrior of legend. And he'd lost control. Again. He had been losing control since the night he'd first met her.

"Whatchya cooking?" she asked, craning her neck in an effort to look around him.

"Don't know," he replied honestly. Reaching over, he flipped open a cupboard door and removed two plates. "You don't have much in the way of nutrition around here."

"I take a multivitamin."

He snorted. "You're going to need a hell of a lot more than a multivitamin to keep up with me, Hot Stuff. I'll tell you that right now."

Scooping the contents of the pot onto the plates, Aidan turned and set her serving before her, then grabbed a fork and passed it over.

Lyssa stared at her plate with wide eyes. "What is this on the salad pasta?" She poked at the little tubes with the tines of her fork.

Aidan turned back around and looked at the can by the stovetop. "Chili."

"And the goopy yellow stuff?"

"Cheese."

"Sliced cheese?"

"Yeah." He shrugged. "The block cheese was moving, so I threw it out."

Her brows rose. Then she speared some pasta and gingerly placed it in her mouth.

He waited expectantly.

"Ummm . . ." she purred, her mouth full. She nodded.

"It's good?" He grabbed a spoon and ate with great relish. It wasn't the best meal he'd ever had, but it wasn't the worst, either.

"So," she hedged finally, her voice tentative, "Tell me about us. And you. And everything."

Shooting a longing glance at the pot, he acknowledged that he'd have to get enough to eat later, when Lyssa was deep in slumber.

Where to begin?

"Do you remember anything?" he asked carefully.

She winced. "Not really, no. It's more of a feeling. Like you're familiar."

He blew out his breath. "Hang on."

Then he fixed her a stiff rum and soda. Setting it down before her, he stepped back and rested his hip against the far counter. His arms crossed of their own volition, and he accepted that he was feeling edgy and defensive. There was no way to explain without sounding like he was a nut. So he just started talking, refusing to cushion things with evasions or half-truths. He knew the tale was unbelievable on its face. It didn't need any embellishment to make it worse.

The whole time he watched her, trying to gauge her re-action, noting how she gulped her drink.

"More," she gasped when he fell silent, setting the glass down with a sharp click on the granite countertop.

He refilled it with a sigh, and waited silently as she downed a third of it in one swallow. "Are you okay?"

Her dark eyes were huge in her face, her creamy skin pale, her hands shaking as she released her beverage and wiped her palms on her satin shorts. Tears welled, clinging to long, dark lashes before slipping free and coursing down her cheeks.

"Lyssa," he murmured, his chest aching at the sight of her tears.

"I'm o-okay," she whispered.

Lyssa winced as her voice broke. Then she cried as Aid-an came to where she sat on the bar stool and cupped her nape, tilting her chin up so that he could brush his lips across hers with heartbreaking tenderness.

"You're trembling." He nuzzled her nose with his. "And your skin is cold."

She knew that, knew she was in shock, but how was she supposed to react when the man of her dreams swore he *came to life* from her dreams? All the hopes she'd been har-boring of this happiness lasting vanished like smoke, and something precious inside her died.

"Oh god!" she moaned, her stomach roiling as she was struck with a sudden, horrifying thought. "This Twilight . . . Is it like another planet?"

He exhaled audibly and tugged her ponytail free. His callused fingertips sank into her damp hair and mas-saged her scalp. She melted, her eyes falling closed. Her breathing was so shallow and the silence so complete that Jelly Bean's purring rumbled like thunder through the room.

"No," he murmured, "It's a conduit plane of existence. Think of it like an apple. Abbreviated space is the hole bored through the center by a worm. Instead of coming out the other side, though, the Elders found a way to suspend us in there."

How could she and JB both be so wrong about him? The man was completely insane. Those oversized clothes . . . *Oh god, what if he was a vagrant?*

"A wormhole?" she repeated. "Are we talking about the same type of wormhole as they have on television and the movies?"

"Yes, somewhat."

"But before you went into the apple," she said slowly, "you came from another planet, right?"

His lips pressed into her forehead. "Yes."

"So you're telling me you're an alien."

"Yes."

"Shit." She cried harder, her heart breaking so completely, she found it hard to breathe. Dropping her wet face into her hands, she gave in to her grief with deep, wracking sobs.

"Shush. I know this is a lot to throw at you. But please . . . you're killing me. I can't stand it."

He enfolded her in his warm, strong arms. She breathed him in, filling her mind with his unique essence, only mildly surprised by how it soothed her. She doubted she'd ever be truly surprised again.

Turning her head, she spotted where her purse was on

the counter and reached for it, withdrawing the pepper pen and clutching it in her hand. *In case of alien, break glass.* The thought of using it on Aidan, of inflicting any kind of pain on him, only tugged her deeper into despondency.

Then the doorbell rang.

She wiggled free of Aidan's embrace, part of her mind wondering how to go about getting someone psychiatric treatment and another part thinking she didn't care if he was insane. There were all kinds of insanity, and Aidan's brand of hot sex and proprietary caring worked for her. She wasn't exactly normal, either. Who was she to bitch about a little mental instability? She was a woman who never remembered dreams and had so much trouble sleeping that it affected her ability to lead a normal life. Hell, Aidan thought she was a prophecy set to destroy him and everything he knew. "The Key" that was expected to annihilate worlds, including her own. Or something like that.

"Lyssa, just ignore it."

"No. No, I have to get that." *Think, Lyssa. Think.*

But she couldn't think when he was touching her. He short-circuited her brain cells.

Needing some distance, she slid off the stool and hurried toward the door. JB jogged alongside her, growling his demon cat growl. She knew Aidan followed, even though he moved silently.

Maybe it was Chad or Stacey. Oh jeez, not Stacey because she'd have Justin with her. Maybe it was Mom! Mom would be excellent. She would start charming Aidan, and Lyssa could sneak upstairs and figure out how the hell her life kept getting worse.

Relieved at the prospect of a moment alone, she opened the door without looking out the peephole. She remembered it only as the door swung inward . . .

. . . and her wide eyes caught the sword swinging downward.

Chapter 12

It was JB's arching spine and bristling hair that alerted Aidan to the danger. The cat was too inherently lazy to do more than growl to intimidate guests. So when JB hissed like a banshee, Aidan's senses went on high alert. As the door swung open, he caught Lyssa around the waist and yanked her back . . .

. . . just in time to miss the downward swing of a sword.

The marble that lined the entryway cracked under the force of the glaive.

"Chad?" Lyssa screeched, limbs flailing. "What the fuck are you doing? You almost killed me!"

A quick glance at the familiar man lunging through the doorway made Aidan's blood run cold. He set Lyssa on her feet and shoved her toward the stairs. "That's not Chad. Go!"

Aidan leaped back several paces to avoid a gutting by the thrusting weapon aimed at his abdomen. With his heart

in his throat over what had nearly happened to Lyssa, he
risked a glance in her direction. She stood frozen. Shock
compounded by more shock.

"Run, damn it!" He landed a brutal kick with his
bare heel to Chad's knee, bringing the other man to the
ground.

"I'm calling the cops!" she cried, sprinting up the stairs.
"You're both insane!"

"*No!*" He jumped, and Chad's glaive whistled through
the air beneath him, the strike aimed to cut him off at the
knees. Literally. "Don't call anyone!"

Aidan was grateful for the loose-fitting pajama bottoms
he wore. They allowed him similar freedom of movement
as his battle dress. Chad, however, was dressed in jeans,
and the heavy, unyielding material slowed him just enough
to slightly mitigate the effect the Elders had on him. Seeing Chad's blank stare and lack of any facial expression at
all, Aidan was certain he was dealing with a sleepwalker.

Determined to keep Lyssa safe, he led Chad away from
the staircase and into the living room. His sword was located there, waiting near the entertainment center. As Aidan
moved to the right, then feinted to the left, Chad pulled
his arm back and made a wild swing. With a rapid spin on
his heel, Aidan caught up his glaive, and before he'd com-
pleted the rotation, he had yanked it free of its scabbard
and blocked the next incoming blow.

The clash of metal upon metal focused him. It was a
sound he'd heard almost as much as he heard his own
breathing. The familiar feel of the hilt in his palm and the
weight of his weapon centered him. It was comforting in a
way only others who lived by the sword would know.

Everything else fell away.

He thrust and parried with singular expertise, recognizing the skill of a Master in his opponent. Which one? Who would come for them like this? Was it Lyssa they wanted, or he? Perhaps both?

Disadvantaged by the fact that he could not kill Chad, Aidan was forced to take a defensive position, a stance he hated and was relatively unfamiliar with. Still, he managed, aware that he could fight for days like this, switching his glaive from one hand to the other when his arm fatigued. Chad was fit, but lacked the stamina and finely honed muscles Aidan had cultivated over centuries. Despite the battle knowledge imparted by the Master who controlled him, Chad's physical form could not be enhanced.

The engagement continued. They were trapped in the small area of the living room and adjoining dining room. Stumbling around furniture, Aidan cursed as he bumped the bookcase.

"Would you fucking *wake up* already?" he yelled at Chad.

But there was nothing Aidan could say, no cajoling or threats that would shake his opponent's position, no sound or facial expression he could make that would inspire fear. Chad was asleep and incapable of being reasoned with, incapable of speech. Sweat poured down the other man's face, dripping from his lashes into his eyes, but he wasn't capable of feeling it.

Aidan kept a running tally of Chad's weaknesses, cataloging them in his mind for use, if necessary. The instant Chad began to move sluggishly and breathe laboriously, Aidan seized the moment.

Moving with tactical precision, he forced the other man to retreat until the backs of his legs hit the low coffee table and he stumbled. Falling backward.

Aidan tossed his glaive to the opposite hand and leaped to the tabletop, his knees bending, carrying the force of his downward descent in his fist. The connection to Chad's jaw was marked with a sharp crack, and then the man fell limp. Truly unconscious, far beyond the Twilight. He lay arched over the table with arms flung wide. His weapon fell from his slackened grip and landed with a thud on the carpeted floor.

"Oh my god!" Lyssa cried. "Did you break his neck?"

Swiveling his head to the side, Aidan found Lyssa standing at the bottom of the stairs, her lips and knuckles white with tension, her outstretched hand shaking violently. He arched his brow at the sight of the object she held, and jumped off the table. "What were you going to do? Parry with your pen?"

Swallowing hard, she sputtered, "P-pepper spr-spray."

His gaze narrowed. "You grabbed that before the doorbell rang."

She blinked.

The implications of her actions made him grit his teeth. He collected Chad's sword and put it on the opposite side of the room.

He retrieved his scabbard from the floor and sheathed his glaive, setting it next to the other weapon with deliberately casual movements. Then he went to her, wrapping his big hand around the one she held out.

"Gimme that," he murmured, prying her nerveless fingers open. Keeping her icy cold hand in his, Aidan side-stepped just far enough to reach the entertainment center. Then he set the pepper spray pen atop it, far from Lyssa's reach.

Her free hand touched his chest, making the muscle beneath it jump. "You're barely breathing hard at all."

Aidan caught her wrist and pulled her hand away. "Were you planning on spraying me with the damn pepper spray?"

Again she blinked huge, dark eyes at him, the irises swallowed by dilated pupils. "Stacey said I should if you wanted to sacrifice me or came from another planet."

"Sacrifice—?" He growled. "And you call *me* insane?"

She frowned. And then burst into tears.

Relenting with a sigh, he tugged her into his arms. His brain acknowledged that she had a right to be wary and to consider self-protection. Another part of him—his aching heart—didn't care about that.

"Did you call anyone?" he asked.

"N-no."

"Good girl." He stroked the length of her spine.

"What's going on?" she sobbed, her voice muffled.

He rested his cheek against the top of her head and told her.

"When he wakes up," he finished, "he's going to hurt like hell and have a nasty bruise on his jaw, but he won't remember any of this."

"I'll never forget it." She sucked in a shuddering breath and rubbed her face into his damp skin in a way that made the ache in his chest worse. "So you told me the truth."

"Of course." He pushed her away and moved to Chad's splayed body. "Listen, I've got to get him to his place before he wakes up. We don't have time to change our clothes."

He dug in Chad's pocket and withdrew his car keys. "I'll follow behind you in his car, then you can drive us both back. Are you okay to get behind the wheel?"

"I think so." She went to the kitchen to collect her purse, and Aidan bent low to heft Chad's body over his shoulder. He found the red Jeep parked just outside Lyssa's garage, tossed his burden into the passenger seat, and moved the vehicle out of the way so she could pull out.

He'd considered the possibility of controlling Dreamers from the Twilight. When he first saw the cavern the Elders used to contain hypnotized humans, he'd thought surely the ability to control the mind in that state would work both ways. It appeared it was true. He wondered if Chad had initiated the connection on purpose—turning to hypnosis to cure some ailment—or if the Elders had the ability to control the human body through dreams. The latter thought was terrifying. It made every single person around them a threat.

Lyssa wasn't safe anywhere.

Lyssa backed out of her garage with more care than usual, then took a long moment to stare at the Jeep and the man who sat so pensively in the driver's seat. She held the steering wheel with white-knuckled force to keep her hands from shaking uncontrollably. Everything she knew about her life had just blown up in her face. An alien invasion wouldn't come by air. It would come from within, like zombies or *Invasion of the Body Snatchers*.

But Aidan wasn't like that. He was warm, caring, passionate. Human.

Just thinking about him made her long for his arms around her. He had come an incalculable distance to save her, leaving everything—*everything*—he knew behind. For her.

She stepped on the gas pedal and drove to Chad's, her eyes lifting constantly to her rearview mirror. Her thoughts were tumultuous, her breathing uneven, and her hands and feet were as cold as ice. She parked her car at Chad's by instinct, her brain too overloaded to record the events. As she slowly recovered from shock, it took her an hour to realize Aidan wasn't talking to her.

He was silent as he arranged Chad on the floor by the bed, simulating a fall that would in no way account for his exhausted muscles and bruised face, but was the best they could do. He was silent on the ride home and on the walk into the house from the garage, even though she'd paused at the door with her hand on the knob, her blood heating at the memory of what they had done there. Only hours ago, yet it seemed like forever.

She'd looked over her shoulder and noted the darkness of his gaze. He had thought of it, too, but aside from the heat in his eyes, he had been distant and cold.

Now, as he stood in her kitchen with a sleeping pill in his palm, she realized this was as hard on him as it was on her. She shook her head. "I don't want that now. We need to talk."

"We've talked enough." His jaw was firm. "You need sleep."

"I'm not tired."

"You're in shock. You don't know what you are." His tone lowered wearily. "Or what I am."

"Aidan . . ."

His eyes closed at the sound of his name.

"Will you come upstairs with me?" she asked softly.

"I can't. I've got work to do."

"Just until I fall asleep?"

"Lyssa." He shook his head. "If I lie down, I may fall asleep. I can't do that. We'll have to sleep in shifts. We can't afford to have me unconscious at the same time you are."

If they slept in shifts, they would never be together.

And she needed him.

She almost told him that all she wanted was him wrapped around her, inside her, making her feel cherished and safe. But she worried that telling him would ensure a negative response. For the first time since he'd walked in the door, she was fairly certain he didn't want to make love to her. So all she said was, "Please."

He growled low and ran a hand through his hair. He gestured for her to go ahead of him and then followed her up the stairs. When she stopped by the bathroom, Aidan handed her the sleeping pill, and she went to the sink as he sprawled on the bed. She looked at her reflection, knowing she looked like death warmed over, but also knowing it wasn't her looks that had dampened Aidan's ardor.

She set the pill on the counter. If she needed it later, so be it. But first she was going to try to get Aidan to talk to her.

Returning to the bedroom, Lyssa crawled on the bed and stretched out parallel to him. Aidan lay on his side, his head in his hand, but when she got close he rolled to his back and tucked her against him. She tossed her leg over his and her arm across his abdomen. He stiffened in response.

"You're mad at me," she whispered, her breath hot as it gusted across his bare chest.

He exhaled audibly and rolled into her. "No. I'm not mad at you."

"Then hold me," she breathed. "I need you."

"Lyssa . . ." Aidan lowered his head and took her mouth, his tongue gliding deep, making her shudder beneath him. She needed this, needed the connection to ground her to him. He was a dream, an alien, a man centuries older than she was. She was a threat, a prophecy, the key to his destruction. The distance between them yawned galaxies and planes of existence apart, and yet he was the yang to her yin, a living puzzle piece that by some miracle made him physically able to fit her, just as males of her own species did. Together they could become one, with no separation at all between them. That's what she needed, *right now*, as much as she needed to breathe.

As her desire for him built, her embrace loosened, her hands moving to stroke the length of his spine. He smelled delicious, even more so than usual because he'd worked up a sweat earlier. The combination of Aidan, adrenaline overload, and testosterone was a potent aphrodisiac.

Endlessly in lust with him, she stroked his tongue with her own.

"Remember the apple?" he murmured into her mouth.

Lyssa stilled. "Yeah . . ."

"That hasn't changed just because you understand now."

"What are you saying?"

"I don't know how long I'll be here," he said softly, his gaze starkly intense beneath the lock of black hair that fell over his brow. "The information I need may be in the books I brought, or it could be back in the Twilight. Right now, we both need to consider my being here as temporary and my eventual departure as permanent."

She swallowed hard. "I thought you said no one has ever gone back?"

"None of the other Guardians had a book by the Elders detailing fissure creation," he pointed out.

"Oh." Sinking into the mattress, her legs slackened and then fell away. "So you're not mad?"

"I am." His voice was low and fervent. "At everything and everyone that prevents me from keeping you." He rested his forehead against hers, inundating her senses with the scent and heat of his skin. "But I'm not angry with you, no. I'm proud of you for taking steps to protect yourself, and I know you trust me. You wouldn't have let me take you without a condom otherwise. You're a doctor and far too smart to gamble with your life like that."

Aidan rolled off her and stared up at the ceiling.

"I don't understand how you could go back," she said, frowning in confusion. "I'm not even sure I understand how you got here."

He turned his head to look at her with a gentle smile. "You've heard of Athena, haven't you? Goddess of Wisdom, who sprang fully formed from Zeus's head."

"That's a myth," she scoffed, but the similarity was startling.

Shrugging, Aidan said, "Aren't all myths and legends based on some grain of truth?"

"So . . ." She stared at his profile, melting inside at how beautiful he was. A large, graceful, and deadly predator sprawled across her bed. She'd watched him through the balusters while he fought with Chad, watched the play of muscles in his arms and chest, the way his PJ bottoms had stretched over his thighs when he lunged forward, and the tight roping of his abdomen as he'd leaped backward. The calculating way he'd studied his opponent had made her shiver, and not just with fear. Just as Stacey said, Aidan Cross was a dangerous bad boy and she wanted to tame him.

Before he could reply, she jumped him, throwing herself over his hard body. He grunted from the impact and stared up at her with wide eyes. She took his mouth so he couldn't protest, her tongue gliding along his lips and then slipping inside. Her fingertips found his nipples and rubbed them lightly. His answering groan was music to her ears.

"It's too late for caution," she whispered against his lips. They were glorious, firm and beautifully etched, but so soft, and the way they moved . . . the way they made love to her . . . "It's going to break me anyway. I think you should make it worth my while."

"I haven't already?" His accent was pronounced, betraying her effect on him.

"I want more." She sat up and yanked her camisole over her head, tossing it to the floor. She cupped her breasts, rolling the aching points between her fingertips.

"Oh, Lyssa," he murmured roughly, his hands rubbing up and down her thighs. "You drive me insane when you do that."

She opened her mouth to say she hadn't ever shown him her breasts and then remembered what he had said earlier. They'd been lovers in her dreams. "I've done this for you before?"

"Ummm," he replied, his thumbs slowly working their way higher, setting her skin on fire.

"Not fair. You have more memories than I do. I have to catch up."

His mouth curved, and her heart beat faster. Catching his hands, she pressed her breasts into them. "Please don't end this," she begged, throwing aside her pride. "I need you. Desperately."

Aidan rolled then, coming over her in a blanket of big, hot, sexy male. "I need you, too." He nuzzled against her throat and slipped a hand up the leg of her shorts. "Too much."

She sighed and wrapped around him again. If she took a moment to think, she would be terrified of the future, but here, now . . . It was heaven.

"Tell me you're with me," she moaned, arching into his fingers as he parted her and stroked across her clit with a feather-light touch of a callused finger.

He kissed her with heartbreaking tenderness. "I'm with you."

It was only for now. But for now, it was enough.

Chapter 13

"I've been looking for you, Captain."

Connor straightened and turned to face Philip Wager as he climbed the porch steps of Aidan's house. Tall and wiry, the lieutenant approached with a long-legged stride that ate up the distance between them. He set a cooler on the bench near the door and then used both hands to tie back his overly long hair with a small black band.

"You found me."

Now presentable to a commanding officer, Philip bowed low. Connor returned the salutation and then arched a brow in silent query.

"Permission requested to speak freely, sir."

"Granted."

The lieutenant took a deep breath and said, "I would have preferred for you to come to me with your questions personally, rather than sending Morgan."

"But then you would have been put in a position you could not retreat from gracefully—defy your commanding officer or betray the Elders. With Morgan, you could easily say no and avoid the discomfort."

Philip snorted. "I've defended your back and saved your life, but you can't approach me as a friend and ask me for help?"

"Every friendship has its limits," Connor said grimly, leaning his hip against the railing.

"Yours with Captain Cross seems to have no bounds."

"He is like a brother to me."

"And I owe him my life, many times over."

Connor sighed and sank into the nearby chair. When Aidan was home, every door was opened wide to allow the breeze to enter. Now the sliding paper doors were closed, barring the interior from enjoying the simulated sunrise. The lack of Aidan's dynamic presence brought an unusual and uncomfortable silence to the place. "He's not the same man you knew, Wager. He's a fugitive who's stolen the Key, and abandoned his men and duty."

"You don't believe that any more than I do." Philip gestured to the bench and asked, "May I?"

"Of course."

Setting his elbows on his knees, Philip studied him with a narrowed glance. With his long queue and stormy gray eyes, he had a renegade appearance to go along with his loose-cannon reputation. Because of his volatile nature, he'd been a second lieutenant for centuries longer than he should have been. "The Elders seriously misjudged you. They'd hoped the promotion would win your favor away from Cross."

"Yeah, and they failed. So they undermine me, assigning

patrols to the Dreamer without my consultation." Connor shrugged. "You got beer in that cooler?"

Smiling, Philip reached inside and withdrew an icy canister. He tossed it over and then grabbed his own. "The captain has kept his woman far from the Twilight, but her own defenses are formidable. The Elders requested a contingent from the Corps of Engineers, and they said the only way to get past that door is if she lets us in."

"Impressive."

"Did you expect Cross to choose a woman who wasn't?"

"Her unusual ability is unnerving, isn't it?" Connor's gaze drifted beyond the porch to the green grass and rolling hills beyond. This was his world, and he would continue to defend it with his life. "Doesn't it create doubt in you? Have you thought perhaps Cross is wrong about her?"

"Of course I've considered it. But he's never been wrong before."

Connor tossed his head back and emptied his beverage in three large swallows. Like Philip, he was withholding judgment on the Dreamer until he met her himself, but it didn't look good so far. "So now what?"

"My team waits."

"Excellent."

"Care to share your plan?" Philip held out a second beer, but snatched it back quickly when Connor reached for it. "Sharing works both ways."

"Cheeky bastard." Connor laughed for the first time in weeks. Aidan had been absent only days, but the mess he'd made of his life since meeting the Dreamer had pretty much killed the humor Connor relied on to make it through eternity. "The less you know, the better for you."

"Oh yeah, and I'm known for doing what's best for me." Philip finished his beer in much the same way Connor had. "You'll need help. You can't go it alone, and I can't think of any other Elite besides you, me, and Cross with balls enough to take on the Elders."

Connor's grin widened. "All right. I need to get into the control room at the rear of the Temple."

"What control room?"

"The one Cross saw before he left." The one Connor had seen briefly in Aidan's thoughts the first night his friend had been gone. They'd met for a moment through Aidan's dream, but the captain had been vulnerable with fever, and the connection hadn't held. The dream had been like nothing Connor had ever seen before. Misty, a bit distorted, like a television channel with poor reception. Whether that was due to the unusual illness or to some genetic differences from humans that altered penetration into the Twilight, he didn't know. And Aidan hadn't returned in a dream state since then to help him find out.

"What's the control room for?" Philip asked.

Grabbing the beer from the other man's unsuspecting hand, Connor chuckled at the scowl he got in return. "Hell if I know, but we need to figure out what exactly the Key is supposed to do, if we want any hope of preventing it from happening. That knowledge should also give us a pretty good indication of whether or not Cross's Dreamer is the Key, or if the Elders have made their first mistake on record."

"Breaking into the Temple sounds dangerous."

"I think so."

"Shit, I hope so. Wouldn't be any fun otherwise."

Connor tossed back another beer, and then belched. "So here's what we'll do . . ."

"Call and check on him, Stace. Please."

"No way."

Lyssa dropped her head back onto the pillow and ran her hand through her tangled hair. She was surrounded by Aidan's scent, even though he was no longer in bed. From the lack of heat on his side, she guessed he had been up for a while. She'd slept in due to sheer physical exhaustion. The man had stamina in spades, his body a well-honed machine. "I just want to make sure he's okay."

"Chad's fine. You said so yourself yesterday."

That was before Aidan kicked his ass. He was an innocent pawn in the battle between her and "the Elders," and she hated that she had inadvertently caused him pain. "Just a quick hi. Maybe you can call about Lady?"

"On a Saturday?" Stacey scoffed. "I might as well start off the conversation with 'Hiya! Lyssa wants to know how you're doing since she dumped you and feels guilty.' Too high school, Doc, trust me. He's a big boy, he'll be fine."

Lyssa closed her eyes, blocking out the view of the vaulted ceiling above her. "I'll give you a raise."

"Right." Stacey blew out an exasperated breath right into the receiver. "That bribe always works. I'm such a money whore."

"You're a single mom. I admire you."

"Flattery will get you nowhere with me. It's all about the money. Though if you can arrange a hunk delivery for me, I'd call it even. How's that working out, by the way?"

"He's dreamy." For real.

"I'm glad. I really am."

"I know you are."

"'Kay, I'll call Chad and try to make some nonblatantly suspicious small talk. I better see you at dinner, though."

Lyssa's fingers pulled the soft, denim-colored top sheet up to her nose to better smell Aidan. She didn't want to leave her home. She wanted to seclude herself with him, keep him, never let him go. "We'll be there."

"See ya then."

The connection was severed. Lyssa hit the off button, then set the phone down next to her. Through the open bedroom door, the scent of fresh, hot coffee drifted up to her. It was such a domestic thing to experience with a man she'd met so recently. But it worked. It made her feel whole and loved, in a way she hadn't felt in years. If ever. Wanting to be with him, she tossed back the covers and pulled on a robe.

As she crept down the stairs in her attempt at stealth, Lyssa hoped she'd catch another display of Aidan's morning exercise routine. Instead she found him yawning and drooping wearily over the jeweled book at the dining table. She padded up behind him and set her hands on his shoulders, kneading her fingers into the tense muscles of his back.

He groaned, and leaned his head back. "Hi," he murmured in that low tone that made shivers run down her spine.

"Hi." She bent and pressed a kiss to his forehead. "Did you sleep at all?"

He shook his head. "No way I'd risk it with you asleep at the same time. I've been checking on you every half hour."

"I thought I was safe once I'd fallen into deep sleep?"

"That's an educated guess." His mouth curved. "In any case, you're adorable when you're sleeping."

Lyssa moved around the chair and slung her leg over his, straddling his lap and wedging herself between him and the table. It was a tight fit, but she didn't mind. Especially when his arms came around her and tucked her closer to all that warm, yummy-smelling skin and ripped muscles. "Find anything interesting in that book?"

"Some things, yes." He sounded weary and disheartened. "Basically I'm just translating at this point so I can look at the whole text at once. Piece by piece isn't working."

"You can't read it?"

"It's in the ancient language. Like most of your words are derived from Latin."

"Ah, gotcha." Her hands slipped along his bare sides, and her lips moved along his jaw, her aim to take both of their minds away from talk of Aidan going home. "You don't have a morning shadow."

"Mmm," he purred, tilting his head to grant her access to his throat. "Guardians don't grow facial hair beyond eyelashes and brows."

"Really?" The doctor in her pulled away in curiosity. "What other physiological differences are there between us?"

"Nothing important." He rolled his hips sinuously beneath her to prove his point.

"I see morning wood is universal." She giggled when his fingertips danced across her hipbones.

"Morning wood is for guys who just woke up. This wood is the kind a guy gets when his woman sits on his lap wearing only a robe."

Kissing the corner of his smile, she got serious. "Have you slept at all since you got here?"

Aidan sighed. "I slept the first night I was here."

"You were sick, so that doesn't count."

"Are you trying to mother me?" The warmth in his eyes made her stomach quiver.

"My feelings are far from maternal. I'm being selfish, actually. You're going to need your strength for sex."

"Oh?"

His eyes lit wickedly and he pushed the chair back. Rising, he set her down on the wooden tabletop and then reached around her to sweep all the books to the floor. The steady thuds and rustling sounds of pages flipping was strangely erotic. Leaning over her, he forced her to drop backward until she lay across the table like a feast. "Sometimes less energy leads to longer foreplay. You'd like that, wouldn't you?"

His tongue licked along her bottom lip. She caught it and sucked on the tip. He shivered, and she smiled, loving that she had that effect on him.

"I need you to have energy," she murmured against his mouth, "so you can help me burn off all the food you've been making me eat. I've never eaten at three o'clock in the morning before. I'm sure it went straight to my hips."

"Ha!" he scoffed, pulling back to give her a mock glare. "You're underweight and you know it. Besides, you needed to eat to make up for missing breakfast."

"Was that your reasoning?" Lyssa pursed her lips skepti-

cally. "I thought you were refueling me for round six. Or
was it seven? You could give the Energizer Bunny lessons
on going and going and going—"

"I'll give you lessons," he threatened, tugging open the
belt she had at her waist.

She smacked at his hands. "No way. Sleep first, then sex."

"But I'm not tired."

"Bullshit. You look worn out." But she was tempted.
Boy, was she tempted. Yeah, she was sore and ached in
places she hadn't known she had, but the pleasure . . .
Dear god, the orgasms were addictive. They blew her mind
and fried her nerve endings. She understood sex addiction
now. Completely.

"I know you want it," he purred. "Otherwise you would
have gotten dressed. And you know . . . I've got more than
enough energy to give you what you want."

"You shouldn't have any energy. You should be spent."
Her head tilted to the side. "Are all Guardians as horny
and tireless as you?"

"Not all, no. I've always had an appetite, but it was easily satisfied." He pushed the edges of her robe aside and
licked a trail from her pelvic bone up between her breasts.

Her back arched upward. "Are you saying I can't satisfy
you?"

"Every damn time," he whispered, his lips hovering just
above a hard, waiting nipple. "You're about to do it again,
too."

His mouth, hot and wet, seared her skin. She gasped
and writhed, but was quickly subdued by his fingers sliding
between her legs. They parted her, stroked her clit, slipped
inside her. He released her breast and growled.

"Fuck, that makes me so hard." He withdrew and slipped two fingers inside her. "I can feel my cum in you. You're soaked with it."

"Yeah," she gasped as he pressed deep. "I told you. You should be spent after last night." Reaching down, she caught his wrist and stilled his movements. "Tell me something. Are we reproductively compatible?"

He went completely still, then took a deep breath. "Would you want us to be?"

His gaze was steady, intense, searching. Deep sapphire pools that were slowly losing the cynicism she'd seen when she first opened the door to him. She made him happy; she had no doubts about that.

The tip of his finger rubbed gently inside her. "Would you, Lyssa?"

The question broke her heart. As she'd lain in bed that morning, a bunch of silly, unrealistic dreams of Prince Charming and happily-ever-after had flooded her mind. The knowledge that he was home with her, making coffee for her, hers to take . . . She couldn't deny that thoughts of sharing her life and a family with him had rushed to the fore.

Tears stung her eyes. "Yes. I would."

It was all she could say past the lump in her throat, but it was enough for Aidan. He cupped her cheek and lowered his lips to hers. "Then let's try."

"What?" Every muscle in her body was strung tight as a bow. "Are you saying it's possible?"

His smile was sweet, but his eyes were sad. "I have no idea. But we can dream."

Picking her up, he carried her to the couch. JB caught a

clue, for once, and leaped from the sofa arm to pad off to a quieter venue. Aidan laid her down carefully, sinking to his knees beside her, his beautiful eyes dark with lust and love. His large hand slid up her inner thigh.

"I can't conceive, Aidan. I take medicine to prevent it."

"In my dreams, you don't." He kissed her knee and then came over her, spreading her thighs, lavishing the attentions of his tongue across her clit until she writhed, before moving higher.

She leaned up on her elbows, watching, shrugging out of her white terry cloth robe one arm at a time. Eager to feel his warm skin next to hers.

"In my dream, this is our home," he said softly, his gaze moving across her like a tactile caress. "We wake up early every morning so we have time to make love. Slowly. My body covering yours, pushing deep inside yours, as if we have all the time in the world. We part reluctantly, kissing each other good-bye before leaving for work. We think about each other all day, and wait impatiently to be together again at night."

He licked across first one nipple and then the other, his hands shoving down his waistband. "We take vacations to private beaches where I watch you play in the surf, laughing, your skin a golden tan. I strip you there on a blanket. Push your suit aside and sink my cock into you. Ride you until you can't take any more. Then I carry you inside and take you again. We share meals together, trials together, life together."

Lyssa's head fell back into the soft cushions as his fingers went to her pussy and slipped inside her. "Aidan . . ." She closed her eyes to fight the tears, but they escaped anyway, sliding down her temples and wetting her hair.

"Every day you say my name just like that. Soft and breathless with desire. And every time I hear it, I love you more. I think of how lucky I am to have you. How well you take care of me, always fussing after me. I soak up every moment of it, because I need you." His voice lowered and grew husky. "So much."

"Yes." Her fingers slipped through his hair as he levered his body over hers, his pendant dangling and glowing between them, his lean hips sinking between her spread legs. The wide, flared head of his cock teased the slick opening to her cunt, making her arch to take more of him. "I need you, too."

"And one day, we decide it's time to have a baby." His hands cupped her shoulders, holding her in place as he eased his cock into her, filling her full with the heated, throbbing length of him.

"Oh god," she breathed, her head thrashing as he didn't move, merely kept her pinned to the couch with every inch of his body. He'd left his pajama bottoms on the floor when he joined her, and the coarse hair on his calves and thighs tickled her delicate skin. She felt the weight of his heavy balls resting against her buttocks, and the tears fell faster.

"I take you like this." He withdrew, the broad head massaging her. He pushed back inside, forcing his way into her greedy, clenching depths. "I fuck you as often as I can. I meet you for lunch and take you in your office. I keep you drenched, soaked with my cum, ready for the moment when you're fertile."

She whimpered as she tightened helplessly around his pumping cock.

"That's it," he purred, his accent thick and sexy as hell. "Tell me how much you like it."

"I love it," she gasped, writhing under a perfect deep stroke. Beneath her calves, she felt his buttocks clench and release as he fucked her slow and easy, swiveling his hips, rocking into her.

Drugged by the pleasure, Lyssa gave herself up to his expertise, her head falling to the side, her hands stroking his back in time with his leisurely, unhurried rhythm. She set her heels on the couch and pushed up, opening herself further so he could drive deeper. Shafting her pussy in long, heavy drives.

The sun continued its steady ascent, the rays of light slanting through the window and warming her skin. She breathed in a shuddering breath, willing to give up everything she had for endless mornings just like this one. He took her as if they had all the time in the world, as if they could do this forever.

Arching his back, Aidan pressed his cock into her deepest point. She came with a silent cry, her cunt rippling along his throbbing flesh, her body shaking with the force of her orgasm.

"Sweet Lyssa," he breathed, moving his cock in gentle nudges, making her climax roll through her in waves. "Just like this. This is how we make our child." He thrust hard and groaned as he joined her.

She felt the warm release of his cum as it flowed deep into her, the hard jerking of his cock making her moan with pleasure. And heartache.

Aching with the force of his orgasm, Aidan pressed his lips to Lyssa's, his mouth hard and his teeth clenched tight as he surrendered to his need for her. He gasped when it was over, his tongue sliding into her mouth, his embrace almost crushing. She sobbed quietly beneath him. He turned his head and pressed his damp cheek to hers, wondering how he would live the rest of his immortal life without her. She would grow old and die, as all mortals did. How would he bear it?

He wanted that dream he'd shared; he longed for it with every fiber of his being. His heart grieved for the loss of the future he wanted but could never have.

But what he'd deciphered in the ancient text that morning left him no choice.

He was going to have to return to the Twilight.

And this was the last time he would ever make love to Lyssa.

Chapter 14

Aidan rolled to his side, taking Lyssa with him. On the narrow space of the couch, they were locked tightly together to keep from tumbling to the floor. His cock still throbbed inside her. Her pussy still milked him gently. He took a deep breath and tucked her closer, struggling to find the strength to leave her.

"Aidan." Lyssa's exhale gusted warmly over his sweat-dampened skin. It shifted through him, moving from his heart to his toes in a tingling ripple of pleasure.

"Mmm?" he murmured, caressing the soft skin of her back. He would never get enough of touching her, holding her, making love to her. The knowledge killed something inside him, that warm spot of hope and peace she'd given him.

"There has to be a way for you to stay."

The lump in his throat was painful to swallow past. He didn't know what to do with this surfeit of emotion. He'd been numb with loneliness for so long, nearly dead inside, caring only for the men under his command. He had respected every woman he'd taken to bed, but the name they spoke was not his. He was "Cross" or "Captain," and the distance between them was vast, even if their bodies were as close as they could be.

"I want to take care of you," Lyssa whispered, her fingers moving through his hair. "I want to make you laugh, make you happy."

"You do." His voice was rough, scratchy like sandpaper.

"I don't want to stop doing those things. You need someone to take care of you."

He pressed a kiss to her forehead. "What a pair we are. You need looking after, too, Hot Stuff. You and I spend so much time taking care of everyone else, we neglect ourselves. You're the only thing I've ever wanted just for me. Selfishly."

What he wouldn't give to spend his life with her, grow old with her, die beside her. Far better for life to be short and sweet, than eternal and empty. But the most he could do for her was ensure her the longest life possible. So she could marry. Have children and grandchildren. *Another man's* children and grandchildren.

The images in his mind were like a knife thrust deep in his heart. Turning, gouging, killing him slowly and without mercy. He crushed her to him, but she didn't complain.

"Can we stay here like this forever?" she asked with a mournful sigh.

He took a moment to control his voice and then spoke as lightly as he could manage. "I think the bed would be more comfortable."

She gave a quiet laugh. It wasn't the full-bodied merriment he loved, but it was much better for his sanity than her grieved tone.

"How about a shower?" he suggested.

"Together?"

"I would love to, but I should clean up the dining room and get breakfast started."

She leaned back enough to look up at him with those big, dark eyes, and he cupped her shoulder blades to keep her from falling. The silent trust she had that he would support her made his smile genuine. Yes, she'd had her doubts about him, but despite them, she had always gone with her instincts, and they'd always ruled in his favor.

"What are you planning to make up for breakfast?"

She'd laughed until she cried when he came upstairs at three A.M. bearing a plate of Chips Ahoy! cookies with gobs of peanut butter smeared on the tops. "What?" he'd asked, grinning. "Peanut butter has protein."

That reply had her falling over with mirth, her lithe body rolling amid the tangled blue sheets. He'd set the plate down on the nightstand and joined her, eventually sitting back against the headboard and pulling her into his lap. She had straddled his thighs while facing him, his cock hard and throbbing inside her. They'd smeared peanut butter on each other's lips and licked it off, making love with cookies and laughter.

He kissed the tip of her nose. "I'll figure out something."

"Okay. I trust you." Her low, fervent tone touched him as few things ever had. With all that he'd told her yesterday, her belief in him said so much.

They separated reluctantly and rose from the sofa. Once

they were standing, Aidan pulled his pendant over his head, tugged her closer, and slipped it around her neck. It settled between her breasts and glowed with an inner fire, an anomaly he'd assumed was attributed to either the journey here or a reaction to this world. It had never crossed his mind that the stone might be reacting to Lyssa.

He pressed his palm over both it and her heart.

"I can't take this," she breathed, setting her hand over his. "It's precious to you."

He shook his head. "*You* are precious to me. Promise me you'll always wear it. I've never removed it. I shower with it, bathe with it. There's no reason for you to take it off. It can't be damaged, and it won't tarnish like Earth metals do. I need to know that this will never lose contact with your skin."

"Aidan?" Her dark eyes were wary and capped with a frown.

"Just promise me. For my peace of mind."

"Of course." She lifted the stone to her lips and kissed it, then rose on her tiptoes and kissed him. "I will treasure it always. Thank you."

"Thank you." He held her tightly to him, his lips pressed hard to her forehead. Inhaling deeply, he tried to imprint the smell and feel of her into his memory so that he would never forget it.

"We'll find a way to be together, Aidan." Her small hands stroked down his back. "I refuse to think that it can't be done."

Aidan knew she felt that way. She survived because she refused to give up hope. That was why he couldn't tell her anything until after he was gone. She would try to stop him from going if she knew he wasn't coming back.

"Get ready to eat," he said, stepping back and releasing her, keeping the careless smile on his face by sheer will-power alone.

Their fingers stayed laced together until the last pos-sible moment, then she took the stairs, and he went to the dining room. Aidan arranged the books in such a way that his purpose and motivations were clear. He couldn't let her think he'd left or was taken. He needed her to know why he was leaving, so that she could live with it. Accept it. Move past it.

She wouldn't notice anything amiss at first, but later, when she looked closely, she would understand.

He saved the note for last, pulling out a chair and taking a deep breath before writing his good-bye.

He couldn't do it face to face. It would be far too pain-ful. Folding the paper, he lifted it to his lips and kissed it, then set it above the open pages of the book he'd stolen from Sheron.

The second book, the jeweled one with the references to Stonehenge and star alignment, seemed to have little or no relationship to the one the Elders kept hidden. If there were answers to be found in that, he couldn't find them. It appeared to present more problems than solutions, like a puzzle that became more complicated the further into it he got.

Without conscious thought, his fingertips drifted over the text he'd translated.

"Beware of the Key that turns the Lock and reveals the Truth."

The words struck him hard, each one an individual blow.

He sat unmoving, his breath whistling in and out between clenched teeth.

The Key wasn't going to open the Gateway to the Nightmares. The Key was going to reveal something the Elders didn't want revealed. That was why they were hunting for it. That was why they wanted it destroyed.

But why the Key was a Dreamer and why the traits attributed to it were so important, he didn't know. And the pendant . . .

His eyes closed on a shudder. There, in the ancient text, he'd found a drawing of the pendant Sheron had given him so long ago. A relic of the old world. A part of the prophecy the Elders had never shared with anyone. The stone would protect her, the glowing reaction it had to her proximity enhancing her abilities in the Twilight. She'd been able to create the door without it. With it, he imagined she would be able to keep Guardians and Nightmares away from the portal altogether. She would finally be safe in dreams.

When he'd first translated that section of the text, he'd been confused as to why something so dangerous would be given to him, a man who was sent out nightly to interact with Dreamers who might be the Key. Why wouldn't it be locked away?

Then he'd read further.

The Key. The Lock. The Guardian.

Lyssa was the Key, as evidenced by the reaction of the stone, which was the Lock. He could only assume that he was the Guardian. And the result of the combination of the three?

"The end of the Universe as we now know it."

Further translation was sketchy. Many of the words used

were unfamiliar to him. But some things were clear. Rupture. Annihilation. To say it didn't sound good would be a huge understatement.

He had to return to the Twilight for answers, and he had to stay away from Lyssa.

Fissure creation wasn't the direction he needed to be looking. He needed to know what it was about Lyssa's ability to see into the Twilight and control dreams that made the Elders so fearful. Why wouldn't a curious Guardian, like him, be an equal threat? And the stone. What was it? What was its purpose? Why had it been given to him?

And what did this all mean? Were the Elders malevolent or benevolent? He didn't know, but he couldn't help thinking that if their cause was just, they would have shared it freely with the Guardians. They'd lied about so much. They said the trip to this world was one-way, but parts of his translation led him to believe otherwise. Why would they hide the ability to travel freely between the conduit and this plane? It was only one of countless unanswered questions.

But, if he was wrong about the round-trip travel, it was possible he could wake again in this world. Aidan's jaw tightened. He couldn't allow that to happen if his presence here jeopardized Lyssa. He would have to prevent it. By whatever means necessary.

The water in the shower upstairs turned off, galvanizing him into action. Aidan washed quickly in the downstairs bathroom, then moved to the kitchen, steeling himself inwardly for the parting that was rapidly approaching.

* * *

Hearing the low, warbling birdcall that said it was safe to proceed, Connor set his jaw grimly and entered the Temple of the Elders. Using comms wasn't possible in a situation like this, where their transmissions would be picked up and used against them later. By necessity, this was a stripped-down mission. His favorite kind.

Philip had taken out the guard at the entryway with a blow dart dipped in tranquilizer. Then he'd retrieved it from the unfortunate man's neck so that no evidence was left behind. The guard would awaken with only the vague sensation of having dozed, perhaps in boredom. Connor would do the same to the lone sentinel in the control room. They hoped their careful planning would prevent them from being both seen and remembered. If they could manage to get some answers and then retreat without being detected, he would consider the engagement a resounding success.

Keeping this objective in mind, Connor moved within the shadows, his senses alert, his steps deliberately planned and timed to avoid being recorded. He entered the middle hallway that led away from the *haiden*. The hall to the left branched off toward the living quarters of the Elders. The hall to the right led to a secluded, open-air meditation courtyard.

So far, so good.

As he walked, a vibration beneath his feet drew Connor's attention to the floor. The stone shimmered and became translucent, frightening him for a moment into thinking the ground had completely disappeared and he was about to fall into the endless blanket of stars revealed. He groped for the wall in an instinctive gambit to save himself, then the view of space melted into a swirling kaleidoscope of colors.

"Fuck me," he breathed.

Arrested by the display, Connor stared agape, wondering if what he was watching was real or a projection of some sort.

Then, knowing time was short, he forced himself to ignore the vertigo caused by the floor and continued on. With each step, ripples of writhing colors spread outward, as if he were walking in a body of shallow rainbow water. Up ahead, he spied an arched entryway and stealthily pressed his back to the wall directly next to it. He glanced inside and saw one Elder bent over a lighted console.

Connor withdrew the dagger at his thigh and held it away from him, angling the shiny blade to catch the reflection of his industriously working target. He would have one shot at this. If he missed, he would give away his position and intent, and set himself up for severe disciplinary action.

So he pulled out his blowgun with his other hand and waited patiently, ignoring the drops of sweat that slid down his temple. When the Elder finally turned away to remove a book from the wall of volumes behind him, Connor filled the doorway, taking the space of a heartbeat to aim before sending the tiny dart flying across the not inconsiderable distance between himself and the Elder.

He then returned to his spot, his gaze on the wildly swirling floor, waiting until he heard the thud of the unconscious Elder falling.

Before he entered the room, Connor whistled, telling Philip that he'd succeeded and to start the clock ticking. The tranquilizer would not hold for long.

"Tell me all your secrets," he murmured, setting his blade next to him on the control panel. Before him lay a semicircular panel of lighted buttons. Above that, embedded in a raised lip, were a dozen small vid screens, each one displaying a view of various Guardians engaged in their assignments. He stared at the display, his mind faltering at the realization of what exactly he was looking at.

All this time, the Guardians had assumed their moments spent in a Dreamer's stream of unconsciousness were private. They were not.

Which means they would have known of the captain's suspicions about the Dreamer. They would have seen the growing attachment between the two. Perhaps they had even fostered it by sending him back to her. They had allowed the relationship to progress because they were aware, not because they were ignorant.

Intrigued and horrified by the thought, Connor set to work, running through the archives with nimble keystrokes, trying to prove or disprove his guess. A quick glance toward the doorway showed him that the hallway floor had resumed its appearance of marble now that he no longer stood upon it. Too many oddities in a world he once thought he understood completely.

All the years he'd spend teasing and dismissing Aidan for his overwhelming curiosity rose up as bile in Connor's throat. Sex and fighting were all he had cared to focus on. How frivolous that seemed now. Life was not as simple as a halfhearted search for a centuries-old prophecy.

Who are the Elders? Who put them in charge? Why the drastic change in their appearance? Where did they learn about the Key? Why do we stop aging? Don't you ever wonder these things?

You ask too many questions, Cross.

Stupid. He never went into any mission without knowing every facet of the situation, yet he'd lived his life without knowing jackshit, as the past few moments had made abundantly clear.

"No more." He rolled his shoulders back, the primary focus of his life switching in one powerful moment of epiphany. "That's all about to change."

Then he heard his name and stilled, trying to discern where the sound had come from. He heard it again, and his wide-eyed gaze lifted to the row of monitors. "Cross."

On the farthest screen to the right he saw Aidan's dream . . . and Aidan.

As Lyssa put lotion on her face, she considered her dilemma and wondered what, if anything, she could do about it. She couldn't help Aidan with the books he'd brought with him since his language was beyond her, but she had noted that the new books he'd purchased the day before had been about Stonehenge. She didn't know why the place held such interest for him, but she would find out.

No matter what she had to do, there was no way in hell she was going to let him just walk out of her life. Not after what he'd shared with her this morning. Her immortal warrior had gone his entire life without needing or loving any woman—until he had found her. Now *she* was his dream, and it was a gift she wouldn't give up without a fight.

Stepping out of her bathroom, Lyssa paused mid-step. Aidan lay on the bed, asleep. She smiled affectionately, her heart swelling with emotion. "My poor darling. Even dream lovers need to rest sometime."

She padded barefoot across her short-pile oatmeal carpet, her hands tightening the fold between her breasts that kept the towel from falling. Standing over her bed, she took in the clothing he wore—loose-fitting black pants and matching vest. Unlike the clothes he'd purchased yesterday, these garments fit him perfectly, hugging him like a second skin to his hips, where the trousers then flared wide for ease of movement. The foreign material and seamless construction reminded her that they came from different worlds.

Her heart in her throat, she memorized his beloved features as they looked in that moment, the hard, angular lines softened by slumber. Aside from the strands of silver hair that lined his temples, Aidan looked no older than her thirty years.

"Gorgeous," she breathed, deeply enamored with his bared arms and golden throat. Bending over, she pressed her lips to his. "I love you."

He slept on.

Needing coffee desperately, Lyssa dressed in a cotton mini-dress decorated with soft pastel flowers. She was halfway down the stairs when she heard a familiar voice calling her from the open front door.

"Lyssa?"

She bounced the rest of the way down. "Hi, Mom." Her hug was exuberant.

"What the hell happened to your entryway?" her mother asked, poking at the cracked and powdered remains of a tile with the toe of her heeled sandal.

"I dropped something."

"A sledgehammer?"

Lyssa laughed.

"Did you just giggle?" Her mother's head came up, and her eyes narrowed. She whistled low. "Look at you! Who-ever your guy is, he didn't waste any time getting to the honeymoon stage of the visit, eh?"

"Mom!" Shaking her head, Lyssa went to the kitchen for coffee, and found a covered plate of Ritz crackers with peanut butter and raisins on top.

"What is that?" her mother asked, her wide eyes an odd contrast to her cosmopolitan appearance. Dressed in a soft gauze multicolored skirt and azure blue tank, Cathy looked fabulous, as always. She moved her hands while talking, making the thin gold bracelets on her wrists tinkle merrily.

"It's breakfast."

"Are you babysitting Justin again?"

"Nope. This is *my* breakfast." Lyssa picked up a cracker and took a bite. It was the best thing she'd ever tasted. Made by loving hands, it carried a heated reminder of their late night snack.

"Ugh." Her mother wrinkled her nose. "So where is he?"

"Where's who?" Lyssa poured a quick cup of coffee, added cream and sweetener, and washed down the sticky peanut butter.

"Don't be dense. I want to meet him. I haven't seen you look so good in years."

Smiling, Lyssa picked up another cracker and walked around the counter to take her favorite stool at the bar.

Her mother followed, a frown marring the space between her brows. "Is he a professor?" She moved to the dining table and looked over the books there. "Or a student?"

"Something like that."

"Why the mystery? I don't like it."

For a moment Lyssa tensed, wondering how she would explain the jeweled book. Relief filled her to see that it was hidden beneath a stack of papers. "You're just nosy."

"Stonehenge, huh? I've always wanted to go there."

"Not me." Not if it meant Aidan would go home. There was so much she wanted to learn about him, so many things she wanted to show him and share with him. He said he knew everything about her because in the Twilight he could see into her mind. She wanted the time to know him just as well.

"Did he go to the store or something?" Cathy asked, looking around. "Maybe he saw your idea of breakfast and decided to get some real food. Really, Lyssa. You can't feed a man a meal like that."

"He's sleeping upstairs."

"Oooh."

Lyssa immediately regretted telling her mother. Cathy was hurrying up the stairs before Lyssa could protest. All she could do was follow and hiss, "This is bad even for you, Mom!"

"Just a peek. I promise I won't wake him up." Her mom paused in the bedroom doorway and froze. She said nothing for a long moment, and then, "Jesus. Is he real?"

"No. He's a blow-up doll. Top of the line."

Her mother glanced over her shoulder with a glare.

"Smart ass." She turned her gaze back to the bed. "Where did you find him, and are there any more like him?"

"He found me, remember?" And thank god he had. Lyssa lifted to her tiptoes so she could see him, too. Aidan Cross sleeping on her bed was the most erotic sight ever.

The two of them were silent, both of them arrested by the glorious specimen of masculinity stretched out in vulnerable slumber. The only sound in the room was breathing, the soft in and out of air in lungs. Her mother took one step into the room . . .

. . . and JB's sudden protective growl scared the shit out of both of them. Cathy jumped and screamed, which frightened Lyssa enough to leap back and screech.

Aidan didn't even twitch.

Lyssa knew her mother could wake the dead with that scream, and her own screech wasn't too shabby in the corpse-raising department, either. Her heart, already racing from recent events, kicked up a notch. Something was very wrong. "Mom, you'll have to leave now."

"Why?"

"Hot guy. In my bed. You figure it out." A hot guy who wasn't moving or reacting to external stimuli.

"I don't know how the hell you plan to wake him up if two screaming women didn't do it. Poor guy. You wore him out." Cathy moved toward the stairs, her hand still pressed to her chest. "That animal is possessed, Lyssa. You'll never catch a man with that beast around."

"Don't worry about that now." Lyssa hurried her mother down to the first floor and then hugged her with more than usual fervor in the entryway, breathing in the familiar scent of Coco by Chanel. In case she wouldn't get the chance again, she said, "I love you, Ma. A lot."

"I know, baby." Cathy's hand stroked over her head and down her back, bringing tears to her eyes. "Will I get to see your McDreamy awake sometime?"

Lyssa set her shoulders back. "I'll do everything I can to make that happen. I promise you that."

"Connor, damn it. Where the fuck are you?"

Just as a Dreamer would be, Aidan was fully cognizant of his surroundings. However, unlike a Dreamer, his stream was degraded, creating a murky glass effect. Connor spent precious moments trying to figure out if he could reach his best friend from the control panel or if he would have to leave. In the end, he quickly erased all the vids of the last several minutes in the Temple, then met Philip outside.

"Cross has returned to the Twilight in the dream state."

Philip frowned, then nodded. "Go to him. I'll take over in the control room and see what I can dig up."

"No way. It's too dangerous. You won't have a second to watch your back."

"Fuck it," Philip dismissed with a snort. "We went to all this trouble. I'm not wasting our efforts. The chances of us getting this opportunity again are slim to none, and you know it."

"So we find another way. An engagement like this can't be done with only one man."

"You're wasting time. And your breath."

Connor growled low and then cursed. He had no choice, he had to go to Aidan, and he knew that once he left, Philip would do whatever the hell he wanted. "You get caught and I'll have your ass."

"Deal. Now go."

Rounding the building, Connor reached the grassy plateau behind the Temple and leaped, gliding swiftly past Aidan's home to the high mountain, then beyond it. Before him spread the Valley of Dreams, wide golden beams rising from the valley floor and piercing the misty sky until they could no longer be seen. The varying streams of unconscious thoughts spread as far as the eye could see. Writhing shadows and wisps of black smoke betrayed the Nightmares who infiltrated the valley despite their best efforts. This battleground was not the hell that the Gateway was, but the stakes were just as high.

He skimmed the edge, traveling as fast as possible, reaching the valley border farthest from the Temple and then dipping over the rise. There, in the ignored stretch of rocky outcroppings, was the flickering beam of pale blue light that represented Aidan's stream of unconsciousness.

Connor had been here before, just by an odd bit of chance. It had been a fluke that the barely discernible light had caught the face of a polished rock at the highest point, which had then caught his eye. He'd noted the anomaly as he exited a mission, and his subsequent investigation had led to them meeting briefly, just enough time to know that Aidan had survived the trip to the mortal plane and to see the barest imprint of the Elders' control room.

Stepping into the cool beam, Connor entered Aidan's dream. His best friend pictured them on the porch of his home, a comfortable place for both of them.

"You have the worst timing, Cross."

Aidan rubbed the back of his neck as Connor approached. "As bad as my suspicions were, the reality is worse."

It was the creaking of the porch step that drew their attention to the Elder who joined them. The deep shadows created by the large hood hid the identity of their visitor, but the way Aidan stiffened set Connor on alert. Not in time, though.

Before he could guess the coming events, the cowl fell back and Nightmares poured from the depths of the robe.

Chapter 15

Connor felt Aidan withdraw his glaive from the scabbard on his back. Yanking his knife free of the sheath strapped to his thigh, he lunged into battle.

Pure fury boiled up inside him, causing his muscles to bulge with the need to tear his enemy apart. He felt it, embraced it, then opened his throat and roared at the Nightmares that swarmed around them.

The sound swelled and then rippled outward. Filled with fury and frustration, his yell was fearsome, and the Nightmares writhed away from it, some of them frightened enough to dissipate into puffs of foul-smelling ash. They screamed their children's cries, which incited Aidan into a frenzy of such magnitude, Connor paused in mid-swing to watch in admiration. There was a reason Aidan Cross was the best of the Elite—he was a badass motherfucker when it came to wielding a glaive.

The Nightmares recoiled, swirling insidiously around them. Pumped up with aggression, Connor leaped toward the shadowy forms with his blade leading the way. Aidan was with him, fighting with vigor such as Connor had not seen from him in many years.

With his focus divided between Aidan and the Nightmares, Connor failed to notice that they were no longer alone with their enemy until it was too late. Before he understood what was happening, hundreds of Elders rushed up behind them, glaives flashing. Soon the entire grassy expanse was hidden by a sea of gray-robed figures and the Nightmares they fought. They spread outward like a growing stain, surrounding the porch and sides of the house.

Connor couldn't figure out what the hell was going on, but at the moment he didn't care. The only thing that concerned him was the Nightmares, and killing every single one of them. With the help of the Elders, that goal was achievable.

There is a moment in every battle when the winds of fate change direction. Warriors of every kind know it instinctively. It comes to them in a rush of adrenaline, a surge of power, a howl of victory.

It was when that moment of triumph arrived that the Elders made their move. Moving as one, they surged up the stairs, overwhelming Aidan in a flood of grasping arms and dragging him away. The captain fought like a man possessed, but he was unable to overcome the sheer number of assailants. Connor roared his frustration and fear for his friend. But he was unable to do anything, trapped as he was by his fight with the remaining Nightmares. He couldn't turn away; he couldn't help.

He could only press on and make a private vow of vengeance.

* * *

Lyssa stared down at the book in her hands and the note that had been set carefully on top of it.

I love you.

She'd never seen Aidan's handwriting before, but the arrogantly slashed letters were his, she had no doubt. Like the man himself, it was beautiful and bold, yet harshly drawn with sharp angles.

Her fingertips followed the lines as she cried. He thought staying with her would place her in danger. He was willing to sacrifice himself out of love for her.

"Aidan." She brushed away her tears, and then gripped the pendant in a fist. "You're not doing this alone, and I'm not letting you go without a fight."

Pushing back from the table with a weary sigh, Lyssa went upstairs to bed. She would close her eyes and pray that she would drift into the Twilight and save him. How she would manage, and what it was she could do to help, she didn't know. She'd spent almost her entire life hiding from the Elders and the Nightmares. Now she had no choice, she had to face them. She couldn't just do nothing; she couldn't leave Aidan suspended like that—his body in one plane, his mind in another. So far, she had gone with her gut instincts every step of the way. She wasn't going to stop now.

Lyssa set one knee on the mattress and crawled over to Aidan. She curled up against his side, her leg over his, her arm flung across his waist. His chest rose and fell steadily, but his heart raced in a desperate rhythm. She pressed her face into the side of his throat and breathed in his scent. It centered her, reminding her of his touch and his tenderness.

He had come through a damn galactic fissure for her. It was time to do the same for him.

Lyssa woke on a blanket on a beach. It took her a moment to orient herself to her new surroundings, but before she could catch a complete breath, the full force of her situation hit her like a bucket of ice water dumped on her head. She leaped to her feet, her hands automatically moving to dust the sand from her clothes. She touched her garments carefully—a miniature, female version of Aidan's black vest and loose trousers.

"Kick-ass clothes," she said softly, lifting her chin. "Damn straight."

Newly armed with memories of the time she had spent with Aidan here in his world, Lyssa was even more determined to save her man. The vision of his blue eyes filled with such desolation and hopelessness made her heart ache.

I'm glad to be here with you, he'd said the day he arrived on her doorstep. His smile had been so filled with joy, it stopped her heart and squashed her common sense like an annoying bug.

"I'm coming, baby," she murmured, heading toward the big metal door that waited just beyond the circle of light created by her dream sun. Taking one last breath of courage, she gripped the handle and pulled the door open . . .

. . . and met eyes of startling gray. Nearly metallic in appearance, they were stunningly set off by tanned skin and a determined jaw. Inky black hair was tied back at the neck and fell past his shoulder blades.

She gaped.

"Your haste in returning gives me hope that you feel the same about Captain Cross as he does about you," the man said.

Her mouth snapped closed so she could reply. "Who are you? And where is he? Is he okay? Is he hurt?"

He smiled and bowed. "Lieutenant Wager, at your service. I'm here for the express purpose of taking you to Captain Cross. Don't worry about that."

Leaning to the side to look around his tall form, she counted at least twenty men behind him, each one uniquely yummy in appearance. She whistled. "Do I know how to dream or what?"

"Cross didn't do so bad himself," the man returned. "What color are my eyes?"

"Gray."

"And my hair?"

"Black."

"So it's true," he murmured, then his amused gaze ran down the length of her body and back up again. "Cute outfit. Right down to the pendant."

It was then Lyssa noted that the other men were dressed similarly but in heather gray rather than the black she wore. It was a uniform. From the look of the various grins directed her way, she quickly deduced that she was wearing a garment reserved for the captain alone. She winced. "Ooops. The necklace was a gift. The rest is a mistake. I'll change."

"No, don't," he said quickly, staying her with a hand on

her arm. "You look great, and the element of surprise is an excellent advantage."

She blew out her breath. "Yeah, well, it's the only one I have." At his arched brow she added, "I'm a veterinarian. If you have a sick pet, you won't find anyone better to handle it than me. But if you want Sydney Bristow, you're out of luck."

His grin widened. "Let's see if you can exit the slip-stream."

"What?"

He gestured for her to precede him, and the other men moved out of their way. "According to the prophecy, you're the Key, and we're supposed to be scared shitless of you. I can't see you doing much damage trapped in your own stream of unconsciousness."

She paused. "What happens if I can't get out?"

"Nothing."

"Okay." Lyssa caught his hand and squeezed it. His eyes widened in surprise. "What's your name? Your first name."

"Philip."

"Promise me, Philip. If I can't help, promise me that you'll save Captain Cross no matter what."

"Definitely."

The word was said with such conviction that she believed him without question. "Okay, then. I'm ready."

For what, she didn't know. But she was as prepared as she would ever be.

With a firm hand at the small of her back, he led her away from the door toward a wall of shimmering blue light. Beyond it, she could barely make out shadowed forms. It was like looking through a curtain of electric blue water.

"Can you see that?" he asked.

She nodded.

"All you have to do is jump out."

"All right. Here goes nothing." Lyssa took a deep breath and leaped.

There was one mistake that everyone who crossed Connor Bruce made more often than they should—they underestimated him. Usually he found grim satisfaction in this. Today was no exception.

"We are pleased that you see our side now," one of the Elders said, a lone voice speaking for the collective.

"Forgive me for my earlier behavior." Connor bowed in a feigned show of remorse. "I'm not a man who likes to be taken by surprise, and I certainly don't like being restrained."

"We knew you wouldn't immediately understand why Captain Cross had to be taken into protective custody. But we hope you remember that our purpose has always been to serve and protect our people."

"Of course," Connor lied smoothly. "No one doubts this, least of all me."

"Captain Cross does."

Connor shrugged, hiding the intensity of his enmity with half-lidded eyes. "The Key has corrupted him, but he's always put his duty before everything else. A small amount of time away from her influence, and he'll return to his senses. He's gone without a romantic relationship longer than any man I know. First loves always screw with your head, but it's only temporary. I'm sure you all know this."

"Of course, and we agree. The captain will be sequestered for a time, and then he will slowly be reintegrated into the community."

"I will be available to assist you with his reacclimation when the time comes."

"Excellent. Your cooperation is greatly appreciated. You may return to duty, Captain Bruce."

Connor's glance swept over the sea of shadowed faces before him. He bowed again and then departed, stepping out to the courtyard where unknowing Guardians mingled completely unaware of the lies they lived with.

The sky was dark, the day long over. A cool breeze blew past him, carrying the scent of fragrant night-blooming flowers. In the distance, the roar of the waterfalls could be heard.

Home.

Like Aidan, he'd been born here and had no memories of the world the Guardians had abandoned long ago. But what was home? Was it a place? Or was it people who cared about you?

He knew he was being watched, so he went straight to the Valley of Dreams. Biding his time was something he had learned to do well during his service in the Elite. He expected it would take a few moments of clearing his head before he could adequately consider all the places they would take Aidan to be "sequestered." His feet hit the ground running, which was why he couldn't stop in time to avoid the lithe blond who popped out of a slipstream directly before him.

He hit her full force and down they went, her screech so loud his ears rang. Clutching her to his chest, he twisted mid-fall and kicked upward, shooting them straight up into the air to avoid crushing her on the ground.

"What the hell?" she yelled, kicking his shin.

"Ow! Fuck."

"Lemme go!" The tiny virago in his arms fought like a pissed-off kitten, scratching and kicking and hissing.

"Stop it!" he ordered in his most commanding voice.

"I'm the Key!" she cried, shooting him a glare with big dark eyes, not the least bit cowed. "I'll . . . I'll . . . put a hex on you!"

Connor noted her garments at the exact same moment she said "the Key," and then he broke out in a grin, which didn't fade even when she caught him on the jaw with a pretty decent right hook.

He shook her and slowed to a hover. "Hey! Quit that. I'm Connor—Aidan's best friend."

She stilled in mid-swing and gaped at him, giving him the chance to really look her over in the simulated starlight. She was beautiful—slender but curvy, with golden tresses that fell haphazardly around her shoulders. Full red lips and huge brown eyes that tilted slightly at the corners gave her classic good looks an exotic cant.

"Oh." She wrinkled her nose, and he could see why Aidan would find such interest in this woman. "Sorry."

"A hex, huh?" He laughed.

She scowled, a facial expression that didn't detract from her beauty at all.

Chortling below them rose in volume and then Philip appeared, nearly doubled over as he hovered in the air nearby. "I think she might have kicked your ass, Bruce, if she wanted to."

"Only because I wouldn't hit a girl," Connor retorted.

"Excuses, excuses." Philip winked at Aidan's lady. "You were tearing him up good, Lyssa."

Despite her recent spate of violence, Connor had to admit he had a hard time picturing her as the destruction of anything. She was so tiny, and a bit too thin. She also had those eyes that were clear and guileless.

She looked down at the ground a good kilometer beneath them and then flung herself into his arms, clinging to him like a vine. "Oh jeez, put me down!"

Brows raised, Connor sank slowly to the valley floor. Her body was a soft, warm weight against his. He blew out his breath, part of him wishing Aidan would return to being a perennial bachelor. The other part of him acknowledged that Lyssa was a hottie with a tough spirit. Some Dreamers came to them in lucid dreams, but never had any of them been able to leave their stream of unconsciousness to walk among them.

As soon as her feet hit the ground, Lyssa stepped back and stared at the blond giant who had scared the shit out of her. Two things struck her at once. One, he was huge—close to seven feet tall, and at least two hundred and thirty pounds. Two, he was just as gorgeous as every other Guardian male she'd seen so far. He also had that same delicious accent.

"Cute outfit." He grinned.

"That's it," she muttered. "I'm changing."

"No, don't," he said quickly. "I bet Cross would love to see you in that."

Her eyes stung at the reminder, and her wardrobe malfunction faded to insignificance. "I need to see him. We need to get moving."

"Agreed," Philip said, all traces of humor leaving his handsome features. "We don't have a lot of time. The Elders have vids everywhere. They're going to know Lyssa's here."

"They took him," Connor rumbled grimly. "I have no idea where."

Lyssa stood stock-still, teary and feeling like a dumb ass. What the hell did she think she could do here? Aidan's men were more than capable of saving their commanding officer. More than likely, she was just going to get in the way.

"I saw where." Philip gestured to his men, who fell into a loose formation. "I watched on the control panel."

"Fuck me," Connor said suddenly, causing everyone to stare at him in confusion due to his low, wary tone.

Lifting her startled gaze to his, Lyssa then turned her head in the direction he was looking.

Revealed by the light cast off from the surrounding slipstreams, a smoky black stain encroached on them in a perfect circle. It widened rapidly, growing by the second.

"What is that?" she asked, her stomach roiling in dread.

"Nightmares." Philip withdrew his glaive. "Thousands of them."

Chapter 16

Lyssa watched the writhing black shadows with wide-eyed horror. They were translucent, their shape no more than a misty fog. A strange noise came from them, a high-pitched squeal that struck her already stretched nerves like nails on a chalkboard. Random words could be heard amid the cacophony, but they were too jumbled to make any sense.

"What are they doing?" she asked, crouching so she could see through the legs of the giants who had formed a protective circle around her.

The men shifted restlessly on their feet.

"They're not doing a damn thing," Connor said.

She held her tongue, but as the minutes stretched out she finally asked, "Is something happening that I'm not seeing?"

"Nothing's happening," Philip muttered. "That's the problem."

She shouldered her way into getting a little better view. "Huh." It was hard for her to reconcile the wake-up-in-a-cold-sweat nightmares with these wispy puffs of smoke. She leaned closer. "Boo!"

They slithered back swiftly.

"Shit." Connor stared at her with wide, wary eyes.

She made a face. "Sorry."

Then she noted how all the men were gaping at her. She blew out her breath and retreated back to the center. Great. Her childish moment was witnessed by all.

"They're attracted to her," Connor said with awe in his tone, "but they're afraid of her, too. I wouldn't believe it if I weren't seeing it myself."

"We really need to figure out what the hell she's supposed to be capable of." Philip turned to the side so he could watch her and the Nightmares at the same time. "I thought her presence would scare the Elders enough to give us a slight advantage. No way would I have guessed this would happen. In fact, I'd been worried about the opposite happening."

"Did you learn anything in the control room?" Connor asked.

"Can we talk about this on the way to rescuing Aidan?" Lyssa's foot tapped impatiently. "At this particular moment, I don't care what it is I'm prophesied to do."

"It's extremely important to us," Connor said, his Nordic blue eyes studying her carefully.

She sighed, chastened. "I know it is. Aidan told me he'd spent centuries looking for me, trying to figure out what it is I'm supposed to do. I appreciate what this legend means to you, and I promise, if you help me get Aidan back, I'll help you figure out how I fit into all of this."

"We need the captain here," one of the men said, his

gaze remaining trained on the Nightmares. "We've never been defeated while he's in command. What good will he be to us if he's in your world?"

A murmur of agreement moved through the soldiers.

"I accept the likelihood of him remaining with you," she assured them with her chin lifted stoically. She refused to cry in front of Aidan's men. "But not like this—with half of him here, the other half with me."

"Perhaps that's it." Connor stepped closer. "Maybe the gate you'll open is not the one to the Nightmares, who clearly don't know what to make of you. Maybe it's the gate between the Twilight and your world."

"No way." Her arms crossed her chest. "Aidan told me your entire Elite force was created to prevent the spreading of Nightmares into my world. I would never jeopardize that."

"Actually," Philip said softly, "The Elite were created to kill you."

She had no idea what to say to that.

"Let's see if they'll allow us to leave without a fight." Connor sheathed his sword and withdrew the smaller blade at his thigh, before coming up behind her and wrapping a brawny arm around her waist. He pushed off gently, slowly levitating them. Lyssa clung to his arm with a death grip.

The Nightmares writhed in frenzy, the noises they made rising in volume, but they made no effort to attack them.

Philip rose, too, as did the men under his command. They continued to hold their swords at the ready until they were some distance in the air. Then Philip gave a command she couldn't understand, and they all returned their blades to their scabbards. "Just beyond the rise, there's a lake."

She felt Connor's nod. "I know where it is. Let's go."

As they glided rapidly through the misty evening, Lyssa studied the landscape beneath them. This beautiful place was Aidan's world. He had spent centuries defending it at great risk to his life. Here he was nearly immortal and he had the power to make things happen simply because he thought of them. Her eyes burned with tears. Earth was not the place for a man like Aidan, she realized. He would find a way back here, and he had warned her—once he left, he would not come back.

Connor's voice was loud in her ear, "If Cross is being kept beneath the lake, there will be no way to approach the area cautiously."

Philip glanced aside at Connor. "You've been there?"

"Not completely. I didn't surface within the cavern. I couldn't. From what I could tell, there's only one entrance and no way to enter with any sort of stealth."

"Damn."

Lyssa winced at the frustration she heard in the lieutenant's voice. "Once you free Captain Cross, what will happen to all of you? Won't the Elders be mad?"

All the men looked grim. It was Connor who answered her. "We know the risks."

"Will they kill me?" she asked, trying to steel herself for the confrontation ahead. Everything was a possibility. She wasn't ruling anything out.

"I seriously doubt Cross will let anything happen to you," he answered dryly.

"And you?" she asked. "And the lieutenant? None of you have any reason to trust me. Hell, I don't even trust myself. I have no idea what it is I'm supposed to do. What if I sneeze and everything blows up?"

His arm tightened around her, which she appreciated immensely because they were really high up in the air. "Do you love him?"

"Desperately."

"And if your existence jeopardizes his?"

"I expect you to take care of it."

His chest rose and fell against her back. "You would die for him?"

"If that's what it takes," she said fervently, the rushing wind making her tears flow across her temple and into her hair. "He risked everything to come to me, Connor, knowing that even if he made it alive I wouldn't remember him. We spent so little time together, but it was enough for him. He wanted me badly enough."

"You want him the same way?"

"Oh yes." She smiled, turning her head to face him, causing her hair to blow into both of their faces. She brushed it back impatiently, and suddenly found it contained by a rubber band. "Did you do that?"

He shook his head.

"Oh man."

"Yeah," he muttered. "Oh man."

They were silent for a few moments, and then he said, "When we get to the lake, we're going to dive straight in. The cavern is quite a ways down, and we need the velocity to get there. I'll warn you when the time comes. Hold your breath and don't struggle. Try to keep your body straight and your limbs tucked in to minimize the resistance in the water."

"Got it."

"I have no idea what we'll find down there. They'll have the area well guarded, and they know we're coming."

"I understand. I'll stay out of the way."

"Good. I would have preferred to leave you behind, but you're presently with the only people in the Twilight who have any desire to keep you alive."

Lyssa's lower lip quivered, and she bit on it. Everyone in this world wanted her dead.

They whizzed over a low mountain and bore down with stunning force toward the lake revealed on the other side. "Follow me," he yelled to the others, then much lower, "Get ready."

She took a deep breath, and instantly found it seized in her lungs as they plunged headfirst into the icy water. Trying not to struggle, Lyssa quickly grew dizzy, her lungs spasming from the unbelievable chill. It felt as if it should be slushy with ice. Just before she passed out, they lunged upward into warm, humid air.

Sputtering and gasping, she was hauled out of the water and thrust roughly aside. Lyssa wiped the water from her eyes and saw the melee their arrival had instigated. Her Elite guards fought with swords against a legion of gray-robed figures who also wielded deadly blades. The space was small and cramped, dominated by a circular computer console and a clear screen of rapidly flickering images. Depending on her angle, she could see right through to the room beyond, a space filled with wide beams of light like the one she had jumped out of earlier. Slipstreams.

The sight of the hallway on the other side of the cavern galvanized her into action. She leaped out of the way of an Elder who was retreating from an Elite sword. Dodging falling bodies and wicked blades, Lyssa crossed the space and made her escape, desperate to find Aidan.

Entering a hallway carved out of the rock, she took off at a run, pausing at each doorless archway to look inside. She heard footsteps behind her and turned, relieved to see that it was Philip sprinting after her. Before her was a seemingly endless row of doorways. Her feet squelched inside her wet shoes, and the loose pants, so light when they were dry, were now a heavy weight against her legs. She wished they were dry, but seemed unable to effect the change.

"Keep going," Philip urged, taking over the task of looking in the rooms on the left. He, too, was still soaked.

The next threshold she paused at revealed a man in a cylindrical glass chamber. She gasped, hope rising, then she realized the dark-haired man inside wasn't big enough to be Aidan. Moving on, she found more men in more glass tubes. They all looked to be asleep. Or dead. "What is this place?"

"Hell." Philip's hand fisted with white-knuckled force around the hilt of his weapon.

They kept going.

Finally she found him, his black garments a stark contrast to the white outfits the other poor blokes were wearing. "Oh my god," she breathed, her stomach churning dangerously. His head hung low, his chin to his chest, his body held upright by no discernible device. Lyssa ran to the chamber and banged on it, trying to find a door or some way to open it. "Aidan! Aidan, answer me!"

The thought that he might be dead made her so ill, the room spun around her.

"Watch out!" Philip grabbed her arm and yanked her out of the way.

A flash of movement in her peripheral vision was her only clue to Philip's distress until a blade whizzed past her, almost severing her arm.

"Christ!" She feinted to the left as the Elder lunged toward her again.

"Kill her, Lieutenant," the Elder ordered, just before he stumbled back from Philip's parrying sword with such force that his hood fell to his shoulders. "What are you doing?" he cried.

Philip thrust her behind him and fought back. "How do I get the captain out of there?"

"He is sequestered for the benefit of all."

Lyssa gaped, horrified by the sight of the man inside the robe. He looked like a corpse, his skin papery thin and wrinkled, his hair a shocking white. He glared at her with pale eyes, and she knew, without a doubt, that he wanted nothing more than to murder her.

"I'll ask you again, Elder," Philip said, nearly catching his opponent with a swipe to the abdomen. "How can we free Captain Cross?"

"I'll never tell you!" the Elder promised viciously.

Lyssa watched in stunned amazement as the two men, so different in appearance—one youthfully virile, the other risen from the grave—clashed in a show of skill that she couldn't help but admire. She retreated step by step as the battle continued, finally coming to a halt with her hips pressed up against the edge of a counter. Risking a glance at what she was up against, Lyssa saw a computer console similar to the one she had seen in the cavern, but a great deal smaller. The writing on the touch panel was foreign, but the rounded slot for a key was unmistakable.

Okay. Taking a deep breath, she ignored the shivers that wracked her body and tried to imagine what type of key she should be looking for. Then she felt it.

Looking down, she was startled to find a rounded key hung from a chain in the center of her palm.

"Holy shit," she breathed, awed at her power in Aidan's world. No need to hunt things down, apparently. A quick check with the lock proved that she had the right key. Now she just had to help Philip get rid of the Elder.

"Got it!" She grinned as she imagined a pitcher with a handle, and it appeared in her hand. Fat at the bottom with a narrowed lip for pouring, it looked exactly like the Kool-Aid mascot. She waited until the perfect moment, then leaped into action, bashing the Elder on the head when he came close enough.

The glass shattered; he made a gurgling noise and then collapsed at her feet, his sword clattering to the ground. Left with a pitcherless handle, Lyssa tossed it aside and dusted off her hands on her wet pants legs.

"Whoa," Philip said, his swinging arm stilling in mid-air.

"Here." She tossed Philip the key, and he caught it in his free hand. "Get Aidan out of that tube."

He moved over to the console. "I'm on it."

Philip powered up the touch pad. A moment later, a loud hiss of air signaled the opening of the chamber, and Lyssa hurried to it just in time to catch a stumbling Aidan.

"Baby," she murmured, her legs spread wide in an effort to bear his weight.

He clutched her tightly to him, straightening, his cheek nuzzling against hers. "You're wet," he noted in a slurred whisper. "And not for the reason I'd like."

"Sex fiend," she retorted, her throat tight with relief. Part of her had been terrified to see him so helpless, this man who was larger than life. Even when he was asleep, there was a taut alertness about him that never let anyone forget how dangerous he was. He had lacked that in the tube. "Are you okay?"

His large hands cupped either side of her spine, pulling her hard to his body until there was no space between them. He held her like that for a long moment, then she felt his head lift and his frame stiffen as he processed their surroundings.

"No, I'm not okay. I'm pissed and freaked out. What the hell are you doing here?"

"Saving you."

"Fuck."

"Can you stop thinking about sex?"

Aidan's reluctant chuckle rumbled against her chest. "Hot Stuff, you drive me crazy."

Her hands slid up his back and into the thick, silky hair at the nape of his neck. She snuggled into him, and then rose to her tiptoes so she could press loving kisses along his jaw line on the way to his throat. As her tongue licked across his pulse, he groaned and trembled. "Lyssa," he breathed, cutting off her air with the strength of his embrace.

"I was so worried."

"I'm terrified. This is the last place I want you to be."

She rubbed up against him, and he hugged her tighter, his hands wandering possessively over her back and hips.

"Captain."

Lifting his head, Aidan gave a nod to the bowing lieutenant. "Thank you."

"Well," Philip began dryly, "our motives aren't entirely altruistic. We're going to need some leadership in exile."

"Who's with you?"

Philip rattled off a list of names.

"I take it this is solely a rescue mission?" Aidan set her away from him, his focus now fully on the situation.

"For the moment. I spent some time in the Temple today."

"In the control room?"

Nodding, Philip said, "I think most of what we need is in there. The Elders have hidden so much from us. Did you know it's possible to move about in her world through a Dreamer?"

"Yes. I knew that."

"And it's possible to traverse planes freely. Did you know that, too?"

"Yes."

"So you can come back!" Lyssa cried, the flood of hope she felt making her dizzy.

Aidan shook his head. "I don't think it's safe to be with you, and until I can be certain that it is . . ." He inhaled sharply and looked away.

Lyssa bit the inside of her cheek to keep from arguing, fighting, and venting her frustration with the unfairness of it all. She and Aidan had never done anything in their lives to deserve this. All this time they'd been waiting for each other, and now they would be parted for reasons having nothing to do with their own actions.

For a long moment, Aidan stood unmoving, his stillness fraught with an underlying tension, as if he was steeling himself for some onerous task ahead. Goose bumps swept across Lyssa's skin even though she wasn't cold.

"Why are you dawdling, Cross?" Connor boomed, jogging into the room. His gaze moved to the glass tube and then back to Aidan. "You're not fuzzy anymore. And you're out of your slipstream. I thought only she could do that."

"Only she can. I'm not dreaming. I'm here."

"What?"

"The Elders retrieved me," Aidan explained grimly. "All of me."

"Bullshit." Connor snorted. "If they could create closable fissures, we would have moved into the mortal realm long ago and left the Nightmares here."

"There's a hell of a lot we don't know. Like these tubes. They're filled with Elders-in-training."

"*What?*" Philip turned away from the console. "No way."

Lyssa frowned, remembering the men she had seen in the other rooms. They didn't look anything like the Elders in the gray robes.

"I want Lyssa out of here," Aidan said roughly. "Take her back."

"No!" She reached for his arm, which tensed to rock-hardness beneath her fingertips.

He looked down at her with icy blue eyes. "To my knowledge, your life is in danger outside of your slipstream. You shouldn't have risked yourself for me."

"But you can risk yourself for me?"

Aidan said nothing, his gorgeous face set in tight, hard lines and his beautiful eyes—the ones that had looked at her with such love a moment ago—were now emotionless. Ancient. "I need you alive, Lyssa. More than I need you with me."

Connor handed his sword to Aidan, then grabbed her around the waist and lifted her off her feet.

As they moved toward the doorway, Lyssa called out in confusion.

"Don't make this more difficult than it already is." He looked away, his jaw tight and nostrils flaring. "Give me something to work with, Wager."

Connor stepped out of the room. "Don't take it personally," he murmured, his lips to her ear. "He has to shut off his emotions or he'll never be able to think of the next move."

Using that impossibly long-legged stride of his, Connor quickly ate up the distance to the cavern. There she saw the Elders restrained in the corner, some injured, others tossing out dire warnings of retribution. Aidan's men appeared unnerved by the situation, but they kept the tips of their swords aimed at the huddle and didn't waver.

At the console, one man worked with rapid keystrokes. He looked up as Connor stepped into the space. "Captain, can you take a look at this?"

Connor nodded, and set her down. "Don't move," he warned.

He took over at the touchpad, and she was suddenly forgotten by Aidan's men while still getting the death stare from the creepy Elders. The air was humid due to the large body of water just beyond the rock edge, but she was cold, chilled from the inside.

The two men at the console worked industriously for long moments, and in the interim Lyssa's attention turned inward, focusing on the need to keep herself together until she was alone. She fought the nearly overwhelming desire to run back down the hall to Aidan. Knowing he was so close was torture. She wanted him with a soul-deep longing she doubted would ever be appeased, but she understood his motives. She couldn't bear it if something happened to him, either, which was why leaving him was killing her. He was going through all this alone, and she wanted desperately to be of help to him.

She was so lost in thought, she didn't immediately notice how unnaturally quiet the room had become. It was only when she felt heat at her back and inhaled the sexy, luscious scent that belonged to Aidan alone that she became aware of the change.

Lyssa stiffened.

"You're still here," he murmured. He stood unmoving behind her, nearly touching, enough that she felt him breathing, slow and deep. She could sense the struggle within him, the fight to keep his distance. Her eyes squeezed closed and her hands fisted.

She understood why they had to part this way—cold turkey. He couldn't afford to let his feelings out. The affection he had shown when he first exited the tube was a liability now. Once a dam was broken, the flood wouldn't stop until there was no water left. She was also holding back, knowing that when she grieved over his loss, the initial despair would last for days.

But she couldn't leave without telling him, at least once . . . "I love you."

The shudder that moved through him rippled across the space between them. His hands circled her wrists, but he maintained that provocative distance. His thumbs stroked over her pulse. "Cute outfit," he whispered back.

A tear formed and then fell, quickly followed by another. Lyssa was grateful that he couldn't see how his reply affected her. Friendly, no intimacy. She opened her eyes, refusing to let her torment be witnessed by the Elders.

"Remember your promise," he said softly. "Don't take the pendant off. Ever."

She nodded, unable to speak.

Connor approached, his demeanor subdued. She wondered what he saw when he looked at them, especially when he glanced away with a wince. Aidan released her and moved to the console.

She swallowed hard and turned her back to him. "Let's go."

Every step away from Aidan crushed her further, until she was gasping in agony. Connor stepped into the water on the shallow ledge and held his arms out to her. Catching his outstretched fingers with hers . . .

. . . she stifled a scream as she was grabbed from behind in a crushing, but instantly familiar embrace. One steely arm lashed around her waist, another pinned her between her breasts.

"I love you," Aidan said hoarsely, his lips to her ear, his

body wrapped around hers with a tangible desperation. "Tell me you know that."

Her hands came up to clutch at his forearms. "I know."

Lyssa almost told him to dream of her. Instead she held her tongue and felt her heart break.

Waking with a start, Lyssa jackknifed upward, her heart racing so swiftly, she felt it against her ribs. Sweat coated her skin, and her chest heaved with panting breaths.

The space beside her in the bed was empty, the pillow still retaining the shape of the man who had rested there so recently.

"Aidan." Tears welled and fell in a constant stream.

Lifting the pillow to her face, Lyssa breathed in the lingering scent of his skin, and cried.

Chapter 17

Stance wide and hands clenched at his lower back, Aidan faced the Elder-in-training in the tube before him, but it was Lyssa's face he saw—wide, dark eyes filled with pain and confusion. He pulled a deep breath into his lungs and clung to his sanity by a thread. Endless days stretched out before him, an eternity without Lyssa.

"Cross, damn it!"

He turned his head, his gaze meeting Connor's scowl.

"Fuck, man," Connor muttered. "I've been standing here calling your name for the last few minutes."

Aidan shrugged, uncaring. "What do you want?"

Connor sighed and ran a hand through his blond hair. "I want you to be happy. In lieu of that, I'd like you to at least not be miserable."

"Did you do as I asked?"

Stepping deeper into the room, Connor nodded. "Aside from Lyssa, no one on Earth knows you ever existed."

"Lyssa's still fighting it?" he asked quietly.

"I'm sorry." Connor shrugged lamely. "She's too strong."

Aidan looked away, his throat tight. It killed him to think of Lyssa being in the same agony he was. He was barely managing to breathe, and she was far more sensitive. It was that empathy that first drew him to her. "Keep working on it."

"Wager's doing his best."

Connor was silent for a long time, then he asked, "Would you forget her, if you could?"

"No." Aidan smiled ruefully. "Better to have loved and lost, than never to have loved at all."

"I don't know about that, man," Connor said gruffly. "I'm kinda liking this side of the fence. To be honest, it looks a lot greener than your side."

Connor left, his footsteps nearly silent on the stone floor. Unasked questions remained heavy in the air long after he departed, and Aidan was grateful that his friend hadn't pressed him to answer them. He couldn't talk about Lyssa now or what he had done while he was with her. It was too painful.

Squeezing his eyes closed, he tried to focus his mind on the tasks yet to be accomplished rather than the piercing ache in his chest. He had no idea how much time passed. It didn't matter.

"Cross."

Moving on instinct, Aidan caught up the glaive resting against the tube before him and spun in a lightning-quick but tightly controlled arc. Sheron barely leaped back in time to avoid being cut in half.

The Elder held up his hands in a defensive gesture. "I am unarmed, Captain."

Aidan's gaze narrowed. "How did you get in here? You weren't with the others."

"You disappoint me. I thought I taught you better than that."

"You taught me enough to hurt you. At the moment, that's all I need to know."

"Really?" Sheron looked around the room. "Then I take it you don't care to hear about how you can return to your Dreamer and be more productive in her world than you can be here?"

Catching a glimpse of a smile in the shadows of the cowl, Aidan lunged forward, pinning his former master to the rough stone wall. His forearm pressed hard against Sheron's windpipe. "When I move my arm, I suggest you start talking."

Sheron managed a slight nod, and Aidan eased up slightly.

Gasping, the Elder said, "There are Earth legends about dreams."

"Get to the point."

"Certain human cultures have worked to control dreams using various items—dream catchers, dolls, or symbols."

Aidan's focus sharpened. "Go on."

"Where do you think the ideas for such items came from? There is a kernel of truth behind every legend."

"I know. And?"

"There are places around the Dreamer planet where the original artifacts that sparked the legends remain. They have been kept there until the Key was discovered. The possibility existed that the Elite would fail to kill her, or be unable to, and the Elders wished to have a recourse."

The blood in Aidan's veins turned to ice. "What do they do?"

"Everything you need to know is in that book you took with you." Sheron's voice lowered, became more urgent. "They'll send someone after those items now. While you're here, they will have someone working against your Dreamer there."

"Why should I believe you?"

"What benefit would I claim by lying to you?"

Aidan arched a brow. "You'd get me out of the way for a while."

"Ah . . ." Sheron smiled. "There is that."

Shoving away from the wall, Aidan raised the point of his glaive. His heart beat in a steady rhythm, his chest rose and fell without labor, but his emotions were nowhere near as calm. "The book says something about the Key, the Lock, and the Guardian destroying the world as we know it."

"Does it?" Sheron asked quietly.

Aidan paused, recalling what he'd transcribed and suddenly doubting the conclusions he'd drawn.

"Vids are everywhere, Cross. Until your men took over the cavern, I couldn't speak freely. As for bringing you back, the Elite would not have commandeered this place if you weren't here, and you will need these tools if you are to have any hope of succeeding. Everything had to happen exactly the way it did. Trust me."

"The pendant?"

"Read the book. It's all there. The Elders are unaware of its loss. Your men here will afford you the time you need."

"You're betraying the other Elders. Why?"

"We all want the same thing—an end to the Night-mares. I just believe that there are different ways to go about achieving that end. I can do nothing without los-ing my position, but you can work in my stead. You may not always understand why I do something, such as with the pendant, but trust that there is a purpose to every-thing." Sheron moved toward the door in a swirl of gray robes.

Aidan leaped to stop him, but as quick as he'd come, the Elder was gone. Vanished into thin air.

As JB grumbled loudly and kneaded her thigh, Lyssa rolled into the sofa cushions and pulled the chenille throw over her head.

"Go away," she protested, hating that he had woken her up. At least when she was asleep, she wasn't think-ing about Aidan. For the first time in her life, not having dreams was a blessing.

A month had passed since they'd parted, and still the pain of his loss ate at her. The intensity of her longing and sorrow hadn't lessened at all.

It was made worse by the fact that no one remembered Aidan at all so there was no one she could share her tor-ment with. If not for the clues left behind—the books, the pendant, his sword—Lyssa might have thought she was fucking crazy. Not that she wasn't close to insanity anyway. Sometimes, in those dark moments when she cried until there were no tears left, Lyssa wished Aidan had cleared her mind, too. Just for a moment. One blessed moment of peace.

JB crawled over her thigh and nudged his head against her. Lyssa withdrew her hand from beneath the blanket and rubbed behind his ears.

He yawned. She cried. Crushed under the weight of her grief, she curled into a ball. Her chest heaved with painful sobs; her heart ached in all its many pieces.

Her mind sifted through her sorrow, remembering blue eyes filled with predatory heat and possessive intent. Remembering a hard, powerful body, and a savagely beautiful face. Phantom touches of Aidan's callused hands moved over her skin.

I love you. Tell me you know that.

She did know that, with a soul-deep surety. It was both a salve and a barb. To have found a love like that, only to lose it . . . Knowing he was still out there somewhere, loving her, and yet they would never be together.

The doorbell rang.

She ignored it. Her mother had stopped by earlier to berate her and order her to go to the doctor. It had been torture to sit up and pretend that she was just tired, and not dying from a broken heart. Finally she'd yelled at Cathy to go away, and her mother had stormed out the front door in a huff, leaving Lyssa to collapse in relief. Going to work during the week was bad enough; dealing with prying visitors was too much.

The door opened and she groaned, snuggling deeper. If it wasn't her mother, it was Stacey, and she didn't want to see either of them.

"Lyssa?"

Aidan's soft brogue caressed her skin like warm velvet. She stiffened, afraid to look. Afraid not to look. Afraid she would wake up. Afraid she had died and gone to heaven, where her deepest wish was granted.

"Hot Stuff." The love and the concern in the beloved voice made her cry harder. Then gentle hands were lifting her, arranging her, scooping her up effortlessly. She curled into the hard, familiar body, crawling over him as he sank into the sofa. Her thighs straddled his hips, her arms circled his neck, her nose pressed to his throat, and she cried against his skin.

"Lyssa." Aidan's hands stroked the length of her spine; his lips pressed kisses into her hair. "Don't cry. I see you crying and it kills me."

"Stacey doesn't remember . . . no one remembers . . ."

"Look at me," he murmured.

She took a deep, shaky breath. Her head lifted, and she met his gaze—dark as sapphire and deep. So deep, with centuries of memories behind them. She cupped his impossibly gorgeous face in her hands and pressed trembling lips to his. "I thought you were gone forever."

"I'm here," he said hoarsely, "and I love you. Christ, I love you too much." He took her mouth, his lips slanting across hers, kissing her breathless. His hands were in her hair, angling her to better fit his kiss. His body stirred beneath hers, growing harder. Everywhere.

Wracked with grief, confusion, and a terrible need to assure herself that he was real, Lyssa tugged up his T-shirt, her hands finding and caressing hot satin skin. He groaned into her mouth and her tongue stroked his, swallowing the sound. She felt his lust rise, felt the effect she had on him as his kiss turned from fervent love to raw, carnal desire.

Her fingers moved lower, to the waistband of his jeans.

"Wait," he said, looking as if that was the last thing he wanted her to do. She brushed his fingers away and ripped open his button fly.

"Hot Stuff . . ." The gritted-out endearment made her nipples hard. It was a sound of both surrender and demand. "Don't get me started," he warned. "I've missed you until I was insane with it. Let me calm down a bit."

"You'll be calm enough in a few minutes."

His cock sprang out into her hand—hard, thick, and throbbing. His breath hissed out when she wrapped slender fingers around him. His clothes didn't quite fit, and from his earlier explanations, she knew why. It was a tiny bit of proof that she wasn't dreaming and she latched on to it gratefully.

She licked the crown.

"Ah . . ." he growled. "Do that again."

His head fell back as her tongue traced the path of a vein. His hands clenched in her hair, tugging at the roots, and her gaze lifted to meet his in surprise. His eyes were nearly black, the blue irises dilated with lust, his cheekbones flushed with desire. With his beautifully etched lips parted on panting breaths, he gasped, "Open your mouth."

She blinked, startled at the harsh order. She was even more shocked when he pulled her closer, one of his hands fisting around the base of his cock and aiming it at her lips.

"Aidan?"

He pushed into her opened mouth, his head falling back as her lips wrapped around him. "I ached for you to touch me like this."

It was then she noted how he trembled from head to

toe, her immortal seducer of such renown. She stroked her tongue lightly across the sensitive underside of the tip, and his back bowed upward with a groan. She was willing to bet that he had never been this out of control when it came to sex.

"*Lyssa.*"

She smiled around her mouthful.

His head lifted, and he stared down at her with narrowed eyes. "You're going to kill me."

She sucked lightly just to watch him writhe, then released him to say, "That'd be a neat trick."

He tugged her closer. "You're doing a damn good job, believe me."

"I felt like dying," she said softly, her lower lip quivering. "Every day for the past month."

"No way." Aidan's leg came up and kicked the coffee table aside. He moved over her, pressing her backward and down, his large, hard body pinning hers to the floor. "How much do you remember about the last time we were together?"

"Too much."

"They're not going to succeed, Lyssa." His jaw was tight and hard, his hands rough as he shoved her dress up and tore off her lace thong. "We're going to make this work."

Her heart leaped at the determination in his voice. "How will we get around the mortal/immortal thing?"

His hand slid up her calf, stopped at her knee, then pushed it aside so that she was spread wide for him. He stared down into her eyes with hot intensity, his callused fingertips drifting between her legs, parting her, stroking across her clit. "We'll take it one day at a time until we figure it out."

As he slid two fingers into her, Lyssa arched helplessly into his embrace. "Wager and Connor are working on it in the Twilight. I'll be working on it here."

Her breathing grew labored as Aidan stroked the sensitive inner walls of her pussy with those expert fingers.

"Working on what?" was all she managed to get out. His thumb was rubbing her clit, his hand flexing as he fucked her. In and out.

Aidan settled more comfortably, his head resting on one hand, watching her, while his other worked her into a state of unmitigated arousal. "Looks like I've got a treasure hunt ahead of me."

As she writhed beneath his attentions, Aidan withdrew his fingers, tossed one jeans-clad leg over her hips to keep her still, then returned to his sensual torment.

"Wh-what?"

His eyes glittered with mischief. "Let's talk when we're done. Next week work for you?" He rubbed a spot inside her that made her whimper with pleasure.

"Don't your men need you?" she whispered, her skin hot and tight, her pussy sucking hungrily at his pumping fingers. A week in bed with Aidan . . . She shivered.

"*I* need *you*. When you left with Connor—" His fingers paused. He closed his eyes a moment, then exhaled harshly.

Her hand came up to stroke his cheek, and he nuzzled into her palm.

"There's a lot to be learned," he said roughly. "We haven't even scratched the surface of what you can do or what you're supposedly going to do. And that damn pendant . . ." He growled. "We'll work it out. As long as we're together."

"I love you." Tears slipped down her temples.

He smiled a purely male smile. "I know."

His naked cock burned like a brand into her hip. Lyssa reached for it, wanting to hold him, love him, give him the same pleasure he brought to her. Her tongue flicked out to wet dry lips. "I thought you needed me to suck you off."

He bent over her and pressed a kiss to the corner of her mouth. "Well, a strange thing happens when you talk about dying—it sobers me up."

Her head lifted as he straightened, her lips clinging to his. "What are you looking for? Will you have to travel?"

"Yes, unfortunately."

"How will we manage?"

Aidan smiled. "Chad stole the sword from an affluent private collector who has been purchasing priceless artifacts through the black market. He recently put out covert feelers, searching for a replacement acquisitions specialist. I'm fluent in every one of the Earth languages and I have firsthand knowledge of centuries' worth of history, so I don't anticipate any trouble getting the job. He'll use me to build his collection, and I'll use him for money and travel expenses."

His fingers wiggled. Her nails dug into his forearms. "I won't remember a damn bit of this conversation, you know."

"I've got all the time in the world to tell you again."

Growling her frustration, she struggled futilely against his superior strength. Her orgasm hovered just out of reach.

With her hips held down, she couldn't work toward it.

"Wanna come?" he asked, with a devilish curve to his lips.

"Yes!"

Aidan chuckled as his thumb pressed against her clit and rubbed in small circles.

Moaning, she climaxed around his thrusting fingers, shivering beneath him, her neck arching with the pleasure.

"Christ," he said in an awed tone. "You're beautiful."

He kissed her again, that slow, deep mating of tongues that made her ache for him. Her hands slipped under his shirt and stroked the powerful muscles that lined his back. He murmured raw, heated sex words as he covered her with his hard body.

She cried out as he thrust hard and fast into her, sliding her upward a good two inches. He anchored her shoulders, and a harsh, edgy sound vibrated from his chest.

"God, Aidan . . ."

His thumbs brushed along her cheekbones, his lips slanting across hers. "Lyssa," he purred, "share your life with me."

"Yes . . ." She pulled herself upward, returning desperate kisses. "Stay with me."

"We'll find a way," he promised.

The hard knot of fear she'd felt upon waking eased immeasurably. Its passing freed her senses, and her attention focused more fully on the place where they joined. "Aidan?"

He nipped tiny love bites across the top of her shoulder. "Yes?"

"Move." She whimpered at the feel of him, so damn *big*. She needed movement, friction, the feel of his large body straining over hers.

"Impatient?" he teased in that lusciously accented voice.

"You have no idea."

He smiled against her skin. "I've been going crazy without you. Now I'm *inside* you, a part of you, connected to you. I damn well intend to enjoy it."

Her eyes squeezed shut on a groan. "I liked it better when you were putty in my hands."

"I've always been putty in your hands." He flexed his gorgeous ass and slipped a fraction deeper, the heavy weight of his balls resting against her. "I'll never get enough of you; I'm madly in love with you. That puts you in control."

"As if I could say no," she panted, her legs wrapping around his hips and urging him to ride her. "You're addicting."

Her hands clutched his back, her fingernails digging into the hard muscles that bracketed his spine. She breathed deep and tightened her cunt around him.

"Fuck," he growled, tensing all over.

"My thoughts exactly!" Lyssa wiggled beneath him, wishing they had taken the time to undress, but too desperate to suggest they correct it now.

He took her mouth, seducing her with deep, drugging kisses. He swiveled his hips, not pulling out, not pushing, just rubbing his pelvic bone against her clit. She came again, the orgasm rolling through her in a brutally intense wave. Tense as a bow beneath him, she tried to gasp. He swallowed the sound with an arrogant grunt as her pussy rippled along his hard, throbbing cock.

"I love you," she moaned, clinging to his delicious body.

When it passed, she was drained, her arms falling to her sides, her legs slipping free until the pads of her feet pressed against the floor.

"Marry me," he whispered, his lips moving against hers.

She kissed him sweetly and smiled. "You betcha. You, me, and more orgasms like that, and I can take over this world and yours."

His nose nuzzled against hers. "Comfortable?" he asked with more than a hint of sinful amusement.

"Hmmm . . ."

"Good. We'll be here awhile."

# Glossary

CHŌZUYA: A fountain at the entrance to the *jinja* where ladles provide the means for guests to cleanse themselves before entering the main temple complex.

HAIDEN: The only part of a Shinto shrine that is open to the general public.

HONDEN: The most sacred area in a Shinto shrine. This is usually closed to the general public.

JINGA: In common usage, *jinja* often refers to the buildings of a shrine.

SHOJI: In traditional Japanese architecture, a shoji is a room divider or door consisting of *washi* (rice) paper over a wooden frame. Shoji doors are often designed to slide open, or fold in half, to conserve space that would be required by a swinging door.

TAI CHI, or TAIJI: An internal Chinese martial art. There are different styles of Tai Chi Chuan, although most agree they are all based on the system originally taught by the Chen family to the Yang family starting in 1820.

Tai Chi Chuan is considered a soft-style martial art, an art applied with as complete a relaxation or "softness" in the musculature as possible, to distinguish its theory and application from that of the hard martial art styles, which use a degree of tension in the muscles.

TORII GATE: The gate to a Shinto shrine (*jinja*), the torii designates holy ground. The gate marks the gateway between the physical and spiritual worlds.

SYLVIA DAY is the multi-published author of erotic romantic fiction set in most sub-genres. A wife and mother of two, she is a former Russian linguist for the U.S. Army Military Intelligence. Her award-winning books have been called "wonderful and passionate" by *WNBC. com*, "Shining Stars" by *Booklist*, and frequently garner Readers' Choice and Reviewers' Choice accolades. Visit with her at *www.SylviaDay.com*.

To learn more about the Dream Guardians, visit *www.DreamGuardians.com*.